THE TIME IN BETWEEN

D0257536

LONDON BOROUGH OF BARNET

Also by Marcello Fois in English translation

The Advocate (2003)

Memory of the Abyss (2012)

Bloodlines (2014)

Marcello Fois

THE TIME
IN BETWEEN

*Translated from the Italian by
Silvester Mazzarella*

MACLEHOSE PRESS
QUERCUS · LONDON

First published in the Italian language as *Nel tempo di mezzo* by
Giulio Einaudi editore s.p.a., Turin, in 2012
First published in Great Britain in 2018 by MacLehose Press
This paperback edition published in 2019 by

MacLehose Press
An imprint of Quercus Publishing Ltd
Carmelite House
50 Victoria Embankment
London EC4Y 0DZ

An Hachette UK company

Copyright © 2012 and 2013 Giulio Einaudi editore s.p.a., Turin
English translation copyright © 2015 by Silvester Mazzarella
Copy-edited by Ben Faccini

The moral right of Marcello Fois to be identified as the author of this work has
been asserted in accordance with the Copyright, Designs and Patents Act, 1988.

Silvester Mazzarella asserts his moral right to be identified as
the translator of the work.

All rights reserved. No part of this publication may be reproduced or
transmitted in any form or by any means, electronic or mechanical,
including photocopy, recording, or any information storage and retrieval
system, without permission in writing from the publisher.

A CIP catalogue record for this book is available
from the British Library.

ISBN (MMP) 978 0 85705 673 3
ISBN (Ebook) 978 0 85705 671 9

This book is a work of fiction. Names, characters,
businesses, organisations, places and events are
either the product of the author's imagination
or are used fictitiously. Any resemblance to
actual persons, living or dead, events or
locales is entirely coincidental.

10 9 8 7 6 5 4 3 2 1

Designed and typeset in Cycles by Libanus Press Ltd
Printed and bound in Great Britain by Clays Ltd, Elcograf S.p.A.

to my sister
so he cannot get the better of her

CONTENTS

Part One
(October 12–17, 1943)

"Each Man is in His Spectre's Power"
WILLIAM BLAKE, *Jerusalem*
(Plate 37)

The Dawn of Things
(October 12–17, 1943)

HE DID NOT KNOW HOW TO SAY HIS OWN NAME IN FULL. When the official asked him all he could manage was "Vincenzo". The official stared at him and made a sudden movement that released a powerful blast of sulphur. Vincenzo held the man's gaze, unable to judge his age, though he had obviously somehow managed to avoid being called up for the war, which probably accounted for the fact that he was now checking immigration documents for the Harbour Authorities.

"And?" the official said.

Venturing the hint of a smile, Vincenzo pulled out of his pocket the worn piece of paper that in these uncertain times had proved as essential to him as the Gospel.

The man took the paper hesitantly, as if fearing something unclean. In fact, it was just a piece of paper yellowed by time and by having been so long in Vincenzo's pocket. With a care more appropriate to an ancient piece of vellum, the man spread it on the table, smoothing its edges like a garment in need of ironing.

Then he got down to reading it.

Now that the first faint trace of dawn was beginning to reach them from the sea, Vincenzo was able to see the man more closely. He was younger than he had seemed at first sight, with a large grey shaven head. Among the prickles on this leathery white surface,

Vincenzo detected the red bites of lice. Which must be why the man was exuding such an acrid smell of petrol and sulphur. Vincenzo instinctively scratched his own head. Then asked himself again how this man, who surely could not be more than thirty years old, had escaped the trenches. He knew he himself had only escaped call-up as an orphan from the First War.

Meanwhile the official finished reading, folded the paper back into four, and picking it up gingerly like a palaeographer, handed it back to its owner.

"Chironi, Vincenzo," the man murmured, copying down the name. Watching him, Vincenzo realised he was being designated. "I only accept this as valid since it is a document officially stamped by a notary, which in these days when so many offices have been bombed, is a rarity. At any other time it would be no more than waste paper," the official pointed out weightily in perfect syntax. "Have you any reference in Sardinia?" he added.

Vincenzo did not understand. "Any reference?" he said. The need for this repetition made it clear that he and the immigration official were worlds apart. Both had pronounced the same word, but their contrasting accents had emphasised their difference. The official's question had sounded gross and heavy; Vincenzo's repetition of it, weak and tentative.

"But are you Sardinian?" the immigration officer asked.

As he spoke, the sun rose. Now for the first time Vincenzo could see that the shed he had been directed to when he came ashore from the ship contained at least a hundred people. Or rather, now that he could see clearly, he became aware of something he had only been vaguely aware of in the darkness when they docked: the astonishing silence. Men, women and children had all been overwhelmed by it as if stunned by gratitude for whoever had saved them from the waves.

The sea had not been calm; they had been tossed about for hours and at one point it had seemed they must find somewhere to make a forced landing. But at about three o'clock in the morning the waves had backed off – intimidated, people said, by the rocky coast of Corsica. So in the shelter of the coast the overloaded ship had been able to proceed unimpeded. Yet fearing the worst, the people still massed together despite the calm, keeping up a silent qui vive, never allowing themselves a moment's rest.

The silence had remained, as though clinging to them, until the very earth itself stopped moving.

The faint smells when they came into the shed seemed no longer to have any relation to humanity. It was a particular smell that Vincenzo was sure he would never forget.

"Well?" the immigration officer asked again.

It took Vincenzo a moment to remember where they were in their conversation: "My father came – from Sardinia. Chironi Luigi Ippolito . . ." he began to recite. Then, afraid he had not made himself sufficiently clear, he poked himself in the chest with his index finger, adding: "Chironi Vincenzo, son of the late Luigi Ippolito."

The man nodded; he had understood perfectly. But what he could not know, since there was no-one to explain it to him, was the fact that the first name, Vincenzo, and the surname, Chironi, had never before been pronounced together by their owner. But naturally the immigration officer, who did not look like a man to be troubled by surprises, would not have fallen off his chair on learning this. Though these were terrible times. And it was even worse overseas, so they said, more than anyone on this raft in the middle of the Mediterranean called Sardinia could ever suspect.

It had been like the end of the world, people said, something inconceivable, a sort of abyss in time and space. Incomprehensible to the human mind. Everything upside down, hell on earth, fire from sea and sky, houses destroyed, forcing humans back to living like the cavemen in picture books, eating cats and dreaming of roast mice. They loved to exaggerate when talking of cities reduced to burning heaps of dust and rubble, as people do who are distant enough to no longer be in immediate risk of losing everything. And people said that throughout the whole of that year 1943 not a single drop of rain had fallen. The sky, they said, had never changed its colour, it had been like a scrap of cloth rotted by caustic soda, syrupy, full of dribbling filaments of storm-clouds that had gathered in the part of the world that the sarcasm of history had named the Pacific. They said the orchards had hurled curses at the imperturbable sky, and that the earth's crust had entombed the seeds in impenetrable petrified clay. Life itself had miscarried in the very heart of the earth, with pallid foetuses of grain, wheat, rye and maize dying as they struggled towards the light in a movement nature herself had decreed feasible but man had now managed to make impossible.

They thought they were exaggerating, these people, but far from it.

From their rock in the middle of the sea, the war had sounded like quarrelling neighbours smashing plates, or a father raising his hand against the son who will not listen to him, or pressing your ear against the wall to hear a wife swearing at her unfaithful, drunken or spendthrift husband. That was how this war had been, a war they did not even dignify with the name of "war". They preferred to call it a conflict, because the War or *Gherra* had been the other one, from 1915 to 1918. Oh yes, that had been a Real War...

Once off the steamship the little crowd of survivors had noticed a young man of above average height, nervous though sober and dry after many days without food. Every inch his father, someone told him, because he wore his uniform like a figure on a fashion-plate and made the girls tremble with excitement. Girls like his mother, ready to fall for the good-looking non-commissioned officers with hidden tufts of hair that popped out like rabbits from a magician's hat whenever they pulled on their peaked caps. If they had cared to learn more, these refugees could have noted the touch of green that came into this man's dark eyes in direct light. A green inherited from the Sut family from Cordenons, now dispersed or escaped into Slovenia, or having perhaps jumped from the frying-pan into the fire, who knows? Apart from this, Vincenzo had grown up a hundred-per-cent Chironi in all respects, if perhaps a little on the tall side, taller than his late father Luigi Ippolito.

The light in the port immigration office had assumed the form of a mournful stroke of conscience. All around him exhausted, dirty, starving people were silent. Unnaturally silent. Vincenzo understood well, having lived the same life himself, that some of those mute people were finding it difficult to accept the imminent brilliance of the new day since, having expected to die inside the ship so violently shaken by the turbulence of the tormented sea, they had come to believe they would never see another dawn. Yet here they were, assembled together in the harbour, thinking back over their family histories and supposing there must be some link between what they had been and whatever they were about to become.

Which was why the only answer Vincenzo had been able to give to the question "First name and surname?" had been "Vincenzo".

It was not surprising that once Vincenzo had succeeded in articulating both his first name and surname, the immigration officer could not miss the look on the young man's face, a look filled with the sort of unwitting awareness given to witnesses of a topsy-turvy world. How could it be otherwise?

When he reached his tenth birthday, the director of the orphanage at Trieste had sent for him and told him that a document, a letter and a small sum of money had been left for him. The document was official proof of his paternity certified by a notary in the year of his birth, and dated May 6, 1916 at the Plesnicar Notary Office in Gorizia. While the letter was a simple note dated 1920, in which his dying mother, signing her name Sut Erminia, begged him that when the time came for him to leave the orphanage in which she herself had placed him for his own protection, he would make his way to Núoro in Sardinia where his heroic father had relatives and property. As for the money, this added up to 275 Italian lire of uncertain present or future value.

"Sí, sí," the immigration official said. "But if you are planning to get to Núoro you will have to wait till tomorrow morning for the post bus . . . Or walk towards Orosei." At this point he raised himself on his arms to look over the desk and check whether

Vincenzo's shoes were up to such a long walk and Vincenzo noticed that the official had no legs. "Of course you may be able to catch the post bus along the road . . . if you see it, stop it, understand? Orosei, is that clear? I'll write the name for you." And without waiting for Vincenzo to answer, he inscribed the word "OROSEI" in ornate capitals on a piece of paper and held it out to him.

Vincenzo grasped the paper and agreed "sí, sí" to everything to show he had understood and that with the name written down he would not be able to forget it; while the soles nailed onto his boots seemed still good enough to carry him quite a long way.

He emerged from the enclosed area of the port with the legless official's approval just in time to greet the light coming directly off the sea.

The earth he was now treading promised to reconcile him to himself, helping to close a circle that had so far remained dramatically open throughout the entire course of his life. Yet he was also aware of the subtle anguish of the dawn reflected in on itself before risking total exposure once again to human judgement.

It was the worst dawn imaginable in those cursed days when a verminous shambles seethed back from land to sky.

Or he could accept the dawn for what it was, and simply leave a mark on the prison wall of History.

The area around the harbour did not seem like a war zone, or at least not like the wrecked dock at Livorno from where the old steamship had set out for Sardinia. There, nothing had been growing but barbed-wire barricades.

Like a skin ravaged by alopecia, a vast, level, no-man's-land now opened before him, and it had to be crossed before he could reach the first modest houses of the district known variously as Terranova or Olbia. In an age of changing regimes, place-names could be more significant to those who imposed them than those who suffered their imposition. Only the little group of buildings around the church had been touched by the conflict with a few buildings destroyed by planes on their way to attack Cagliari. It was only a minor port, but whether as Olbia or Terranova, it had been visited occasionally by a de Havilland Mosquito or a Messerschmitt Bf 110, or both, streaking greedily through the sky. The variegated scales of the church cupola looked as though they needed propping up on one side. A mere nothing compared to what, in this belching of reason, was happening all round on other islands and across the sea.

It took Vincenzo Chironi a hundred steps to cross this no-man's-land, and hardly more to cross the little deserted streets of the built-up area and reach a sponge-like hint of countryside.

This bleak space was covered by dry moss that squeaked underfoot like stale bread. A few rocks interrupted the order of things. There, between hills and sea, the light was still uncertain as a dazed sun struggled to shake off the previous day, which for Vincenzo had been his third at sea after his twenty days' walk from Gorizia to Livorno, during which he had risked being mistaken for a deserter at every step. He could no longer remember how many times he had had to prove he was the only son of a widowed mother and a war hero decorated on the Bainsizza Plateau. That exemption from military service was his only documentary history, together with the notary's certificate and his mother's letter. But now, standing on a rock to note the exact point from which the new day was dawning, he told himself this would be the beginning of a new life. Leaping in the air like a child and dropping back to earth again, he smiled and walked on. Walking faster now, he remembered the most important thing was to keep the sea on his left. Never mind whether he could see it or only hear it, it had to stay on that side: "Going south, the sea must be on your left, going north it would be on your right, because the other way round would mean the opposite, is that clear?" That was how the knowledgeable immigration officer had put it before writing down the word "OROSEI" for him, so that if he ever got lost – and of course these people from the mainland always say they understand and then of course never do – and after Orosei anyone could show him the way. Post buses go from there to Barbagia, the man had said, and then on to Núoro, which was of course where Vincenzo had to go.

Vincenzo had seen the place-name Núoro for the first time on an old Austrian map, trustworthy but too out-of-date to print the name in the bold type reserved for major inhabited areas. This seemed credible for a world likely to be populated by obscure tribes and bloodthirsty brigands. But it had been the home his father had left in May 1915. And if Vincenzo's calculations were accurate – not forgetting he had been born at seven months – he must have been conceived in August that same year. But where? Who could know? The relationship between the Sardinian soldier from Núoro and the peasant girl from Gorizia probably had not been love at first sight or eternal love either. A wartime relationship. Their names, Chironi Luigi Ippolito from Núoro and Sut Erminia from Cordenons, were probably never printed in bold type. Even so, something must have linked them sufficiently to cause the lightly wounded Luigi Ippolito Chironi to make the most of a short leave to hurry to the Plesnicar Notary Office at Gorizia and officially acknowledge the fact that he had become the father of a newborn son. A unilateral act presumably, since no mention was made anywhere at the time of the Sut woman named as the child's natural mother. Nor do we know who would have informed Chironi that he had become a father. But something must undoubtedly have induced him to take that action which perhaps involved righting a wrong. And it is a further fact that when the child reached the age of ten in 1927, the Plesnicar notary went in person to the Collegium Marianum at Trieste to hand over the proof.

The director of the orphanage, Padre Vesnaver, had sent for Vincenzo and asked him to sit down since he had something important to tell him. It was then that Vincenzo saw the small map of Sardinia for the first time, as the director showed him on the map exactly where the place called Núoro was. Then, reading in the boy's eyes anguish rather than enthusiasm at the thought of having to travel to such a distant world, a place that scarcely even seemed to exist, he assured the boy that he did not need to go there immediately.

In fact, it had taken Vincenzo fifteen years to decide. And now that scarcely credible location was almost upon him.

After walking for an hour with the sea dozing on his left and clutching in his hand the piece of paper on which the direction he must head for had been written so beautifully, Vincenzo found himself in an extensive area of hills the colour of a cow's back or purplish pressed grapes, where the earth had been ploughed up by bombs jettisoned by exhausted homeward-bound fighter-bombers, though lingering traces of dusty green could still be detected.

The white road took him to a small oasis of young oak saplings. He stopped and listened to the air, which had been motionless since early morning over sea and land, sand and rock, which are after all the same thing in different forms. In that teeming silence he noticed the light sound of a fountain and looked around to see exactly where it was coming from. Pushing his way through saplings scarcely taller than himself, he became aware of an unpleasant smell of shadowed damp earth, and a rivulet gushing from some rocks . . . It smelled of incandescent iron, as if the trickle of water as it crossed live rock had captured heat from the friction of centuries, fortress-like granite suddenly yielding to obstinacy. It was not easy to collect water in his hands, so he took a large leaf, dusted it till it shone like wax, painstakingly filled it with water, and drank. Then he dug round the base of the rock, used more leaves to prevent the earth swallowing up the whole rivulet, and sat down. He searched through the leather bag he was carrying and pulled out a badly folded shirt, a rectangular box and a small waterproof wax container.

Taking off the shapeless jacket and sweater he had worn for the crossing, he pulled the shirt he was wearing over his head, sniffed it, and did the same with the clothes from his bag. Checking that enough water had gathered at the foot of the rock, he took what looked like a piece of amber from his waterproof bag. As he was not wearing a vest, the morning air made him shiver, transforming his bare skin into rough citrus peel and his nipples into cherry stones. Contact with water gave the amber fragment a smell of camphor, lard and ash, and as soon as it began to froth he rubbed it under his armpits, round his neck and over his ears. This ritual, restricted though it was, made him feel more comfortable. Running this virtually dry soap over himself seemed to free him from the whole human race and the odour of their bodies, as though Adam, once condemned for earthly evil but now forgiven, had been given a chance to return pure in his nakedness to Eden.

After making an effort to rinse himself, Vincenzo fingered his bristly cheeks. He had long been used to shaving without a mirror, able to recognise the contours of his face from touch. This was how he had discovered how to shave his high cheekbones and strong jaw, and that his razor needed to negotiate a deep cleft in his chin; and how whirlpools of hair swirled on his neck. Now, feeling his face with his left hand, he continued with the other to work the damp soap into a froth, which he spread with quick circular movements over his cheeks. He took his old razor out of its case. It needed sharpening, though if used with care it could still do its job. The main thing was not to shave against the grain and not to overstretch his skin. He had obviously not been able to learn about this from his father, who had scarcely even seen him. He crossed the whirlpool of hair on his chin with ever quicker movements, as if tempted to shake the blade. Since his childhood he had thought of himself as ugly, but there was no point in dwelling on that now. At the orphanage he had been judged a wise child and later a studious youth, so that thanks to Padre Vesnaver, it had even been suggested he might graduate to the local seminary. Everyone expected him to hear the call, and looked forward to seeing him in a cassock. That had seemed an obvious development.

As for his present shave, his touch revealed rough work, but by the end he felt reasonably satisfied.

Having spread his shirts out to dry, he put on the one that smelled cleanest. The world had been dragged unresisting through the cesspool of war, and he had always imagined peace would be like a river running in sunlight and bathing the land with dew. But not here, where the putrid water emerging from a gloom of karst limestone was failing to irrigate the fields.

He realised he had lost weight. Adjusting his shirt he fastened what was left of his leather belt and looked about himself. Then collected his few possessions, and with the sea breathing on him from the left, started walking again.

He crossed hard, crusty earth like a gradually rising dough of fired clay, while not far away a luxuriance of withered asphodels cut into the horizon. A more diffused light was now pervading the world like a cloud of dust. It was well into October, but he was sweating.

They said that in that particularly cursed year, all the winds, both the hot sirocco from Africa and the cold *tramontana* from the north, had stopped blowing. Everything seemed to contribute to a need for silence. Only a brief undertow of burned earth under his footsteps kept him company. The vegetation consisted of a carpet of moss, so brown as to be almost red, like the liver of an enormous beast waiting for inspection by some titanic religious diviner. If there had ever been trees along his path, there were none now. It was scarcely a road, merely a track of uneven depth bordered by wilted leaves and branches, with an occasional uprooted trunk or tuft of roots still obstinately clinging to the floury river bed from which they had once sucked life.

Reaching the top of the rise, Vincenzo was aware the previous day had given him no sense of the shoreline, only a sort of blundering awkwardness of intent resolved by a vague, indecisive luminosity. Perhaps an infinite prolongation, an offshoot of land reaching to the opposite shore, an obvious negation of the whole island; in fact there was nothing but the ocean reaching as far as he could see, pale and dull like the sky above and the mustard-coloured earth that pressed against it. Apart from the little copse behind him where he had washed, there was still no vegetation along his path except myrtles growing no higher than his shoulder, thistles and umbelliferous plants . . . and not a single house anywhere. Perhaps, if he looked more carefully, he would be able to see the point where land and sea met and shared virgin beaches as white as perfect teeth. Perhaps beyond this confused whirl of colours something might exist that could be defined as living and capable of reaction, because at the moment everything seemed catatonic.

He decided to follow the path down to a foul-smelling area of rocks. It was a clay-like space inside which he had the feeling, indeed the certainty, that to die on that very spot and at that very moment would be a suitable end for anyone who like him had been conceived for no purpose other than to show disrespect for loneliness and despair.

Even the lack of air became visible in that space where granite rocks were still reflecting the heat of recent summer. Like huge sponges, these rocks had absorbed sand and salt and so were now giving off a putrid breath. He kept his eye on the path which further down dived into a gorge that seemed no wider than a horse's groin and continued for three or four hundred metres, but the viscera he had been sucked into seemed infinite. The air was unbelievably damp, as if the rock walls were two mouths brushing against each other and exchanging breath and saliva. Barely aware of what he was doing, he speeded up until practically running, and came out into a surprising space: a little stretch of level ground rich with maples whose foliage was already beginning to turn orange. The path seemed to have completely vanished under a thick blanket of bright yellow dried grass. After the reeking breath of the rock tunnel, these trees gave him new heart, as did the sky, now once more infinite and no longer a mere strip above his head. Opening his arms wide, he sat down on the ground, dead grass rustling like raffia under his body. From where he was sitting the sea was invisible, but he was reasonably sure he was still heading in the right direction. Centuries seemed to have passed since the immigration officer at the port had told him how to get to Núoro. He looked up at the sky for a clue as to the time of day, but it could not help him, any more than could the light in which he was barely able to cast a shadow.

In this emptiness he suddenly heard a bell ringing, as if kilometres away across the valley a diligent sacristan were summoning the faithful to church. He leaped to his feet, but he could see no chapel, nor any other sign of human habitation. The insistent ringing continued, no longer seeming so far away, but more like a distressed animal separated from its flock. He turned to see a billy-goat spring from the stinking guts of the rocks from which he had just himself emerged, followed by a man.

The animal was aware of Vincenzo's presence even before it saw him, and stopped with its hoofs planted only a few metres away. The man was old and small, very gaunt and apparently blind, and he held on to the goat by a tuft of hair beside the animal's tail. A miniature Polyphemus searching for Nobody.

The old man's blindness did not stop him studying the area where the animal had hinted a stranger might be found. He pointed straight at Vincenzo's face and spoke. Not understanding a single word, Vincenzo shook his head. The goat shook its head too. The old man signalled to Vincenzo to come closer. When they were less than a metre apart, Vincenzo realised the old man barely came up to his chest.

He was dressed in a filthy vest without buttons and ample shorts of the same material, which made his legs seem even thinner. Instead of trousers he had a dark skirt made of coarse compact material, held by a strap that passed beneath his groin, like a horse's bridle. His feet were bare. Tiresias in person, Vincenzo thought. But the long, untidy hair spread out over his neck like Absalom's would have trapped him in a tree in the forest of Ephraim if he had been forced to struggle against his father David. And he had a long beard like Moses when God was dictating the Ten Commandments to him.

It seemed promising that the old, blind man was speaking with a toothless grin, but whatever he was saying, Vincenzo could not understand it. The goat listened to this exchange between humans with the superior attitude of one who had never attached much importance to words. The man reached out his hand to find Vincenzo's face and smiled when he realised the difference in height between them. For a few more minutes they attempted to understand one another: the old man clearly asking if he was hungry and Vincenzo in turn asking the old man if he had anything to eat. They were speaking what must have been the language of the labourers, slaves and architects who built the Tower of Babel. Eventually the old man pulled some cheese and sausage from the bag on his shoulder and they both sat down; Vincenzo ate, and the old man listened to him eating while the goat moved a little way off to graze.

With food in his stomach, Vincenzo ventured a more direct approach. Pulling the piece of paper the immigration officer had given him from his pocket, he read aloud, letter by letter: O – R – O – S – E – I, pronouncing each letter as if addressing a deaf man rather than a blind one. The old man nodded, apparently unsurprised. Then nodding again, he offered Vincenzo something to drink from a bottle made from a dried pumpkin. This turned out to be a strong but acid wine. Then getting to his feet, he produced a guttural sound from the darkness he inhabited and the goat ran to him. When he sensed it was close enough, he reached out to grasp the fleece near its tail, and started walking, ignoring Vincenzo, who followed.

They were crossing a small hollow when, for the first time that morning, Vincenzo became aware of other living creatures. Small buzzards were darting over the rocks, close enough to the beaches to eliminate any suspicion that there could be a conflict between sea and mountains. Vincenzo, as a Friulian, knew he must give up such assumptions now he was in Sardinia. He could see this for himself as he took in junipers and firs growing together. In a concentration that forced nature to express itself synthetically, but also in an established perfection of universal genetics. It was not that gulls must fly down near the coast and buzzards up among the peaks, but that they were doing it so close to each other, leaving less room for the same unchanging mechanisms to operate, or so Vincenzo told himself.

The idea seemed reasonable in this obvious adjustment of dimensions: small trees, small hollows or clefts, low mountains and small men. The older land is, the more it is concentrated, formed from clots calcified aeons ago in Pangaea; whereas new and ample lands, on the other hand, are the subtle and delicate epidermis of something newly born and exposed to every kind of transformation. They are spaces where the mechanism, which still has everything to learn, becomes hair-splitting, refusing to accept what is unfathomable and believing everything that happens to be quantifiable and entirely predictable. It is old age that abandons belief in this perfection, demonstrating in the very fact that it exists that there can be no perfection in a body that consumes itself. Like a land which thousands of years of winds have reduced to its lowest terms. In the end, if you look at it carefully, this illusion of invulnerability is the most impermanent feeling any man can have, since it can only last as long as the power of the senses, the response of the flesh, the speed of a synapsis. Then this concentration becomes saturated with experience, with awareness of itself, so that the mechanism, worn out, begins to contract. To Vincenzo the land was in every respect like the old blind man now walking ahead of him guided by his goat, a tame animal surrendering its primary function – reproduction – in favour of a higher function. A qualitative leap that in that short space, more ancient than antiquity itself, had been granted to this ignorant beast to transform itself from nothing, an inferior being with no special purpose, into the sense of sight for a man who lacked it. All this was possible, because of something that Vincenzo instantly understood, that in such a place processes that would normally require thousands of years could come about in the twinkling of an eye.

So he came to the conclusion that there was nothing extraordinary about the fact that gull and buzzard were able to fly so close to one another, assuming that they were able to understand their own flight to be in perfect proportion to that miniature sky.

The rocky part of the land developed into a couple of kilometres of winding bends. The level area that had seemed so compact turned out instead to be bristling with little gorges full of brambles that the goat and the old man avoided with the skill of bats negotiating obstacles in total darkness. Vincenzo placed his boots in the steps trodden first by the goat's hooves and then by the old man's bare feet. They went on like this in silence for two hours or more: hoof, bare foot, boot. All around them life became increasingly frenetic with huge crows, tiny rodents, slithering snakes and young wild boar. What Vincenzo could hear with his ears in no way corresponded to what he could see with his eyes. Rustlings emerging from inside oily rock roses, short ripping sounds from the leaves of wild olives and carobs, and hisses from frothy asparagus ferns. Occasionally, a torn animal corpse would reveal some secret struggle for survival. A vital impurity expressed against a tomb-like silence of purity. Absence had cleansed everything, reducing both man and land to silence, creating an apparent need to return to the restless bustle of promiscuity. With this restatement of life the air was suddenly becoming breathable. As if the gates of the Earth had suddenly been flung open at the end of that rocky gorge.

The sea obstinately persisted on the left, and Vincenzo sighed as if only then entering his father's home. Seen from that height the water was beginning to take on a consistent colour, veering between green and blue. It was clear that the immemorial coming and going of the waves had worn the granite down to produce those narrow beaches of extremely fine sand. There was no longer anything hostile about that clearly defined sea; it seemed as if tamed for ever and so close that Vincenzo could almost reach out and caress it. But the old man gestured no, not to go that way, forcing him to turn his back on the coast below. Instead he and the goat led Vincenzo to a sheep-track shaded by very tall brambles without a trace of late berries. This sheep-track led to a wider path apparently used regularly by carts and beasts of burden. A little further on, the road forked.

The goat stopped at this point, as did the old man in the thousandth of a second it took him to complete the step he had already started. To Vincenzo's astonishment, the blind man indicated the road heading for the hills on the right rather than the sea on the left. This confused him: had the old man not understood that he needed Orosei? But the old man seemed absolutely certain: "*In cue nono*," he said, shaking his head and pointing with a dry finger at his own chest. That gesture, rather than his incomprehensible words, convinced Vincenzo to choose the steeper and more tortuous road to the right. So he started walking in that direction aware of the look on the goat's face and the old man's sharp hearing that continued to check whether the unprepared "*istranzu*" was still doing as he had been told. Turning every so often Vincenzo saw the two still standing motionless until a thicket of rock roses and myrtles hid them from view.

The road led straight to an area of spurge scrub, which the heat and drought had transformed into what appeared to be birds' ribs and cannulas made of glass. As he crossed this morgue, "bones" snapped beneath his feet at every step.

The countryside gradually opened into wide concave fields like nets stretched to cover an abyss, and crossing it meant venturing over a varying level of brushwood, which was up to two metres deep at the centre, before it rose again towards the opposite side, overlooked by a few cork-oak trees with foliage as dense as enamel. He continued to worry about leaving the sea behind rather than keeping it close beside him. But an infinitesimally light breath of air, a fragrance of trodden grass and the occasional distant pealing of a bell convinced him that he was at least heading for a place where life was struggling to wake again from its comatose sleep. Without ever letting the path out of his sight, he doubled back to the left, reaching the perimeter of an estate marked by a dry wall. Beyond this wall – no more than a metre in height – was a modest grove of olive trees, not well tended but rich in fruit. Moving forward another few metres, he kept the wall in view as if following the bank of a river. This vision of water reminded him that he was thirsty. He stopped, suddenly conscious of two unconnected facts: one, that his throat was burning with thirst, and two, that he was entirely alone, unconnected except that it was the intense discomfort caused by the acid sausage and salty cheese that was reminding him with a painful pang how alone he was on this Earth, how different from all the strangers he had been meeting – the legless official, the blind old man with the goat, and even the shape-less mass of stunned refugees with whom he had crossed the sea.

Every noise seemed to have been interrupted. A period of heavy waiting had petrified the olives. Vincenzo was as distressed as he had been when as a child he had assumed the whole world must have been responsible in some way for his lonely upbringing. This made no sense because, however much he tried, he had no memory of his earliest childhood. He had always imagined that his mother must have been thrown out of her home when she fell pregnant. During his years at the orphanage, this belief became a permanent reality. "Such things are errors," Father Vesnaver had murmured. Errors, of course, but even so, what appeared to be the truth did not change and could not change. All Vincenzo Chironi had inherited had been his name. And even that had only reached him after some delay. He knew as much as anyone could ever know about loneliness. It was like someone greeting you from a distance in the station, on the street or at the market and you responding automatically, but when that person came nearer, you would realise he or she was not the person you thought they were. That was how it felt.

He was standing still in the middle of the sheep-track, as if trying to remember something that had slipped his mind, when the sound of a nearby shot made him jump. He threw himself instinctively to the ground, then crouched against the dry wall. Another shot exploded with the theatrical force of an ancient firearm. After a third shot, Vincenzo decided to announce his presence. "Hey! Hey!" he shouted, "there's someone here!"

The shots stopped. A sound as of trodden hay was followed by a man running into sight from the other side of the wall, a double-barrelled gun in his hand and an expression of terror on his face.

Vincenzo held his arms wide. "There's no problem," he protested, "I'm alright."

The man was only a little older than himself, but almost too terrified to speak. "I swear that in all my life . . ." he began.

Vincenzo burst out laughing. He was familiar with that kind of embarrassment, but also with the problems it could cause. "Don't worry, Father," he said.

The man looked squarely at him, conscious he was wearing nothing to show he was a priest, despite the fact that he was one. "Do we know each other?" he asked, worrying this might be some parishioner he had lost touch with.

Vincenzo shook his head.

The man hesitated a little longer, then said, "My name is Virdis, and I'm a priest; I don't believe you come from round here." He used the polite form "*lei*" which had become the custom even in Sardinia during the Fascist period, which is to say over the previous twenty years, especially when addressing people from the mainland.

"Yes and no," said Vincenzo, with a touch of elation.

The priest continued to stare at him, assuming an expression that had served him well a thousand times when encouraging some local rascal to confess to wrongdoing.

"Vincenzo . . . Chironi," said the other, introducing himself.

Now the priest seemed genuinely disoriented. "Chironi?" he asked. Vincenzo nodded. "Chironi from where?"

"From Nuòro," Vincenzo answered firmly, stressing the second vowel, but beginning to feel this person reaching out to him from so far away must, in fact, be someone he knew extremely well. "But I wasn't born there."

The priest's expression changed to that of someone indicating he had understood when in fact he had understood nothing at all. Vincenzo, for his part, smiled, happy to imagine the man had understood even if he had clearly not understood a thing.

"We're nowhere near Núoro here," the priest stated. "Do you have relatives there?"

"Yes . . . at least, I think I do." Suddenly things were beginning to fall into place. "But if you have anything I could drink, I'd be grateful," he suddenly blurted out, having noticed a water-bottle hanging round the priest's neck.

The man offered him the bottle without even waiting for him to finish the sentence. Vincenzo tried to control himself and to drink calmly, but he had not realised how thirsty he was and could not help gulping down the contents. The man, whose name was Virdis, watched with a paternal air that confirmed he really was a priest. "It's boiled water . . . malaria . . . You did well to take this road for Núoro, the one by the coast is quicker, but more dangerous, the epidemic's getting out of hand and quinine is rationed if you can get any at all. It's been a long summer."

"That was good." Vincenzo gave the bottle back almost empty. "Thanks."

Virdis ignored his gratitude. "I think I've shot a hare," he said, gesturing vaguely towards the olive trees. "Are you hungry?"

Twenty minutes' walk took them to a little church, no bigger than a chapel, dedicated to Sant'Antimo. The lonely illuminated perfection of the curved apse, the small lace-like rose window, the low door that aspired to be a portico, and the solitary bell set high up in the roof; all gave the little church a curiously impressive appearance. Further on, a group of modest houses, some clearly long-abandoned, formed a closed courtyard. The priest beckoned to Vincenzo to follow him into what appeared to be the least dilapidated home.

"In times like these," he began, but had to struggle with the front door which had stuck shut. He did not continue until it finally came open: "The Curia instruct us to go on with our normal duties, but at the same time they advise us not to live in malarial districts. This is not my parish, you understand." He waved vaguely towards the sea. "And down there it's a disaster, you can't count the sick, and babies even come into the world already infected with malaria. In one single month, I buried six parishioners and four newborn infants . . . that's how it is. The men die goodness knows where, while the old are swallowed up by poverty or fever and children are born with faces like skulls. That's it. You need strength to survive round here. But in Núoro it's different. The air's good and there's a medical centre for anyone brave enough to use it." Vincenzo listened in silence. "You must excuse me, I know I talk too much, but I haven't spoken to anyone for months. Life makes much more sense to me than death." He ventured a timid smile. Vincenzo smiled back. "We have water here," the priest continued. "Outside, right behind the house, there's a drinking fountain, I don't recommend drinking from it, but you can use it for washing. I'll do some cooking now, alright?" he added suddenly, as if afraid his intrusiveness might frighten his guest away. Vincenzo encouraged him with a gesture of gratitude and went out.

They ate stewed hare with wild fennel. The priest chewed slowly, savouring each mouthful and depositing small portions on the side of his plate. The stewed meat had the consistency of hot seafood, Vincenzo decided, hardly remembering how to chew after being used for so long to preserved cold food. The thing was not to let the hare slip straight down your throat.

"Try not to eat too quickly," Virdis said, as though addressing a young altar boy. "You do know, don't you, that digestion starts in the mouth?"

Vincenzo nodded, deciding this must be a saying as dear to priests as a formula from the Eucharist along the lines of "Eat everything, but chew slowly, savouring every mouthful." He nodded, but was careful to slow the action of his jaws, like a child worried about being caught out.

The priest studied the half-naked San Giovanni that faced him, whose leanness had a dry, massive, quality about it, as though his muscles had been chiselled out one by one. The stranger was eating with his head down, face curtained by his dark forelock. It must be something to do with the fact that he is so tall, Virdis mused.

Vincenzo lifted his head from his plate, continuing to chew for a little before swallowing which made his prominent Adam's apple leap. "There's a little wind now," the priest went on. "Your clothes will soon be dry."

In fact, not long before he sat down at the table, Vincenzo had done his first real clothes wash for two years and had spread two shirts, three pairs of socks, two pairs of trousers and two pullovers like ghosts over the bushes in the courtyard behind the priest's house. And he had been able to wash himself with enough water to feel clean. And now this hot food.

Not far from the table, in a shadowy part of the room, dozing on a folded sack, was a large dog that had given no sign of interest in anything happening around him. Virdis nodded in his direction. "Murazzanu," he announced as if making a revelation. "He's nearly twenty years old now, can you believe it?" Vincenzo peered into the dark corner where the animal lay, breathing heavily. "You have no idea how many times he has saved my life . . . as you know, I'm a hunter." He waited for his guest to acknowledge this statement before going on. "Once a wild boar attacked me from behind." Here the priest allowed a long pause for emphasis, so that it occurred to Vincenzo that probably he should always remember to stop whatever he was doing to allow Virdis to continue. "I turned just in time to see a massive animal of at least a hundred and fifty kilos about to charge me. Have you ever seen a wild boar charge?" Vincenzo shook his head. "Well, I was certain it was the end of me, so I addressed the Lord and said, 'Very well, if this is what you have chosen for me, Lord, so be it,' at which point, detaching himself from the other dogs who had run into the thicket, Murazzanu was suddenly there. A lovely animal in those days, as young sheepdogs from Fonni usually are – and he threw himself on the boar which was twice his own weight, grabbing it by the scruff of the neck – like this." And the priest grabbed his own neck. "The boar stopped in his tracks to shake the dog off. I managed to get away, but I could not possibly have shot the boar as the two animals were locked together in a cloud of dust. Then the rest of the pack ran up and that was that. But when we were loading the cart with the '*sirboni*' – that's what we call 'wild boar' – what do you say?"

Vincenzo, unprepared for the straight question, had to spend a moment searching for the word: "*Sanglàr*".

"Strange," the priest remarked.

"To me, what you say sounds strange," Vincenzo said.

Virdis laughed. "But anyway," he went on, "we were loading the boar onto the cart when I noticed Murazzanu was lying on the ground. Disembowelled!" Virdis waited for a reaction from

Vincenzo, who began to feel cold but could think of nothing to say. So Virdis went on, telling the story more for the sake of hearing his own voice than for any other reason. "Well, there was Murazzanu on the ground with his intestines spilling out. What would human instinct tell you to do in such terrible circumstances?" This seemed like a question, but, in fact, Vincenzo suddenly understood that he did not need to say anything. "Instinct would have urged you to kill that poor magnificent dog to spare him terrible suffering, but no. I was a chaplain in Libya, and I know a thing or two. So I loaded the dying dog on the truck with the dead boar, while all my fellow-hunters called me mad and told me to 'spare the poor animal unnecessary suffering!' But I told them, 'leave me alone! If I can get him home alive I'll save him just as he saved me!' I knew they were all thinking 'what sort of gratitude is that?' But some things are stronger than I am; a voice was telling me to save him and I had to obey it. In fact, when we reached the village, he was still alive, breathing heavily and with his guts steaming. I knew Dr Muroni, the local village doctor, could treat animals as well as humans – we buried him five or six years ago, God rest his soul," he added, crossing himself. "Anyway, I took the dog to him and without a word he pushed the entrails back into the hollow under the ribs and pulled the lacerated edges of the stomach hard together, telling me to hold them firmly in place. Meanwhile Murazzanu was sucking in air as if through a drinking straw, poor creature. He'll never make it, I thought, this can never hold . . . Meanwhile, Dr Muroni, like a tailor, had threaded a large needle like a hook with surgical twine. 'The animal's exhausted,' he said to reassure me, 'so by now he'll no longer be in pain, but let's finish the job anyway and then we'll see whether he can get through the night.' I agreed, and the doctor began sewing. The stretched skin of the stomach squeaked at every stitch and hissed when the thread slipped in the hole. The dog seemed unconscious, breathing very softly and occasionally whining, but no worse than if he had merely lost his voice. After about twenty minutes, the sewn edges were still roughly in place and the restored entrails had regained their warmth in the dog's body. Well, all that was sixteen years ago . . ."

The fact is that the priest Virdis had indeed talked a lot and not eaten very much, and eventually seemed rather to lose interest in his subject. After emptying the bits he had left on the side of his plate into an old chipped bowl, he got up and took this to the dog, bending over him, gently stroking his snout and offering him the succulent, fatty and tender bits he had selected. Murazzanu touched the food with the tip of his tongue, and then slowly began to chew. "My poor friend," murmured the priest. "He is completely deaf and has cataracts in his eyes. If he were human he'd be more than a hundred years old now," he said, returning to the table. Vincenzo licked his own fingers to taste the remains of grease for himself. He felt more satisfied than he had done for ages, feeling a warmth spreading inside him. "It's not physical hunger that matters," the priest continued as if talking to himself, like some subterranean river running for several kilometres deep in the belly of the earth before suddenly re-emerging. "The point is not so much physical hunger . . ." He seemed to search the air around his face for the right word. "Not physical hunger but immaterial hunger. There," he concluded, deeply satisfied as if the concept had come into his mouth with the right flavour and freshly cooked.

39

"People don't think of God, they only think how much they need God, because you can receive God anywhere, He is a guest who will be satisfied with any available space – a bed, a chair, a table, even a lamp. You know what they teach, don't you?" Vincenzo could think of no appropriate reply. He was sliding without resistance into a listlessness as subtle as a caress on the nape of the neck. "I'm thinking of the wise virgins, I mean." Vincenzo's eyes were closing. Virdis studied him as though seeing him properly for the first time. "You're tired," he said, calmly and firmly. From the depths of his digestive stupor, the young man nodded.

When he woke it was pitch dark. The shirt he was wearing was not his own: wide, but its sleeves too short and shoulders too tight. He could not remember lying down, only leaning his head on a cushion. After giving himself a few minutes to get used to the darkness he looked about himself. He was in a simple room that contained the bed he was lying on, a chair piled with his clothes (shabby though now clean and dry) and a trivet with a wash basin and jug. A crucifix emphasised the austerity of the bare wall before the bed. And the silence. Or rather, to be more accurate, when his hearing began to emerge from sleep too, Vincenzo became conscious of a frenetic calm in the surrounding countryside; a chirping, scratching, breathing and fluttering of parallel lives of plants and animals from land and sky, from sea and rock. From far away scarcely noticeable bursts of sound reverberated like pockets in the air, but in the midst of all the nothingness they seemed so distant as to suggest that there must be a battlefield somewhere. It was barely believable, but after the simple paradise of eating hot food and sleeping in a clean bed, he could scarcely believe such a back-to-front world could really exist. Yet so it must be.

Vincenzo had had a dream in which he himself featured though somebody else had been there too, in that he had seen himself objectively in it. The kind of dream that survived only through its dominant emotion, like a song survived by only the merest trace of its tune. He felt sure that what he dreamed had somehow related to infancy though not necessarily his own, or perhaps it had been his own infancy as seen by himself after reaching adulthood, as if recklessly entering the machine of time he had met himself still wearing swaddling clothes. A dream of illustrated registers, of astral exploration. Of books read by candlelight, with the odd black and white image before each chapter. The kind of image that can give substance to otherwise disembodied heroes, whose names are difficult to pronounce and who experience utterly improbable adventures that are all the more beautiful for that reason. Vincenzo had dreamed that his reading had saved him. And that during his short life he had at least been able to rummage in a library, possibly a small one but nonetheless real and full of stories, like Father Vesnaver's library in Trieste. And this apparently unrelated dream had revealed unsuspected relationships as solid as the proof of a theorem in Pythagoras, because it had been another Father, the priest Virdis, who had provided substance for this by lending him this very bed on which he had been able to enjoy his first deep sleep after months of darkness. The whole of the library in Trieste had fitted into two large cabinets with glass doors just behind the rector's desk at the orphanage. That being how life is, things can mix together in an apparently unrelated whole which later, surprisingly, turns out to be connected. Vincenzo, in the obscurity of this unfamiliar bedroom, tried to latch on to details just as when, as a child, he looked over Father Vesnaver's shoulder to read the words on the spines of those books shut away behind glass doors regularly polished by the nuns whose work it had been to clean, keep house and cook at the orphanage. That was how *Treasure Island*, Jules Verne's *From the Earth to the Moon*, and *The Count of Monte Cristo*, the titles he could see most easily, had become more than books, more than mere stories, but evidence of another world waiting to be explored. As soon as he had permission, these were the first books he would read.

"Not even the thunderstorm could wake you," Virdis murmured, appearing from the darkest corner of the little room.

Vincenzo gave a start. Now on the point of waking fully, he believed the priest must have been watching him for hours. "How long did I sleep?" he asked, realising someone else must have dressed him in these unfamiliar clothes and put him to sleep in this strange bed.

"About two days," the priest said simply. "I even dreaded the worst. Especially when the thunder and hail started."

"Two days," Vincenzo repeated. He sat up and swung his legs from under the bedclothes. "But I must go now!"

"Where on earth do you want to go? You'll find nothing anywhere but night."

Vincenzo looked round himself again. "Two days. Two days."

The priest nodded. "Murazzanu died last night," he said as if talking to himself. "Poor creature." He moved to sit beside Vincenzo. "Everything's dead here, everything, and this rain doesn't help. Autumn never comes, the temperature won't drop, the rain's a mere buzzing of insects. I feared the worst for you too when you didn't wake, but then I noticed your breathing was regular and told myself you must have been very short of sleep." Vincenzo felt sluggish; not even the cold bite of the floor on the soles of his feet helped him regain full consciousness. "The hail seemed to be trying to empty the sky. I ran out to get your clothes, they're dry now. I used to be able to count on Filomena, who would have ironed them, but, poor woman, she too died a couple of months ago."

"I had a dream," Vincenzo announced. And in that rarefied calm after the storm, his voice echoed uncertainly as though he still had to explain something he needed to do.

Virdis stood up as if waiting for Vincenzo to continue, then realised the young man had nothing further to add. "These are not good times for dreaming," he reflected, as if complying with some unknown duty to play his part in a conversation that had never even begun. "Hungry?" he asked, a few seconds later.

They buried the dog. It was a dark, harsh morning, dull as a slab of slate. Unnaturally sultry, bringing bronchial misery even so soon after dawn. Vincenzo struggled to dig a hole in the heavy earth near the drinking trough, the spade striking sparks from stones buried in the hard clay.

"There," the priest Virdis said, "yesterday it hailed, and the humidity still won't give us a moment's peace, but the earth remains as hard as bronze and can't absorb a single drop of water, that's it." He spoke as if wanting to acknowledge that even in the horror that the world had become, the earth itself still had a point to make by retreating into itself and rejecting hope.

Vincenzo, striking yet another blow with the spade, decided these blasphemous conclusions of utter hopelessness, especially from a priest of the Church, were merely expressions of bitter grief at the loss of such a deeply loved animal.

The dog, tied up in a jute sack, was laid gently at the bottom of the hole. Once resting on the bare earth, which was darker than the surface earth, the sack waited to be covered with the quiet respect due to a corpse that was no longer a living body but mere insentient flesh. The priest struggled to hold back his tears. A light wind rose and whirled about like a deep and stubborn musical note. Vincenzo looked up at the sky which was hanging over them as if waiting to bury all humankind under a greasy shroud. He had still not managed to finish filling the grave when more rain began falling. They got back into the house just in time to avoid being soaked to the skin.

The wind had got stronger and the heat more asphyxiating. As in the theatre where a surgeon operated, there was a pervading smell of iron and essential oils, wet hair and cadavers, excrement and medicinal herbs. It was as if the corpse of a deer or mouflon sheep, trapped on the rocky floor of a ravine – a creature surprised by death in its search for wild herbs or fleeing a predator, and whatever dampness it had once embraced in the secrecy of the wilds – was now being exhaled in the form of vapour from the earth. Where humanity had finished up was a mystery, rotting while other more important matters took shape, as it waited for a fragment of space, enough to reach out a hand for that shard of earth that, though not dying of war, was nonetheless dying from it.

"This is no blessing at all," the priest announced, noticing that outside the windows the rain was beating down mercilessly. "I said Mass at Budoni yesterday," he interrupted himself, distracted by how vigorously the leaves of a quince were resisting the downpour. Vincenzo said nothing. "This is no blessing at all," Virdis repeated. "More a celebration by ghosts. Yesterday, four people died at Budoni . . . and at Orosei, and all over Baronía they say it's even worse. You need to find the safest place to get past, of course." He hesitated, then seeing that Vincenzo had not understood: "Núoro, isn't it? Núoro you have to get to?" As if waking up, Vincenzo agreed, yes, that was exactly where he had to go. "Well," Virdis went on, "in that case we must do things properly. I should have a map somewhere. An atlas," he said, moving in the direction of his own room.

Vincenzo watched him leave, suddenly transported back sixteen years, to the rector's office in Trieste.

"Sit down, sit down." Father Vesnaver, director of the Collegium Marianum had said on that occasion. "There are one or two things we need to discuss." Vincenzo had lowered his head waiting for the director to continue. "Connected with your past and your future, I have here two documents handed to me by the Plesnicar notary in Gorizia. Which is where you were born." The priest stopped to look at him. "Doesn't that interest you? It's you we're talking about. As your tutor authorised by my duty to this Holy Institute, I studied these documents before I sent for you, and decided it is time you knew their contents. You have nearly reached your eleventh year now." He placed a sealed sheet of paper on the table.

According to the rector's summary, this document proved without a shadow of doubt that a father had emerged from the suburban notary office, altering Vincenzo's status from "father unknown", to "son of . . ."

"I don't want to change anything," Vincenzo had murmured, without lifting his head.

Father Vesnaver had shaken his own head. "*Tu son un casier . . .*" he had said, not investing the statement with any great solemnity. "Blockhead! A father, have you got that? Your name is Chironi, Vincenzo Chironi, do you understand?"

Vincenzo had nodded, but then resumed counting the stripes in the pattern on the floor beneath his feet. He had taken care not to let the sole of his shoe touch the lines that edged the regular pattern on that particular piece of floor and was now doggedly trying to memorise the indeterminate number of brush strokes that had gone into it. In effect, he said yes, but what he meant was no.

After waiting for a reaction that did not need to be either an absolute yes or no, Father Vesnaver jumped up and turned to the two cabinets with glass doors that contained his library, taking out a wide but slender volume. "Atlas," he said, placing the book on his desk.

The word was marked like a scar on its leather cover. Vincenzo finally raised his head. Atlas, the giant who carries the world on his shoulders, the one who bears the weight of this world on which we tread. Here was the entire known world set out in marvellous reproductions on thick pages. Italy completely surrounded by sea, slender like a dagger and apparently close at hand, and the island of Sardinia, which was now part of it. Father Vesnaver's index finger pointed to the island as if the finger of God had decided to sink it. Then Vincenzo saw the barely marked name of a place that was scarcely more than a village: "Nuòro," the rector pronounced stressing the second vowel, and indicating a place that seemed a mere nothing: "Here!"

Vincenzo's heart nearly missed a beat as he hazarded "No", while trying not to cry.

Father Vesnaver smiled as far as his remarkably inexpressive face allowed. "No need to decide anything now. You may go."

*

This memory disturbed him. But the atlas belonging to the priest Virdis was utterly unlike Father Vesnaver's atlas; this one was as chunky as the other was slender. Virdis consulted it with unmistakable efficiency. It showed alternative roads to the one indicated to him after his arrival at Olbia, or Terranova as it had once been known. Vincenzo pretended to follow, but could not shake off his uneasiness as he felt the old refusal rising again deep inside him. He was back to being the child studying the pattern on the floor. "What's the matter?" Virdis asked. Vincenzo said it was nothing, really nothing. "First there's nine kilometres of country roads before you get to the road for Lula, which to be honest is not much better but wider. Carts pass there, even the occasional lorry if you're lucky. Going through Orosei is out of the question. You can't even be sure the postal buses still go there, things are so bad. They do get quinine and pyrethrum from Núoro, but not nearly enough. Best to take the high roads and keep away from the valley." He pointed to the hills with his finger and covered the lower ground with his palm. "A rough road and twice the length, but safe."

In the afternoon a strip of blue cut a slow fissure in the calloused expanse of dark cloud, slipping beyond the sea as if giving access to a manhole. The priest had ridden his donkey to a parish a little way down in the valley and was now heading back for the high ground and home.

The night sky above his head was luminous with stars. Beautiful, with a pitilessly simple total beauty, like a bride's smile, or the pride of a boy knowing he will become a man, or the expression of someone who knows they are loved. A human beauty, rather than impersonal beauty, just as a little earlier, in the mud and rain, every kind of human ugliness had been on display. So few nights are like this one, Virdis reflected, deciding its perfection had brought him the moment for reconciliation with whoever had decided his much-loved dog must die. Dismounting his docile donkey, he kneeled on the damp earth, crossed himself, and prayed, asking God not to ignore the infinite love he had given through his just actions. He asked God to remember every single occasion when Murazzanu had looked at his master in the same way that Virdis, a priest by vocation and not out of any mere sense of duty, had looked towards God. He begged God for pardon and sweetness in return for his own bitterness, to sew up the wound and replace the beating of his heart with the brilliant diffused light of that sky. Then he climbed back on the donkey and gently struck the animal's rump to set it moving forward again.

It was late when Virdis reached home. He could see the pale light of a candle shining through the little kitchen window. Like the wise virgin, he thought. Coming in, he smelled fried lard. On the table, covered by a plate, was what seemed to be a substantial potato and cheese omelette. It was still hot. As he sat down to eat, he realised he could not stop himself putting a few tender mouthfuls aside for Murazzanu.

The young man was to leave the next morning, now that pelting rain, clearer intervals, funeral rites and recovery had already consumed the best hours of the present day.

Vincenzo got up before dawn, having prepared his things the night before. He dressed and tidied the bed, trying to make no noise. He heated a little water in the kitchen, and shaved with care, studying his face in the mirror on the trivet. He looked to himself like a complete stranger. Thinner than when he had last felt his face while shaving blind; the face that looked back from the mirror was gloomy and shadowed, but thoughtful and wise with unimaginable wisdom.

He had had another dream, but not as memorable as the first. The razor made a sound like ripped cloth on his face. Under the blue shadow of his beard his skin was very white, its childlike quality clashing with his tense expression. Now the two faces, one reflected in the mirror and the other looking at it, seemed like father and son. If he had ever known his father, he would have been able to see the extent to which he had inherited the serious frown of Luigi Ippolito Chironi, hero of the Carso and – according to the official statement of the notary – his natural father. And he would have been able to be confident that this paternity had marked him with a perfect mould of expression and form: forehead, mouth and nose an exact replica, eyebrows and hairline identical in colour and tone, an ivory pallor with hair so black it was almost blue. But his eyes were different, a luminous green, which with his slightly prominent ears and slender wrists he had inherited from Erminia Sut of Cordenons, his peasant mother.

Now he remembered his dream, or it may have been the figure in the mirror that reminded him of it.

He had been waiting as a child in his mother's arms at the top of a tower, when they were joined by a man like him in every respect, except that his head was concealed under a gleaming helmet. Yet even as a child he could recognise his own adult self by the jaw, and the neck enclosed within the formal collar with its glittering braid. He had dreamed that his mother and his adult

51

self were in conversation, and when he told her he would rather die than see his family go to ruin, she replied he would not die because now he had a son. And in the dream his mother asked the soldier – of whose face he could see little apart from very white teeth – whether he would like to take his son in his arms. The soldier said yes, but when the woman held out the child to him, the infant suddenly burst into tears, terrified because his father had no face. The man, understanding the child's fear, gestured to the mother to wait while he took off his helmet.

It was this serious face that was now staring so thoughtfully at Vincenzo from the mirror.

When he returned to the kitchen with a towel round his neck, the priest was sitting in the corner where only two days earlier the dog had been dozing. As Vincenzo finished drying himself the priest said having a proper shave had made him look five or six years younger; he had not realised before how young he was. Then, passing from one thing to another, he remarked how much he had enjoyed the food Vincenzo had left out for him the evening before. Vincenzo shrugged and said, oh, just a few potatoes and an old piece of cheese he had found in the kitchen. Just some *frico*, a simple dish well known where he came from. The priest said yes, but it was so good.

A few more words, until all that was left was for Virdis to make sure that Vincenzo had understood the instructions he had been given the previous evening, under the teeming rain, about how to reach Núoro without catching malaria. Vincenzo said yes, he knew he must choose the longer but safer route. Virdis then encouraged him to get going quickly because the morning hours are always precious. In fact, by then Vincenzo was already standing in front of the door, his bag bulging with newly washed clothes and a few provisions for the journey.

"You'll learn," the priest said suddenly. Vincenzo, about to open the door, stopped. "What?" he said, without turning.

"If you live here, you'll learn what suffering is. Both the curse and the blessing islands bring, which is that you have to leave them and then always have to come back again . . . in suffering."

Vincenzo thought he understood this perfectly. "These are terrible times," he said, as he opened the door.

"They are," the priest agreed. "It would be good to be able to stay here and pretend the rest of humanity doesn't exist, and that everything that happens out there is just an unsuccessful attempt to achieve something, an error that can be rectified."

"I ought to go now."

Vincenzo went out without closing the door, and the priest's gaze stuck to him until his tall figure vanished beyond the low dry wall that bordered the olive grove.

The smell of the morning took him by surprise and terrified him. He was seized by a deep panic, but for no clear reason. A sad yet at the same time more tranquil turbulence hung round his chest like a wet shroud. For an instant he lost his nerve. Once he was sure he was out of the priest's sight, he stopped. The sky above him was darker and more wrinkled than the surface of a peat bog. An impossible sky, stinking almost nauseously like the skin of a pachyderm. Looking up, he stared at the mass suspended over his head and marvelled at how it could stay suspended without a pillar to lift it clear of the ground. There was something so elementary in this mixture of gas, earth and water that put him in mind of the night of the world. It could have been the first sky the world had ever seen, Vincenzo thought. Because he was certain there must once have been an actual moment when a human being had first needed to be aware that there was a sky above him, a real moment, but are not *all* moments potentially world-changing? That was it, he was thinking of a moment which certainly must have existed, in which whoever then inhabited the Earth passed from having no experience at all of what surrounded him or her to a time when, too astounded to be surprised, he or she had first lifted their eyes and become aware of the sky. Of course, he or she would not then have called it sky, but given it no name at all, but even so, like it or not, it would always have been there, and always would be there. Always. Vincenzo lived the moment again, almost as if born in that moment. Because that unhappy turgid mass of muddy clouds, more livid than dark, was nothing other than the tangible expression of his uncertain progress. But he could not have been more certain that he had never seen anything like it before. Never a sky like that one.

Torture by Water

MICHELE ANGELO CHIRONI GOT UP VERY EARLY. IT WAS his seventy-second birthday, and the sky was dark. He had opened his eyes an hour earlier because the sound of rain on the roof had woken him. Outside, in the yard, the water was having fun with metal buckets and tin cans, either because rain sometimes likes to express itself as if human, or perhaps because humans sometimes suppose non-human categories of sound to be human.

Michele Angelo was a blacksmith, and had been long before he realised his unrelenting confidence in working with this material brought him more misery than happiness. Or both in equal quantities, though happiness and misery, even when they seemed not to differ in any respect when weighed against one another on the scales, are very different when they involve the flesh. So it was really cursing good fortune to claim that during those seventy-two years happiness had never visited the home of Michele Angelo, blacksmith of Núoro in Barbagia, but it was equally impossible to say how far the deaths of nearly all his children and of his son-in-law and granddaughter, and the mysterious disappearance seven years earlier of his wife, Mercede, might have counterbalanced his remarkable professional success. So that, left alone now with one surviving daughter, he had decided he could not close his account with destiny until he closed the business from which both his happiness and misery had sprung. For five years now no living soul had been allowed near his forge and anvils. He had even placed four lemon trees in pots to the right-hand side of the courtyard to bar the entrance to his workshop.

Yet the forge had been the stage for a magnificent professional life that had been the very epitome of hard work. A place of voices and glances, of incandescent metal tempered by water, in the same way that Michele Angelo assumed he had tempered his children. But that cannot have been a job well done, as he told himself in the torrential rain of that dark gushing dawn.

Deciding he had spent far too long in bed mulling over negative thoughts, he got up. He had taken to sleeping on his wife's side of the bed. This was because the bedclothes on her side were still impregnated with the secret smell of his woman after forty-seven years of nights together. He recalled the sorry catalogue of his extinct bloodline. On that side of the bed Mercede had suffered her first and last childbirth pains. On that side, too, the district's professional wailing mourners had been ready to deplore her death when her life seemed endangered by the birth of Marianna, their last child.

Michele Angelo first slept on that side of the bed when he realised Mercede would never come back, a day when he was overcome by a sleep so deep it was closer to profound unconsciousness, as if a vital part of himself had decided to leave him as flaccid as an empty sack. He had felt as though his flesh had left him, while his muscles had insisted on detaching themselves from his bones, extreme weakness precipitating a silent battle between two parts of himself: his intimate self and the self he had so suddenly lost. So he had dragged himself to the bedroom like a dying man gathering his last strength to deceive all the dear ones surrounding him into supposing that, contrary to what they thought, he was nowhere near death. But he only just managed to reach the bed, the only marriage bed he and Mercede had ever wanted, even when they could have afforded a more comfortable one. And here he had let himself go, pressing his face against a pillow still fresh with his love, recognising the sweet yet acrid perfume of his wife's hair, still black despite being worn down for years by her hairbrush . . . he remembered the particular fragrance where the curve of her nape met the beginning of her neck, where vigorous and still youthful tufts of hair had continued to escape whenever she had tried to roll her locks into a plait. He had remembered the form of her still slender body under his, weightless as a shell.

They told him he slept solidly for three days, through nights as merciless as the snapping shut of a trap, without giving any sign or trace of hope. Already a very old man at sixty-five, a widower unable to weep for his wife, since no-one could be quite sure that Mercede was dead.

At the very moment when Vincenzo was emptying the last spade-ful of earth on the grave of the priest's dog and running for the house to escape the rainstorm, in Núoro, Michele Angelo was reflecting in front of a spent fire how unremittingly cruel life had been to him while at the same time he was obstinately insisting on living or at least surviving.

"The trouble with you is you're too robust," Dr Romagna had said one day on his way out to the courtyard gate, which as always was ajar.

Michele Angelo had shrugged indifferently. "That's as may be, doctor. But I have pains all over my body."

Romagna offered his ambiguous professional smile. He knew his patients tended to divide into two categories as mutually hostile as Montagues and Capulets: those who were never well and those who were never ill. A roundabout way of saying he had learned a thing or two when it came to infirmities.

Michele Angelo seemed to know how to keep illness at bay, just as throughout his life he had always known how to keep everything at bay. Even pain. Even having to accept so much loss in his family.

Now he sat before the dead fire while outside the rain continued to fall and Marianna, arms crossed, sat silently behind her father. Then she went to the French window that overlooked the courtyard, drew back the curtain, and crossed herself, terrified at the sight of the livid sky. Neither spoke. Father and daughter were capable of existing silently together for days on end in that house filled with ghosts. In the kitchen where Luigi Ippolito had announced he was going to the War – his "Gherra", the "First War", the Real War – not this one.

This was also where, thumping the table with his fist, Michele Angelo had put an end to the schooldays of his other son, the time-waster Gavino. Later that same table had been spread with trays of sweet cakes and steaming cups of coffee for Marianna's wedding. And there too for a few hours, even the little white coffins of the twins, Pietro and Paolo, their bodies collected in fragments from a clump of bushes, had rested before their funeral.

All dead, Michele Angelo recalled. As he did every day.

*

At that very moment, Vincenzo realised he could have stayed longer with Virdis, since there was no guarantee that he would find anything in Núoro. Another ferocious night followed, with planes skimming the ground and adding even more terror to the skies. Michele Angelo, opening his eyes, cursed the ever-vigilant consciousness that watched over his bed. Then, turning towards the side where he had formerly slept, he was relieved to find he was not there. He no longer existed now, his body stretched out in Mercede's place, which was all that mattered. It really was all that mattered, because this failure to find himself was the answer he had been trying to find for seven years, the knowledge that disappearing was the equivalent of escaping from pain.

Michele Angelo became conscious of his own disappearance just when Vincenzo was packing his things, all the while trying not to disturb the priest Virdis, who was awake in any case.

"Torture by water," Michele Angelo murmured into the silence around him. Stability could only be achieved through radical change. If you immersed incandescent magma in a bucket of water it would puff and whistle and solidify.

Fundamentally, that was how he had come formless into the world, not forged by love until his eyes had first met those of Mercede. For years a hammer had beaten his body, trying to force him to give way. But he had resisted until Mercede decided to leave. And even after she had gone it could not be said he had yielded. Despite all the evidence, despite every recognition, he had continued to resist the mirror of water that could have ensured him a definitive state. This was why he could not say, why no-one could state, that Mercede was dead. She had gone out and never found her way home again, that was the most anyone could ever claim. Overlooking the fact that she had gone off barefoot in her nightdress with her hair undone; and also the fact that a few scraps of torn cloth had been found near the gorge at Gorroppu; and also that six winters and seven summers had now passed since then, and that the last winter had been an exceptionally hard one, with constant frost, heavy snow and torrential rain, and that even if she had survived the cold, she would have had no chance of avoiding wild boar. And even before she vanished, she had never ventured far from home, and had never previously had any experience of living outdoors, and finally, that after Luigi Ippolito's death she had never been the same, but had decided to make the best of things because her daughter Marianna had found such a suitable fiancé, a *podestà* or mayor; no less, and was about to be married, and even after the wedding Mercede still battled on until she learned that Marianna's daughter, her own grand-daughter Dina, was also dead.

The magnitude of those tragedies only made sense in relation to the fact that in other respects fortune had been so good to the Chironi family and needed to make them pay dear for this generosity. In the case of the others fortune had been no different, tragedies following in any case. Without stubborn resignation it seemed impossible to come to any satisfactory conclusions about such a world. Michele Angelo remembered the dream of the Pharaoh who saw seven fat cows and seven thin cows, and how Joseph had interpreted it: "Seven years of great plenty, and then seven of famine." That would maintain the balance of things: one must always be ready for bad times when things are going well. But such elementary wisdom cannot but crumble at the first hint of reality. What if abundance and want share the same bed and plenty of food is available, but the mouths that should be eating the food have disappeared?

Then you lose your head, and love is no longer enough. If the facts cannot be known, it must mean they never really happened at all. The breath that revives the flame is the same breath as gives substance to life. The words Mercede and Death can never be pronounced together in the blacksmith's house; no human being has the authority to say "Mercede is dead", and no-one can claim with authority "it is not possible for Mercede to have survived". That was how it was.

This was yet another day when Marianna tried to persuade her father to come out with her and he said no. He did not want to see anything beyond the courtyard. He had no wish to visit a town he no longer recognised, especially as some people were already beginning to call it a city.

The tragedy of the refugees had accidentally launched a form of prosperity for that previously forgotten part of the world. The bombardment of the ports had led coastal folk into the jaws of the barbarian cave-dwellers, among them smart people from Campidano and less sophisticated ones from Gallura. Some were vaguely equine in appearance with Castilian jaws, while others were fairer and more Tuscan in appearance. Most refined of all, if merely beneficiaries of minor prosperity, were those who had lived in mansions on the southern coast and in the diocese of Capo di Sopra where the late baroque was still in fashion. Now, exiled to this barbarian midland bondage, these people had to be patient, accepting the locality for what it was and the people and buildings for what they were, but at least they had found houses that were still standing, while, one had to admit, the surrounding country-side was magnificent. Even the air was good, and so was the cheese, even if the locals had no idea how to make wine, their variety being heavy and quick to turn acidic, and when transported it clouded with bits and pieces so you had to leave it to stand before you could drink it at all. That was how these city people from the South and North of Sardinia saw it, assessing these shepherds from the interior as coarse in every respect and requiring delicate treatment, if they were not to darken in an instant and for no obvious reason such as an accidental lack of tact, a word too many or out of turn, or a careless glance – people liable to switch in an instant from joy to pain or from laughter to tears.

Most of these refugees were renting large houses from the Mussolini period that had already long been empty. Or low buildings thatched with reeds, where people could share vast rooms with their animals, but had no other facilities than the surrounding countryside. The richer refugees had bought and improved their houses, while a few had even transferred their entire businesses to Núoro.

With the horrors of the abyss raging all around them, these people had taken refuge in a sort of rustic Switzerland, where they could argue about the distribution of spoils, and dream of expanding towards the hill district of Istirítta and building a major new church dedicated to the Madonna delle Grazie.

In this settlement of intelligent people, whether Fascists with human faces or melancholy Communists, the spectre haunting the rest of the world was little more than a shadow. Threatened by a resurgence of suffering, these people were concerned with their own immediate future. They understood that eventually there would be no more major vendettas, only desultory ones, because even the most powerful political ideologies are not important enough to generate endless recriminations. Their feuds would be restricted to trifles. Nothing more than that.

The "Final Solution" had been in action for nine months by now, but the elderly local solicitor whom circumstances had elevated to be *podestà*, or mayor, had no idea what might or might not physically constitute a Jew. For him History could be summarised as changing the colour of your shirt. Just a few years later, walking down the Corso with his wife on his arm, people would point him out without malevolence and even with a certain affection as having once been a great Fascist.

Clearly this was a slump, part of a downward turn. Only ten years earlier the world had been full of cudgels and truncheons, gonads and testosterone; a system of institutionalised power. But after a war too many, and a certain lack of equipment, all the puffed-out chests had turned to pathetic flab. As for self-sufficiency, the people of Núoro certainly could not be accused of having given too much thought to that. Here, the only self-sufficiency was what had grown out of the nightmare of the times. People still ate their own bread, cheese and vegetables, and continued to drink their own appalling wine. Just so.

Michele Angelo dreaded discovering that Núoro had been transformed into an Ithaca he could no longer recognise. He knew the district had never yet been able to boast any bard with a voice able to mediate between the town and History. And intuition told him that without that, people and places could not be immortalised. As far as he knew, as far as he could remember, Homer's Ulysses returned to find his home island unchanged after being away for twenty years. The crafty son of Laertes found nothing changed, not a single house that had not already been there when he left for the walls of Troy two decades earlier and nothing growing that had not been there before, not even a single extra animal in the herd of goats grazing down at the water's edge.

But the voices that penetrated his half-closed courtyard were singing a different song: a story of vanished vineyards, like the one at Ponte di Ferro or the one on the hill just above Seuna; of new roads; of a new market where the convent orchard used to be, and of new people, some who had come from the mainland and opened new shops; wine-sellers who had closed old taverns and others who had opened new ones; and of houses being built on land where previously people had never even grazed goats.

The very opposite of poetry.

For some reason the blacksmith could not understand, everything around him seemed bent on rejecting eternity.

Every time Marianna tried to get her father to leave the house, it was because she wanted to attract his attention to things he particularly did not want to notice, determined not to accept how ruthlessly new times were swallowing the old. If Mercede had still been with him the courtyard would still have been open, because she was the only reason he had accepted so much change even in his own body. That was the point, even though he was hardly aware of the fact himself, the one thing that Michele Angelo Chironi had really understood was that outside, beyond the shade of the quince tree, the persistent drip of the little fountain and the dusky corner where the hydrangeas flourished, everything both good or bad that mattered could still be found – apart from Mercede herself.

The portion of sky over the enclosed garden changed with the seasons, just as leaves and flowers and light changed. Even in that restricted area, completely isolated from the outside world, there was infinite variety. Rhododendrons and dracaena surculosa gave the evening air its particular scent. Here a sad languor emanated from walls saturated with thick smuts from the chimneys; and tiny frogs no bigger than a fingernail flourished in leaks from the watering hose, on the spot where people crouched on iron stools to pluck capons and peel broad beans. From that viewpoint you could see the Gran Carro or Plough or whatever you liked to call it, because the place where it came to rest when its work was done was in the portion of sky over the very centre of the yard. It was in that exact place, too, that March filled the afternoons with a somnolence which spread through the laborious silence of that beautifully refurbished kitchen. Even the forge – when there was still someone working there to give it life by creating unfinished gates, sections of balconies, and wings intended for chimneys and railings – still filling the space now dominated by four lemon trees in pots, proved that nothing was really as permanent as it might seem.

You could lie down under a September sky full of stars, drunk on the passionate perfume of a perfect night, and wake in a suddenly cloudy November with your nostrils still full of the same melancholy perfume. You could never trust the sky, but only your nose. You had to learn to live in harmony with the firmament, looking inside yourself for survival. Michele Angelo could not imagine that he had never known anything different from this; by unblocking access to the forge and keeping the gate to the courtyard ajar, he had given meaning to his refusal to abandon all hope as meaningless. He had concentrated his feeble surviving energies on preserving some sense in a life that otherwise risked having no sense at all. Because it was only in that context that he could claim to feel really safe.

Torture by water had been acid, terrifying and instantaneous. Just below the surface of the cold water he had for a moment lost his breath; but now, under the apparently changeless sky, he felt in control and no longer feared anything.

"Why not come for a short walk?" Marianna said at his shoulder.

She did not wait for her father to answer.

And as she had expected, he did not answer.

Ulysses Returns to His Homeland

VINCENZO SPENT THE WHOLE OF THAT MORNING WALKING. The higher he rose, the harsher the climate. Naturally, it was not a case of climbing mountains, for these were more than hills with the sheep-tracks at some points dwindling into mere clefts between rocks. Even the vegetation changed: no longer dry and crackling, but turgid and smooth, with leaves slithering silently past his body and resisting him rather than falling apart at the slightest touch. The warmer he felt, the more quickly he walked. For two hours he saw no living creature, apart from small families of partridges, chattering suspiciously and running for safety at the sound of his footsteps. He wondered at the strangeness of birds that would hurry urgently forward as if they had too much to do when in fact all they needed was to survive. And it occurred to him that, seen from above, he too must give an impression of inexplicable urgency with his rapid steps, concentrated gaze, diffidence and obsession with detail.

A series of dry noises somewhere in front of him distracted him from these wider thoughts, so he increased his speed exactly like the partridges to get off the path and see what was happening.

Half-hidden by a loop in the sheep-track, a woman was chopping at a plant. The dry blows he had heard were those of a blade hacking at the arid flesh of a very tall bush covered with yellow flowers.

Deciding to show himself, Vincenzo ventured forward cautiously as if into a room full of sleeping people. The woman seemed not even to notice him.

He was within a few paces before she heard him and finally turned. Looking her in the face, Vincenzo saw she was not as young as he first supposed.

"*Buongiorno*," he said.

"*Buongiorno*," the woman answered, put off her stride by the accent that proved him an outsider.

"You don't come from round here," she stated, trying to take refuge in the most neutral Italian she could manage.

Vincenzo nodded, thinking how often recently he had been faced with what was not so much a question as an assertion.

The woman cleaned the strange knife she had used to attack the bush by wiping it first on one hip, then on the other. She was dressed as Vincenzo imagined a local woman would be dressed, her hair hidden by a handkerchief in much the same way as the peasant women of his homeland, with whom she shared an unexplained lineage that made her familiar as well as strange in Vincenzo's eyes.

"I have to get to Nuòro," he said eventually, seeing the woman had returned to her work.

"Enula," she said inexplicably. Then repeated "enula", making it clear she was referring to the enormous plant she had just been attacking with such fury. "Nothing to be done," she went on. "This stuff ruins the honey. Nice flowers, but the bees go for it and ignore better plants, and this plant does not make good honey, it doesn't

69

hold and ferments . . . it won't do." The plant bowed as if before an acknowledged divinity. The woman gazed at it as if waiting for it to breathe its last, then seized the whole plant and hurled it with remarkable force into the middle of the sheep-track.

Vincenzo jumped out of the way to avoid being hit. The woman felt no need to excuse herself for the fact that the stranger had happened to be standing exactly between her and the area she had chosen for collecting the twigs. "Is this the right way for me to go?" he asked, preparing to move on.

The woman adjusted the handkerchief on her head and waved the knife to indicate yes.

Vincenzo watched her start on another flowering plant, then left her behind.

For another twenty minutes or so he walked gently downhill along an excavated road that grew gradually wider, its borders marked by fragrant bushes that here and there invaded the road itself. The sun, not bright enough to blind him, had placed itself at a theoretical zenith, the shade it cast shrunk to a patch of bitumen. Vincenzo judged it must be about one o'clock. Or perhaps that was what his stomach was telling him. He looked around for somewhere to sit down to eat some of the meagre food Virdis had given him, then heard the rumble of a motor from behind him. The nose of a small lorry appeared round a curve. As he dodged out of the way of the passing vehicle, he noticed the driver was the woman he had just left. She braked with a loud grinding sound. "I go as far as Lula," she said, continuing to stare ahead, serious and concentrated. Vincenzo was not quite sure if this was an invitation to get in, but the woman waited for him to go round to the passenger side and open the door. The first thing he noticed was that she had wrapped her long skirt round her thighs to keep it free of the pedals. He scarcely had time to close the door before she drove off. "I have to keep the engine running," she said as though forced to explain something though having no wish to do so. Some things are not worth discussing, such as the accursed maximum permitted speed which she was exceeding and which was forcing her to make as few stops as possible with her engine running, and so on. All in all, it was already a huge concession that, having once started her lorry, she had ever stopped at all to allow this stranger to get in. This whole unspoken discussion sat like an uncomfortable third person inside the cabin to be tossed about between the driver and her passenger. Vincenzo's instinct told him this was not a person to talk to unless she started the discussion herself, so he said nothing.

From his perch high up in the lorry the land looked gentler than it had seemed from the road. The vegetation now seemed not so much desiccated as naturally solid, in no way docile. Superficially soft, but essentially metallic and immobile. It would have been no surprise to hear it tinkle at each breath of wind. Every now and then, at the barely smooth edges of the road, small ravines seemed to froth with rowan trees. Everything was turning pewter or chalky grey. The already pale sun was now screened by sparkling mountain crests with shaggy valleys and smooth peaks.

They climbed a further six or seven hundred metres to a clearing, where a natural terrace opened to the surrounding countryside. The woman swerved rather roughly, stopped the engine, got out without a word and stretched, raising her arms and fists to the sky, like a priestess cursing some obscure divinity from a mountain top. Vincenzo waited a few minutes then got out too. From that position the earth seemed about to pass from solid to liquid with rigid karst walls from which the mountainous stretch of road they had just crossed had been excavated; a hilly zone dense with arbutus and rock rose at the foot of the hills, an undulant plain with occasional orchards and a village. And further away, the sea.

They stood in silence. The woman seemed constantly about to speak, but each time appeared to change her mind. When she finally did open her mouth it was to ask him if he was in a hurry.

Vincenzo looked at her with surprise. "No," he said. "No hurry."

The woman seemed to approve. "I always stop here. In any case, the rest of the way is downhill so we'll be able to do it in neutral." Vincenzo ventured a smile and the woman realised he had not understood. "Do you drive?" she asked with her usual impersonal frankness.

"No," Vincenzo said.

"Then there's no point me wasting time telling you what 'neutral' means," she said, returning to her contemplation of the countryside below.

"Well," Vincenzo ventured, "usually when people don't know things they have them explained . . ."

"That's true, too," the woman agreed, pointing at the lorry. "But do you know anything about engines at all? I can tell you this is a 1924 model, a Fiat 505, and that it can deliver up to 30 horsepower, does that mean anything to you?"

This time it was Vincenzo's turn to accept what she said, if only up to a point: "But I'm someone who likes to learn."

The woman wasn't listening. She went to the lorry where she had some wooden boxes stored with jars. She picked one up. "Good honey," she announced. "We have to eat, don't we?"

They divided what they had, he providing stale bread and cheese, she honey and water. In order to be able to eat more comfortably, she had knotted her handkerchief behind her neck to keep it off her face. She could not have been much older than thirty. Her hands were dirty with oil, like those of a mechanic or someone who worked with motors. She had been left alone, she told him, in an empty house in the middle of the countryside, with a neglected vineyard, twenty beehives and a lorry. Her husband had been sent somewhere in Russia in the summer of 1941. And Russia, she had learned, was an unspeakable place. His last letter had reached her in November 1942 from the Don Front. The Don was a huge river in spite of its short name – did you know that?

Vincenzo listened without saying anything because he was not sure it was really to him the woman was speaking.

So she had had to manage as best she could with what she already knew and learn everything else. Driving the lorry, for example, and carrying the honey as far as Lula to sell or exchange it; and she had to do men's work because when there are no men left it's up to the women to make ends meet. Anyway, she had no children, and if children had come, her husband Antonino had been taken away too soon to have been able to be of much help with them. Taking a leather wallet from her pocket, she pulled out a small photograph and for the first time turned directly to Vincenzo. "Here," she said, holding out the photo to him, as if they had been childhood friends. It seemed as if, lacking anyone better, she had decided to make the best of this person whom fate had happened to throw in her way.

Vincenzo wiped his hand clean on his jacket before delicately taking the photograph. It showed a young boy, his hair glossy with brilliantine. He had that dreamy quality that comes to good people not yet burdened by responsibility. Vincenzo tried to imagine the world that might have faced that youth at that moment when his image was stamped on film. Perhaps he had been with the girl he was going to marry, or his mother who had bought him the neat shirt he was wearing open over his jacket collar in the American style. The atmosphere was what you might expect in the city studio of an overworked photographer.

The boy's face, caught by surprise, seemed to imagine a simple future; there was nothing complex in his pose, and even less in his expression. He was simply, transparently, Antonino. As uncomplicated as the design of a funnel spout, or the illustration of a bee in a children's A.B.C. book.

Antonino's ordinariness had the perfection of any unknown soldier, perhaps now lost in a shell-hole, buried under unimaginable quantities of snow, or fallen while being forced to march in light shoes on feet swollen with frostbite. In Russia it was always winter, a place where terrible things happened to soldiers who never returned. A place where, they said, even the weather made war, with eternal ice and a merciless incessant cold wind. Where voracious women snared our men in tents, after digging them out moribund from the snowdrifts that edged tracks trodden by platoons and battalions, to imprison them for ever in warm little pockets of paradise.

Truly terrible times, with human beings reduced to slaughter-house meat in places with unimaginable names.

Only a few days before, during the crossing to Sardinia, Vincenzo had heard terrible stories of the martyrdom of Stalingrad. No-one on board the ferry knew quite where the city was. Even with a map before them they would not have been able to point to it; they only knew it was in Russia, and that was enough.

The fact of its being in Russia defined it exactly enough; every-one knew it was in Russia and had something to do with Stalin, the Man with the Big Moustache, and with the butchery of the universe. Sons were said to have grown so numb in the eternal ice of that winter of humanity that they ate their dead fathers. And girls had given birth to children spawned in horror, half-human half-beast. And soldiers had been known to save the last precious bullet for themselves. In any case, none of these people would have caused the Man with the Big Moustache to lose much sleep. In a world whipped by winds which, they said, could sweep away anything that might come between them and whatever unknown place they might be trying to reach, and refusing to go at all always the ultimate possibility. Ah, such stories! With the sea shouldering the ship's keel, they had seemed nothing more than whisperings from the poor souls being tossed about on board. And at the very centre, the place where they needed to arrive, the festering origin of those ferocious days when the devil in person, in shining helmet and boots, had found himself faced with a full array of saints in bare feet and torn clothes, poor soldiers on both sides in the war, frozen stiff as they ate excrement and drank urine. As if in the antechamber to a nightmare, or the unmitigated nightmare itself. Those who told the story always told less than they knew; behind the facts, behind the terrible suffering of the people they talked about, something beyond all telling remained concealed.

In this infinite plot in which one thing relentlessly recalled another, Vincenzo wrapped things unsaid in a cloak of sleep, including memories not directly connected with his own wretched life, like the time when Jewish children began to disappear from the orphanage, or when soldiers who had lost their uniforms were trying to hide in cellars, and when people began to test the endurance of their bodies beyond reason, as if their souls had suddenly fled to goodness knows where. As they neared Sardinia, between waking and sleeping as the movement of the ship gradually grew calmer, Vincenzo told himself that for every major story from that abdication of humanity, thousands of lesser tales could be derived, like fragments of a curse. He himself could have spoken about slaughter in places where names and languages had changed. Where he came from, for example, a cradle made from the quality wood of what had once been an Empire and had now disintegrated into Chaos, its language spent in an uncertainty of meaning. How can you tell that story, eh? How could he tell his own little story of one single worm on this Earth? About his father having been a soldier, a hero, and his mother dying young and, perhaps, who could know, the place where he might find previously unknown relatives. He was twenty-seven years old now, and had lived twelve years in an orphanage and then seven in a seminary . . .

Suddenly Vincenzo realised the woman was waving her hand to have her photograph back. He returned it hurriedly, as if caught doing something wrong. She seemed sorry now that she had lost control of herself, and resumed chewing in silence. Not a good idea to share personal matters with strangers.

"So you want to get to Núoro," she said in an offhand way, as if to lighten the silence. Vincenzo swallowed and nodded. "At Lula, you'll be nearly there. From here it's about forty kilometres, perhaps a little more. I don't often go there myself."

An elderly shepherd passed by, guiding a few thin grey sheep. His greeting seemed only for the woman, who answered with a toss of the head. "In fact, I have little need to go there; why should I?" she continued when the shepherd had gone. Then she leaped to her feet, shaking handfuls of crumbs from her dress. "Where do you come from?" she asked unexpectedly.

"Friuli," Vincenzo answered with a touch of anxiety.

The woman looked puzzled. "Is that in the north of Italy?"

"Yes, in the North," Vincenzo said.

"But you need to get to Núoro," the woman said, as though to confirm that the stranger with whom she had just shared her food knew absolutely nothing.

"Nuòro, yes. I have relatives there. . . name of Chironi."

"Chironi," the woman repeated as if to herself. "Which Chironi?"

Vincenzo shook his head helplessly. "My father's father is a blacksmith."

The woman's face lit up. "Ah, Chironi, those people! Michele Angelo Chironi, the master smith! I've met him, he did some jobs once for my husband." The faint trace of a smile appeared on her face. "Ask him if he remembers: say Antonino Podda and his wife Giovanna – that's me. People from Janna Murai, say that and ask if he remembers us." She said the last words as if anxious to establish her place in the story.

"I'll tell him," Vincenzo said, intending not to.

It was developing into a heavy afternoon. As they freewheeled downhill Vincenzo understood without a shadow of doubt what travelling "in neutral" meant. Partly because the lorry gave the impression of being out of control as it gathered speed, and partly because Giovanna Podda explained the phenomenon from a psychiatric point of view. While the outside world slithered past, she explained that "going in neutral" was travelling without rules: "Like when a horse takes over, you understand? Like when it goes completely mad – but don't worry," she added, noticing Vincenzo growing increasingly tense. "In neutral means you don't switch on the engine, just free the wheels and leave the rest to the slope. That way you save fuel. Then to stop, you either turn uphill or switch on the engine. Got it?"

Increasing speed turned the rocks, bushes, shrubs and trees rushing past the windscreen into a mere flash. Vincenzo pushed himself back in his seat and braced his feet against the coachwork. The woman was amused. "Not suffering from travel sickness, I hope?" she asked, seeing her passenger go pale. Vincenzo had no idea whether what he was suffering from was travel sickness or not; he had had so few chances in his life to ride in a motor vehicle. Perhaps if he'd been called up it might have been different, because in the army you learn more than you need for war, and if you come out alive you could even have learned a trade. But he, Vincenzo Chironi, had never been called up, because his father had been a decorated war hero.

Hurled about, in spite of his attempt to anchor himself by clinging to the dashboard, Vincenzo tried to hide his rising panic, until the gravel on the road surface made the lorry vibrate almost to breaking point. The woman did not seem unduly worried, her voice cracking as the vehicle bounced.

When she unexpectedly swerved up into a side road, the lorry slowed and came to rest with its nose in a natural lay-by and its back perpendicular to the roadway. Vincenzo got out at once. The woman followed and asked if he was alright. A huge valley lay close in front of them, like a green polychrome basin at the foot of the steel mountain behind them. It was now a spring-like October day, the countryside looking as if it had never heard of the agony of the world; the only visible sign of humanity a bright white shrine.

"San Francesco di Lula," the woman said. "We'll find someone here to take you to Núoro."

A man in early middle age was packing crockery and glasses on the back seat of a car parked between the church and the nearby lodgings for pilgrims. Several women of various ages were helping him, on their faces the contented but melancholy expressions of people after a party when everything must be cleared away.

Giovanna Podda went up to the little group who hurried to greet her. She gestured towards her lorry with the honey for Lula and pointed at Vincenzo; the women turned as one to stare at him as though at a rarity, and indeed there were few young males with them.

Giovanna Podda spoke sharply and confidentially to the man and he responded with a shrug.

When she broke away from the group and rejoined him,

Vincenzo felt the priest Virdis' prophecy about Suffering already coming true. The woman explained a feast in honour of the saint had just ended, and that the prior's family were cleaning up ready to prepare for the next celebration in May. The man was loading up things that had to be returned to Núoro, after which he would come back to fetch the older women, while the rest would travel in Podda's lorry. Vincenzo was too busy, apparently overcome by a sensation of ingurgitating phlegm, to listen. It was just as Virdis had said. They would now entrust him to this small plump unknown man, and the new day would introduce him to yet another stranger. Yet again he would have to get used to a present with no definite future, like everything else around him, like life itself, which seen from this point had even begun to seem to be verging on the liveable, even if likely to consist mainly of women, children and old people. When Giovanna Podda held out her hand to say goodbye, Vincenzo's lips trembled with emotion: another parting, another fragment of life slipping past, as if his urgent need to survive was constantly forcing him to try to reassess himself.

But it was, perhaps, the very fact that he had reached the country he was aiming for that had caused this melancholy that required each new experience to be abandoned as soon as it occurred. This was perhaps what Virdis had been trying to say, having himself just lost the living creature dearest to him: "You have reached a land where everything is ancient, where taking and leaving can require thousands of years," this was what he had been trying to say. "Pain is precise, but happiness is vague and dreamy. Because the one is an armed warrior, and the other a young girl."

He thanked Antonino's infertile widow Giovanna Podda, and climbed into the car.

*

The man at the wheel, whose Italian had clearly been learned at school, explained it was not a long road but an awkward one, because they had to start by going down into the valley, then climb again to reach Núoro, involving six or seven kilometres of hairpin bends. After that he stopped talking.

Seen from the car, the countryside began to loom over them again, even if the hilly slopes they were crossing were unusually bare.

"Beautiful countryside," Vincenzo observed as they began to climb. The oak saplings were becoming denser, almost a forest.

"She says you don't come from round here," the man said, perhaps feeling he should make conversation. Vincenzo closed his eyes. "Beautiful but too quiet," the driver added unexpectedly. Vincenzo turned to look at him." There used to be lots of sheep and you'd hear cowbells, but now there's nothing, nothing at all. With this war there's no-one left. No shepherds, no men to do the work.

Vincenzo nearly answered back, but if he did not do so it was mainly not to risk causing further disconnection.

They remained silent a little longer, then without taking his eyes off the sharp curves racing past them, the man asked: "But where exactly are you from?"

Vincenzo took a while to answer. Beyond the windscreen an area of high shaded country was beginning to take shape. He waited till the car had passed a section mostly concealed by roadside trees. "Friuli," he said.

The man gave a nod as though he had understood, and asked, "And where are you staying exactly?"

The hint of a smile crossed Vincenzo's face, but he just said, "Very far away."

This answer seemed to satisfy the driver, who shook his head vigorously. From his point of view "very far away" must have seemed an extremely precise explanation.

As the car climbed and swerved round hairpin bends among holm-oaks, that very far-off land suddenly seemed near. When Vincenzo could not help sighing, the man looked at him and said, "Should I stop?"

Vincenzo nodded. The car moved forward another few metres, enough to reach a small clearing right at the apex of a curve.

They got out. Vincenzo excused himself, but the man shrugged as if to say he had no reason to apologise. He explained it was not far to Núoro now, but the last bit could be difficult for anyone who suffered from car sickness. Vincenzo spread his arms as if to dismiss this, but could not explain the real reason for his sudden disquiet. It was as if he had been too slow to meet a punch in the stomach. "Friuli . . ." he continued with no apparent connection. "You must have heard of it, you sent so many men there. You must know where it is!"

The man grasped Vincenzo's tone, between resentful and desperate. "They sent us there," he answered sharply. "No-one wanted to go. We had no choice."

Vincenzo interrupted: "I meant no offence." But the man seemed in no way offended, just surprised, as if Vincenzo's "very far away" had been evidence of a sudden tenseness in his passenger, something he was ready to accept. So, controlling any hostility he might have expressed in different circumstances, he rummaged in the car for a bottle of red wine.

They drank two or three draughts straight from the bottle. It was a very dense, heavy wine, but it had the desired effect.

"Guiso Giovannimaria," said the driver, introducing himself and offering his bottle for the third time.

"Chironi . . . Vincenzo," Vincenzo said, accepting it.

The man indicated that made sense, and held out his hand. "Call me Mimmíu," he said, passing straight from the formal "*lei*" to the informal "*tu*".

The afternoon continued grey but clear, as if everything were entirely under control apart from the sky, which at that altitude was tending to lose colour.

Exactly where they were heading was a mystery. Mimmíu seemed to read his mind: "You don't see it till the last moment," he explained turning the wheel without restarting the engine. "It's a place that lurks round the corner like a thief. After several kilometres without knowing when you'll get there, it's suddenly in front of you after the last curve. Not far now, anyway. Giovanna Podda told me to leave you at Sa' e Manca, which is the cemetery. It's no distance from there to the blacksmith's house, all you need do is go straight on as far as the Rosario church . . . but keep straight on, that's the important thing, then you'll see the place in front of you, a high wall with a wooden gate. Can we go on now?"

Vincenzo agreed and knocked back his last mouthful of wine.

The hairpin bends ended at a place with the wonderful name of Valverde, or "Green Valley", and to Vincenzo no name, no matter how apparently banal, had ever seemed more fitting.

The first person who claimed to have recognised him was Palmira Serra, who had known all the blacksmith's children. It was all rather scary. As she was coming out of the cemetery, who did she see in the street? Luigi Ippolito Chironi, no less! God strike her dead if it wasn't him. So tall and handsome, looking lost as if he couldn't even remember where he lived. The women she told this to thought Palmira must have gone mad, because how could Luigi Ippolito Chironi, who had died in 1917 in the War, the First War, have come back on his own two feet and even younger than when he left? That was impossible, of course she must be wrong. But there she was insisting, she couldn't possibly have been wrong. Deaf? Well, she was a bit deaf, but there was nothing wrong with her eyes, despite her age.

While everyone was teasing her, the object of their mockery walked past, looking lost and unsure of himself. It certainly was Luigi Ippolito, back like Lazarus from the dead, his face as pale as ever. A young boy, preserved from the worms of decay, and utterly unchanged, but for the dark patches under his eyes.

Even the sceptical ones had to cover their mouths not to swear. "It is him," they nodded. "It really is him."

Vincenzo walked past this knot of flabbergasted women without noticing their surprise, as he was desperate not to forget the instructions of Mimmíu, who claimed to have left him just outside the blacksmith's house, as Giovanna Podda had asked him to.

His entry to the town, directly from the open countryside, seemed to suggest there had to be some clear demarcation between man and nature. The road he had been following so far was like a caesura dividing gardens from the odd vineyard. Further off, to his right, a wall isolated the new cemetery on a hill. After that the vegetation shrank from nothing to small gardens and an occasional livestock enclosure, with cobblestones beginning to appear in the street if not emerging from the earth itself like cochineal insects on an infected branch. Here the sides of the street were lined with the first (or last) houses, white and close together, their roofs made to measure and without shutters, buried in layers of moss that followed the regular undulation of the tiles, round their tiny doors and windows. The smell everywhere was of manure and soot. He knew he had to follow this uphill stretch to the end and then move straight on to where the houses crowded even more closely together. In fact, further off still, he could see more dwellings higher up, the tops of trees visible above their compact walls. For plaster, they had made do with quicklime thrown over naked stone.

Still ignoring the women staring at him, Vincenzo walked on without turning until he found himself in front of an open space near the back of the church which must have been the one the driver had called the church of the Rosario. There was a cul-de-sac that was really not a street at all, more a recess in the wall surrounding a very large courtyard. At the end of this recess, a gate led into the courtyard, and the house beyond the courtyard had to be the one he was looking for.

*

As always, Michele Angelo had left the gate to the courtyard half open. Here too, the autumn was like summer. Vincenzo was disturbed by a subtle anger, as though a strong silk thread was being tightened round his neck.

Before going back into the house Michele Angelo shook his head at the lemon trees obstructing the workshop. He always did this to chase away regrets and to avoid admitting to himself that he had not made the most of the happiness that had come his way. Nothing very much admittedly, but there had been enough.

"Then you leave the gate open as usual, and I have to go and close it," Marianna grumbled, seeing him come back into the house.

"I didn't forget," Michele Angelo answered. And that was all he said.

"You never forget to open it. But closing it, I have to remember," she said, letting her shawl slip from her head as she prepared to go out.

Discussions on this subject always ended in the same way. Marianna knew perfectly well that for the last seven years, her father had deliberately half-opened the courtyard gate every afternoon, and she also knew well that the reason he did so was to make it possible for anyone who had gone out to come back in; Gavino perhaps, or even Luigi Ippolito. Or Mercede. Back from the world of the dead.

Rather than involve herself in an absurd discussion, Marianna never said a word, but waited until her father had gone to bed before going out to shut the gate herself.

So time passed in the Chironi kitchen, like a pale imitation of a life that had once existed. The survivors, father and daughter, were paralysed in a fixed purgatory of repeated gestures.

They were never afraid to discuss the dead, talking of those who, each in turn, had left this Earth for a place that must be better in every way. Sometimes they talked of the outside world beyond the courtyard and even beyond the sea where another war was still thundering. News apparently aping History and grimacing at destiny.

Vincenzo hesitated a long time in front of the gate. Now that he had found what he was looking for, he had no idea what to do next. He was prey to conflicting thoughts. What if whoever was living in the house did not recognise him? Or took him for a criminal? Or a liar? They would be right, he reflected, stepping back. But I have my documents, he remembered, immediately moving forward again. Luckily he could not be seen from inside the gate, since anyone watching him going backwards and forwards might think he had gone mad. Indeed he felt mad, exhausted and mad, as if he had gone on pilgrimage in the hope of a miracle only to realise that miracles come solely to those who believe in them.

The feeble evening light contrasted with the storm it contained. Vincenzo looked up at where the clouds were lining up, barely perceptible but ready to dissolve in an instant, and was shaken by a resentful nervousness exacerbated by irritation with himself and his own indecisiveness. So while the cords grew tighter across the sky and threatened to snap, he decided to walk to the gate and lift his hand to knock.

But at that moment he heard footsteps from inside the courtyard and only just flattened himself in time against the outside wall before the gate was slammed once, then again, just as though someone from inside the house had realised he was there and about to knock.

Then silence.

He stayed motionless, getting his breath back, until the last strand of cloud above him dissolved; then tested his own capacity to continue standing without leaning against the wall.

Eventually he decided to go back the way he had come and make for the countryside, now looking for absence rather than presence as he crept along the lanes.

It was not difficult to reach an area sheltered by trees and far enough away to make even the modest public lighting in that area as yet scarcely visited by modernity seem significant. Nevertheless the night still appeared to him so ancient as to be immodest, full of obscenely naked stars in an absolute virginity of space restricted to the voices of prehistoric animals and the fruit of extinct plants. But he was too tired now to worry about his failure. Hungry too, but no hungrier than he had been so often in recent years. He looked for somewhere to spend the night in a dark abyss of unconsciousness, under that sky that seemed to vibrate with an unstable and febrile quivering, as if the stars were so precariously suspended as to be about to throw themselves down on him.

He spread his jacket on the cold and dry though soft and mossy ground, and stretched out on top of it.

He woke suddenly, though it only took him a moment to realise where he was. Getting to his feet was more difficult, like the very first man on earth when he understood he had two legs to stand on but no experience of balance. He staggered, as if he had woken in a room on an unfamiliar bed. The night had disappeared and the stars gone to reveal themselves elsewhere. He gave his jacket a good beating before putting it on, and this calmed him. He felt serene for no particular reason, and just as previously he had feared the worst, he now convinced himself he had nothing to worry about at all.

Retracing his steps to his father's home, he again found the gate ajar. Doing his best to keep silent, he pushed it and entered the courtyard.

It was as if time had stopped. The silence within had an indisputable certainty, as if even the sap in the crowded plants had decided to percolate silently, and the insects to fly without motion and hum and buzz without sound. This silence reassured him. It seemed right that this house, the home of his family, should be silent. Four lemon trees in enormous terracotta pots blocked the entrance to a building that filled the courtyard to the right, while every other available space seemed crammed with bright, luxuriant, motionless vegetation. Threading his way through this forest he found a French window leading to what looked like a large kitchen.

And knocked.

Hearing the knock, Michele Angelo started, and turned to tell his daughter, without saying a word, not to stand there as though rooted to the spot, but to go and see who had come in.

But Marianna was not there. She had gone on an errand. The knocking came again, louder this time.

Michele Angelo reached for the rifle he kept hanging beside the fireplace; a rifle no-one had fired or even cleaned for many years. Then, gun in hand, he went to the door.

Through the glass he could see a man in a torn jacket, trousers too wide for him and baggy at the knees, and a shirt that had once been white.

But nothing can be white anymore in these dreadful times of change, Michele Angelo reflected.

"The gate was open," the man said.

Michele Angelo needed only an instant to understand. He lowered the rifle and opened the door.

When Marianna came home she saw her father sitting at the table with someone who had his back to the door. She immediately caught the eye of the old man who seemed to be finding it difficult to attract her attention to the miracle that had only just appeared to him in flesh and blood. But her uncertainty lasted barely a moment, because when she walked half round the table and looked the stranger in the face she instantly understood the wonder Michele Angelo had not been able to express.

Words from Puccini's opera "Suor Angelica" came to her mind: "How painful it is to hear the dead mourn and weep!" For her brother, Luigi Ippolito, killed in the war and buried under the war memorial at the cemetery, had come back to life and was sitting at her table, in her kitchen. She struggled not to cry out because no words could have conveyed what she was feeling.

They were hunter and prey, the old man and the stranger. Hound and game. But the prey watched the hunter as though knowing him well. Facing one another, wrapped in each other's gaze, with only the table between them. Motionless, bloodhound and mouflon sheep, rifle and deer.

Despite the gun, the prey had not fled but had advanced to face the hunter and, as in a fairy tale, had been the first to speak.

Telling how he had been the child, born at seven months, of a Sardinian officer who had met and fallen in love with a Friulian peasant girl. And how he had grown up in an orphanage.

His soft voice was full of strange sounds. But though his words sounded so different, the movement of his lips was familiar.

Marianna watched his lips, riveted by their perfect similarity to those of his father.

Michele Angelo could hear himself in everything. He would have thought, if it had not been pride to think so, that History was beginning again. He too had been snatched from an orphanage before he could live.

The man must certainly have a lot to say, but he was content for the moment to describe how after walking for many days he had boarded a ship at Livorno, bound for Terranova or Olbia or whatever the place was called. To the old man he seemed younger than he looked, a tall, lanky youngster with a clear skin and concentrated gaze. He had towered over his fellow-travellers, poor families with few possessions, struggling for the benches, including soldiers with no identifying insignia or shoes, and children supervised by nuns and Red Cross workers. As he well knew, everyone who reached Sardinia that day had left a terrible inferno behind them. The last terrible rites of a war that had re-created the Apocalypse on earth.

This lonely man, who had fled devastation, told how he had promised his mother in his heart that if she died he would seek out his father's family while she, for her part, had promised him that if he did find them, he would not suffer from cold and hunger.

Which was why the first thing he had done on disembarking had been to go to the port immigration office to ask how to get to Nuòro, where, he believed, what was left of his father's family still lived.

He showed Michele Angelo his documents just as he had shown them to the port official, identifying himself as: Chironi Vincenzo, son of Chironi Luigi Ippolito and Sut Erminia of Cordenons, born February 15, 1916, paternity confirmed at the Plesnicar Notary Office, Gorizia, May 6, 1916.

Michele Angelo smiled and wiped his eyes. "Vincenzo, Vincenzo Chironi . . . Chironi," he repeated.

Part Two
(1946–56)

The mind is its own place, and in itself
can make a Heaven of Hell, a Hell of Heaven.
JOHN MILTON, *Paradise Lost*
(Book 1)

The Visible World

MICHELE ANGELO SPENT THE WHOLE OF THAT FIRST YEAR going around and showing off this newly discovered Chironi. Marianna went out more often, reverting to blouses and skirts she had not worn since the days when, as a *commendatoressa*, she had still officially counted for something. That is, before her husband, Commendatore Biagio Serra-Pintus, had been killed during an attempted kidnapping. She had been identified as a serious Fascist, but this had been seen as entirely excusable. Then with the war over, all those who could, needed to forget. In any case she had never taken any notice of what people said about her, and now she wanted to compensate this close relative for any privation he had suffered.

Once the initial excitement of the arrival of this new Chironi had passed, first at home and then throughout the entire district, peace finally seemed to have settled in, even to the extent that Marianna began pretending to complain about it. To Michele Angelo those days when there really had been something to complain about seemed blessed.

Happiness now assumed the limited dimensions of those who, presented with a colossal victory, have no wish to humiliate their opponents.

Because the return home of this unsuspected grandson and

nephew, a stranger and long unknown, meant that everything, absolutely everything, could start again. People even began whispering that the blacksmith would soon reopen his forge and that the business would pass on to this young man from the mainland, who was said to have had some education. As for his resemblance to a father who had died in the war, this had to be taken as indisputable proof of his identity, something that could not be ignored and as such, a credit to the modesty with which the survivors of the family had accepted the slings and arrows of fortune.

Vincenzo quickly got used to his aunt's adoring gaze. And the disbelief that made his grandfather touch him or brush against him every time he passed close.

Father and daughter began discussing the fact that she was treating a full-grown man like a child and that he was still finding it difficult to accept that his grandson existed at all. Occasionally, feeling guilty, he would revert to stirring the cauldron of the past by claiming that this new opportunity, this life now reborn in their home, must simply be yet another joke of fate, promising more suffering rather than joy.

From Michele Angelo's point of view, the purgatory he had shared with his daughter up to then had been no blessing. Rather a stagnation, a somnolence or torpor from which it seemed impossible to wake.

That he should feel this distrust was understandable. Less understandable for Marianna for whom the arrival of Vincenzo was a rebirth and a prize. Water to revive a desiccated root and sugar to sweeten a great bitterness.

*

After barely two years of looking at each other and sizing each other up like hunter and prey, there could be no doubt of the existence of love, though at times it seemed more like distrust. Vincenzo found it hard to accept that this place where fate had brought him was his home. He told himself he had never really belonged anywhere, except the institute where he had spent most of his life.

Michele Angelo understood this, and knew how to interpret it. He himself, at the age of nine, had been rescued from an orphanage, and found himself in the house of Giuseppe Mundula – the man who brought him up and trained him to be a blacksmith – in the same way that Vincenzo now found himself here. But it could not be the same for Marianna. She lived as women do on this earth, never wavering when faced with love. And it was abundantly clear that Marianna was in love with her nephew.

Sometimes the power of the bond she felt for this grown man, this boy, this child, frightened her. Occasionally she was able to understand the nuances that had tied her to his father, her brother. So she talked to him about this as often as she could. Sitting at the table she remembered the day when her "mamma", the grandmother Vincenzo had never known and who today would have been so happy to know him, the day when they had gone with his father Luigi Ippolito, then younger than Vincenzo was now, to see him off to the war front in the post bus, in his smart new uniform and with the anxious concentration of someone about to embark on something at the same time wonderful and terrible. She had not yet been fifteen years old then. But she could remember everything, absolutely everything: the particular light of that morning, the smell of petrol, the determined yet also hesitant expression on her brother's face . . . I don't know if this boy can understand that . . . And Vincenzo seemed to show that yes, he could understand. After all it was only a few months after that, not even a year, before he was himself conceived . . . And Marianna's voice broke as she reached the point where she had to describe how they said goodbye and Luigi Ippolito, resplendent in his new uniform, told her to be sure to look after the old people, speaking with that firm sweetness he had, a sort of distracted concentration, that seemed simultaneously attentive and absent-minded. Because Vincenzo's father had been educated, so he knew things could exist in more than one place at the same time, not like ignorant people who cannot understand divided attention. No, Luigi Ippolito had still been there at that moment, but it was as if he had already gone. And then he spoke in that strange voice, which was his own but at the same time someone else's voice too. Do you understand? Vincenzo nods and smiles. Marianna is excited, the look on his face is just how his father looked: then and on other occasions. At this moment and in this light, he would only have to glance in the mirror to see Luigi Ippolito. Oh, how can she not consider it a blessing, this opportunity life is offering her? Vincenzo gets up obediently and goes to the French window to study his reflection, but sees nothing he doesn't expect. He has put on a kilo or two since he came, but nothing more than that; like a succulent plant finally getting enough water.

Beyond the windows, the little forest in the courtyard has grown more dense because now it is late spring and everything is flowering, growing while you watch. Seen from there nature seems over-exuberant, unwilling to accept moderation: writhing jasmine violent in its smell; the hydrangeas Marianna keeps in the shade but which overflow their designated space, and the miniature meadow of aspidistras, their enormous blooms nothing if not the flower of flowers; all this together with invading passionflower hedges that will produce oval fruit, and those flesh-like flowers that seem to bear within them the instruments of Christ's martyrdom. Did you know that? Vincenzo shakes his head. Marianna runs into the courtyard along paths only she can see to pick one of these flowers which she brings to the attention of her prince. You see? Look, the hammer and nails used on the Cross. And those intense blue hairs are celestial rays to welcome the blessed to Paradise. So much in a single flower, can you believe it? Just think how perfect nature is, replicating herself in everything in such immense and constant variation from such small beginnings. Yes, yes, that's the fact of the matter. Vincenzo knows it well, himself from a place no less sober than magniloquent. He has certainly understood from the first that concentration is the key to this place that has now accepted him. Concentration in the sense that what starts small can suddenly grow exponentially and visibly. He can imagine birds of paradise, hummingbirds flying among the foliage in the courtyard, and dwarf monkeys resting among the branches of the plum-tree or the laurel; mambas slithering over the beaten earth and vicuña llamas climbing the surrounding wall. That would be entirely logical. Anything could happen in a space so limited yet at the same time so immense. Not to mention the processions of ants climbing the trunk of the quince tree as evidence that, at the top, honey-producing parasites were nesting among the new sprouts. Thus these marching armies, heading for honey produced by invaders, are evidence beyond any possible doubt that the tree which appears so luxuriant is, in fact, a victim of disease, just like in the world beyond the courtyard. This is something Vincenzo can understand. He has studied and he understands. Like the swarms of bats swirling at dusk in dark circles, a sign that the buzzing delirium has not quietened down while the outside world is racked by the terrible wounds inflicted by Anopheles mosquitoes and Dociostaurus locusts. The senseless human war has fizzled out from sheer weariness, but its ramifications are still obstinately being fought over: neglected fields, abandoned livestock, and ravening insects. Millions upon millions of mosquitoes have infested the coastal districts with malarial fevers that have been raging for years and reached chronic proportions; not only that but now, driven by hot winds from Africa, locusts have arrived in clouds compact enough to cut out the sun.

Now, standing before Marianna, Vincenzo embodies what she has invisibly nurtured beneath the ashes for years. He is proof, here and now, that she did well to fight on for so long. Never surrendering when carnage was raging on all sides. There were so many things she could have told this nephew: her own life story that had made her a high-profile Fascist in people's eyes, for example. She could also have tried to explain how frenzied events in the world around her had presented her with two options: "take it or leave it". She could have tried to tell him how she had been led to marry a man she did not love, about the miracle of giving birth to her daughter, and the horror of seeing that daughter shot dead in her arms.

As it was, he had already heard the story from Mimmíu. Thanks to him, and to his certified lineage and exotic background, Vincenzo had been accepted as a member of the community in Núoro.

Occasionally he had imagined this must involve a club so exclusive that he must think himself exceptionally fortunate to have been admitted to it. Yet it had also been Mimmíu who had told him his aunt was a "top Fascist" and why she was respected nonetheless.

This happened by chance, in a bar, when a youth barely out of adolescence had walked past them.

"That's Nicola Serra-Pintus; he's almost related to you."

Vincenzo had looked at Mimmíu with curiosity and a certain amount of trepidation at this unexpected news. "Almost related to me?" he repeated. Mimmíu shrugged and refilled his drink. "His uncle married your aunt," he said. "They were an important family but short of money, they had spent everything, have they never told you?" Vincenzo shook his head. "A pragmatic marriage between people with status and people with money. Because your folks are really well off. Have they never told you that?" Vincenzo stuck out his lower lip. "Anyway, the man was well in with the Fascists," Mimmíu went on. "They appointed him *podestà* of Ozieri, except that he never got there." At this point he interrupted himself. "I have to go," he said. "Have to be up early tomorrow morning because they're looking for people at the Agricultural Inspectorate to help with the battle against the locusts, haven't you heard about this?"

Vincenzo had heard.

Marianna shuddered at the thought of her garden being taken over by locusts. Vincenzo noticed. "You had a daughter," he said. Marianna answered with her head, hoping he would notice in the glass of the French window. "She would have been twenty years old now," she whispered.

The silence grew heavier, as if aunt and nephew were frozen in some kind of submerged conversation. A paralysis broken only when they had to move to let Michele Angelo slip past them on his way into the house.

He had been in the workshop. A good many months had passed and he was mulling over the idea that even there life might begin again. Yet he went there alone for fear someone might guess something of the sort and see it as a challenge. So, in silence, since Vincenzo and Marianna seemed to have plenty to discuss in the kitchen, Michele Angelo decided to look round the workshop. Pushing past the lemon plants to get to the space between their pots at the entrance, he had put the keys in the lock and waited, paralysed in that absurd position for a long time before finally opening the door.

First he noticed the smell. His ageing sight seemed to fail him until his lungs had fully absorbed the dry, pungent odour of iron. An instantaneous image of furnaces and sweat came to him, of sounds of ringing, frizzling and blowing, then cold and hot together, ice and incandescence, blackness and light, softness and hardness.

At that moment, Michele Angelo wanted everything except to see. Because he knew when his sight finally returned, no further escape would be possible. In fact his sight did suddenly return and what he feared did start moving towards reality: a ferociously painful need for that particular solitude, silence and stagnation. Dust had subtly misted the tools, as if it too wanted to help soften that terrible vision of what had once been force but was now inert, spent power, formerly alive but now conclusively dead.

Michele Angelo sat down, realising why, during all this time, he had never found the right moment to speak to his nephew about his idea of reopening the forge. He had always known it, but the idea had become reality in this way, too painful to contemplate.

Gavino's gloves were still in the place where he had left them on the rack.

They never had much to say about that other uncle, Gavino, who in the photographs looked fairer and more strongly built than Vincenzo's father. In fact, they said as little as possible about him. Yes, of course, Vincenzo knew he had died at sea on the way to Australia, an open and still bleeding wound. He had never been at the front, but had fought his own war nonetheless, that was what they said at home, and it had to be enough.

Those abandoned gloves had once protected Gavino's hands, which had been strong and beautiful; now drowned in the far northern sea off Scotland, so it was said. Those gloves were the only proof that this wonderful man had ever trodden the earth at all. A grieving spirit, restless and kindly. Strong, but at the same time sensitive. Michele Angelo remembered when Gavino had taken his mother to see the sea. Yes, that had been Gavino's idea.

It had been a few days before Luigi Ippolito left for the front. Gavino had said that at all costs he must take his mother to the sea. Just like that, "at all costs". Luigi Ippolito had arranged it in the way he had, with that look of his that was at the same time half-present and half-absent, and had agreed, yes, they must take their mother to the sea. Mercede had protested violently to begin with: no, what a lot of trouble, to go all that way for no good reason. But that evening, when they got home again, her face had changed. How she loved her sons that day – and it really was love.

Michele Angelo sat down on the stool facing the forge, the stool on which he had so often sat waiting for the iron to heat from orange to white.

Only his sense of hearing was still unsatisfied now in that workshop full of unnatural silence, the unnatural silence of something greater than mere physical space. He suddenly felt a tear without being able to do anything to stop it, but he was not exactly weeping. It was more a realisation that what had been invisible had found light again. Like a secret discovering its voice.

So he wiped his cheek with the back of his hand, gave a last look around to assure himself that nothing, absolutely nothing, had moved, then stood up and walked towards the door. The time was not yet right, he decided, so he must wait a little longer before speaking about the workshop, a little longer.

On his way back into the house he noticed Vincenzo and Marianna standing in front of the French window in the kitchen.

"Where have you been?" Marianna asked, as if feeling she should know.

"Out," the old man said.

"But you've been sitting somewhere," his daughter said, "your trousers are all dirty."

Michele Angelo did not answer, but ran his hand over his backside to brush the workshop dust off.

Both fell silent. It was Vincenzo who spoke first.

"Tomorrow morning, if that's alright, I thought I'd go to the Agrarian Inspectorate, they need people to fight the locusts."

Marianna immediately protested he had no need to do that

sort of work. Thank God, he could take his time, no-one was putting any pressure on him.

Michele Angelo, like God bringing Adam to life, raised a finger to interrupt her. "What time will you need to be woken?" he asked, and said nothing more.

Mimmíu and Vincenzo formed part of the same team, which also included Nicola Serra-Pintus. The area assigned to this team was defined by the letter D, and ran from the Pratobello valley to the plain of Ottana. An in-land region, containing both hills and plains. You were not aware of any desolation at first, you had to look closely to see it. From a distance the land seemed golden and fertile, a newly harvested field of grain caressed by a gentle breeze. But what had seemed to be newly harvested ears of corn turned out to be swarms of locusts teeming as far as the eye could see in a single vibrating monochrome. The earth was chirping loud enough to deafen; all you could do was listen, blending the sound to the terrifying sight. Such enormous numbers were heaped up together, that they could not avoid being squashed beneath the workers' boots. People had described this, but it was something else altogether to experience the fever of an earth completely submerged under the dry squeak of carapaces crushed at every step. It reminded you that each individual was an extremely fragile crisp crackling insect, the distinguishing feature being their sheer numbers, as innumerable in that relatively restricted space as stars in the sky, if not infinitely more. You did not need to be an expert to tell the difference between the so-called cross-shaped locust that went for cereals, and the Moroccan locust that preferred orchards and vines. And to judge by the dominant gold colour there were also some of the Levantine variety, which scarcely needed to fly at all, because delivered already pregnant all round the Mediterranean by ships from the vast fields of Africa, a plague in the form of a noxious cream-like cloud, deposited by the wind on any land emerging from the sea. The plagues in the Bible must have been like this, never intended to meet humanity until humans themselves helped spread them.

The Agricultural Inspectorate made the most of each person's individual abilities or qualifications in its teams. Mimmíu, with his driving licence, was allotted a lorry adorned with the words "War on Locusts". While Vincenzo was allowed to join the same lorry from which, carrying a shovel and wearing rubber gloves, his job was to spread bran and one per-cent sodium arsenic to which the locusts seemed to be especially partial. Ahead of their lorry, the plain had already been surveyed by explorers and team leaders, who placed huge quantities of as yet unopened capsules in the fissures of dry walls and even inside prehistoric nuraghic ruins. This was a clearly defined process: first seed-layers spread the poisonous mixture, then *piroforisti* or incinerators turned flame-throwers on the dead and dying insect bodies, then cleaners swept up the mess, and finally specialists laid a smoke-screen. All to make sure no larvae could survive.

Vincenzo shared his first day in the lorry with a youth from Mamoiada who at each dose of bran and arsenic cried, "*Manicàe*", followed by "*Crepàe*", which he repeated thousands of times, with a separate exclamation for each shovelful. The boy hated this work, and would have preferred flame-throwing; he kept insisting that for him nothing in the world was more disgusting than the locusts, nothing at all. Perhaps for this reason, the next day he was replaced in Vincenzo's lorry by Nicola Serra-Pintus.

Nicola Serra-Pintus was small and well-built, one of those people who always look diffident no matter whom they are talking to. "We are almost relatives," Serra-Pintus said for no apparent reason while they were working. Vincenzo decided this remark must have been addressed to him, since no-one else was present. "You're that foreigner, aren't you?" Serra-Pintus went on before Vincenzo could think of an answer. Again, the youth had spoken as if anxious to blame him, though this time he waited for an answer.

"Yes," Vincenzo said. "I'm the foreigner."

Nicola nodded as though to compliment himself on his brilliant intuition. "Then we're almost related," he concluded, returning to his work.

They went on for a while in silence, then, deciding to introduce himself more formally, Vincenzo struggled out of his heavy rubber glove before wiping his hand and holding it out to his semi-relative.

The other did the same. "Nicola," he said, shaking Vincenzo's hand. "My uncle Biagio was married to your aunt."

"Yes," Vincenzo confirmed.

"An ugly story," Nicola said, taking care not to be on the wrong side of the wind as he threw the poisonous mixture onto the ground. Vincenzo said nothing, but Nicola misinterpreted his silence. "No," the other said. "I didn't mean it was an ugly story that your aunt and my uncle were married, I meant all the rest. The attempted robbery, and the way my uncle and his daughter were killed."

"We never refer to it at home," Vincenzo said, hoping to change the subject.

"Yours has been an unfortunate family, certainly very well-off but unfortunate," Nicola remarked, apparently unaware of Vincenzo's increasing unease.

Luckily Mimmíu knocked from inside the front cabin as a signal that they were about to make a stop.

They washed their hands despite the fact that they had been wearing gloves and tucked into bread, cheese and wine. The wine was warm, having been stowed under the vacant passenger seat. They ate in silence on an immense carpet of hundreds of thousands of locusts. That evening Vincenzo returned home exhausted. Marianna prepared him a bath-tub full of steaming hot water, before moving away to let him undress.

When he had washed and dried himself, he joined his aunt and grandfather in the kitchen. They waited to hear about his day, dumbfounded at the news that the situation was getting so desperate that they were having to hurry to deal with the larvae rather than just concentrating on the flying insects. He told them the front was now only six or seven kilometres from their home. And that the area of the crossroads to Mamoiada was a disaster, just a desert of bare earth.

Thinking of her plants, Marianna looked through the window at the courtyard, while Vincenzo tried to reassure her by telling her in detail how the infestation was being dealt with by teams working from north to south. This puzzled her. Michele Angelo explained that from north to south meant that the disinfestation had started in the areas nearest the main town and would then move towards the Campidano district. This did not reassure her, because someone had told her that there had already been small invasions of insects at Marréri. Vincenzo, with his new authority as a disinfector, claimed isolated spots could easily be controlled. Michele Angelo confirmed this and said no-one would be so cruel as to threaten her plants. Marianna sighed and filled a bowl with wholesome soup for her menfolk.

Nothing visible could frighten Marianna. What she feared was what she could not see, imponderable things. Now that life had given her a second chance, she had no intention of letting the opportunity to make an impression of some kind pass her by. Everyone knew the sort of life she had lived and what her public, though not her private, tragedies had been. Widowed in an instant, and then what? What could you call a mother who had lost her little girl? A reverse orphan? Or is there no word for it, because there is nothing natural, nothing acceptable, in a world where parents outlive their children. No vocabulary anywhere would have a term for this. Only something from the subterranean world of monsters – we all know that well enough but have to pretend we don't, purely out of an instinct for self-preservation. We pretend such things cannot exist, when the fact is that they do.

For instance: in what corner of our hidden hell did they invent a locust invasion? It occurs in the Bible, which proves such things really can happen. Someone thought up that particular scourge, like the toads, the plague, the war, and the premature death of eldest sons. Disobedience exacts punishment; Marianna needed to make sense of a pattern that had stripped everything from her and now she had to some extent make up for it with the arrival of this unexpected nephew, this substitute for a son. So when Michele Angelo criticised her by saying she was making too much of the boy – he always called Vincenzo "the boy" – she would say he wasn't a boy and she would never, never relinquish her fair reward after having suffered so much. She said she would always stay up waiting for him if he was late, and would turn the whole of Núoro and its suburbs upside down if he ever asked for anything that she could not find, she said she would treat him like a husband but, she told herself, only as a legitimate way of possessing him, of making him unable to detach himself from her since she would be the only person to give him everything, absolutely everything, without ever expecting anything in return. That was how she should have treated the husband she had supported against her will. She knew now how much that particular failure had cost her, all the worse for it having been voluntary and deliberate in every respect. She said this but at the same time denied it. But it was clear to Michele Angelo how much she had forced herself to live in silence with the ghosts of her unhappy life.

"Eventually he's bound to go," he told her at a certain point with reference to Vincenzo, but she refused to listen. Her thoughts turned again to Suor Angelica and how in the opera her aunt the Princess goes to the convent to tell Angelica that her younger sister can marry now and that this will finally restore their family's honour, but the aunt fails to inform Angelica that her own, illegitimate, child has now been dead two years. Marianna never hated anyone in the world more than this aristocratic aunt who had taken away her own niece's child, banishing the mother to a convent and then rejoicing in the fact that the product of this sin had died a premature death. Marianna cannot bear the story because, in effect, the involuntary nun is forced to live in the real world while her hypocritical aunt is not. "He will need to live his own life," Michele Angelo said, referring to Vincenzo.

"His life is here. Don't ruin everything now! This is where he belongs."

"His life will be wherever it takes him."

"No, that sort of talk will drive him away."

"You're the one who'll drive him out if you cling to him like this."

"No-one has ever clung to him . . ."

"This is not good, Marià! Why do you never listen to other people?"

"I have no reason to listen."

"Though the fact is you must listen."

"No. I must go and water the plants, the wind is drying the earth . . ."

And that was all.

The story of flame-throwing through Ottana, house by house, hencoop by hencoop and church by church, took up most of supper. Vincenzo enthusiastically reported how useless it had been trying to stop the villagers continuing to beat the walls of their houses with dry twigs. He described how an inferno of locusts covered the buildings like a swarm of bees. But with the arrival of the flame-throwers, shining warriors of the faith entered to repel the forces of evil. Those lads with their fuel tanks on their shoulders had been heroic. Most of them too young to have been called up for the war, but at least they now had a chance with weapons on their shoulders against a winged enemy.

The flames licked the houses with immediately effective incandescent tongues. The crackling and whistling of the insects as they burst at the touch of fire was an extraordinary sound, with a scent like the crust of toasted bread. Charred locusts fell in heaps on the yards and pavements of Ottana. Black and shiny as cockroaches, reduced to firebrands and often not quite dead, they writhed in dark mounds until the local women swept them into heaps that could grow a couple of metres high.

Vincenzo loved reaching the point where he could describe these immense heaps waiting to be set on fire for a second time until they were nothing but volatile dust.

Then he rose to his feet and lifted his hand above his own height of one-metre-eighty to make clear that even the smallest of these heaps must have been at least twenty centimetres higher than he was. Marianna covered her mouth, her usual way of expressing astonishment, while Michele Angelo shook his head and smiled, cheerfully warning his grandson: "If you go on like that she won't be able to sleep tonight."

A few minutes later, Vincenzo is getting ready to go out. It is already dark outside. Marianna looks at him as she expects an explanation. Vincenzo does not understand or does not want to understand. Michele Angelo watches them tussle but does not intervene. He would like to be able to talk about some real work for his grandson, a real future. Particularly his idea of reopening the forge. The boy is strong and would learn quickly. But he is held back by the realisation that Vincenzo has never seemed to want anything. There is something about him the old man cannot understand. Perhaps it is a mainland streak, some mystery inherited from his mother's side. Michele Angelo is pondering this when Vincenzo gets up and says he is going out.

Marianna waits until he is on the threshold before asking why on earth he wants to go out at such a late hour. At this point Michele Angelo decides that he must intervene, telling her like a child to be quiet and mind her own business, because the boy is old enough to decide for himself.

This skirmish discourages Vincenzo; "It's not absolutely necessary," he says, and prepares to go back to his place and sit down again, adding, "Tomorrow's a rest day, so we thought we'd all get together."

"Yes, of course," Michele Angelo says approvingly. "Off you go and let her say what she likes." Then he looks his daughter straight in the eye: "Does anyone ask questions when you go out?"

When Marianna goes out, it's always to go to the other house, the one in via Deffenu. She keeps it clean, even though no-one has lived there for more than ten years. Its placid silence makes it seem as if its occupants can only have been away a very short time. She goes in like a professional cleaning woman, as though the house, both the private and public home of a *podestà*, had never contained anything personal to herself. This is far from the truth. Everything has been preserved from time immemorial to ensure it is never forgotten because oblivion, for Marianna, would mean the destruction of a part of her life that still has meaning for her.

She cleans meticulously, even ferociously, as if dust has the power to obliterate anything not kept bright and clean. Her reward is to be able to remember how everything was. The consolation of being able to prevent any person or object coming between two different parts of herself. So, time after time, she cleans each room and each corner of each room and every object in it, including the large hall with its central table and two oriental-style vases that gives access to the studio of her late husband, Commendator Serra-Pintus, with its three chairs of local design and acceptable quality where those who wanted to see him would wait. Then there was the so-called "bay", a blank area full of closed doors, leading on the right to kitchen and dining-room, straight on to bathroom and laundry, and on the left to the bedrooms.

The great size of the apartment was a consolation, a clearly defined space, big enough for people to get lost in. The only room she did not love was the studio because, she told herself, it represented the dull vacuity of the man she had married. And perhaps, she regularly told herself as she dusted the otherwise untouched volumes in the walnut bookcase behind his formal desk, all this clarity, this false transparency, this careful brightness and cleanliness, was nothing more than a way to punish herself for not having been strong enough to refuse to marry him.

The room of Dina, her little girl, still carried a barely perceptible hint of milk and talcum powder. Before she started doing anything in that room she had to sit down. It was always the same because in that room she needed to breathe differently, and sitting down enabled her to adjust her lungs to the airlessness that characterised it. When her breathing achieved the right rhythm, she would get up and begin to dust the pale chest of drawers that contained the wonderful white clothes her little girl had worn. They had not been discoloured by time, simply because time was never allowed anywhere near that room.

In fact, they had never lived long in that house. But its obvious reality had made it impossible for her to pretend that nothing much had happened there. The reality was that a lot had happened. Though in what had been her child's room she was conscious of a sort of supplementary desperation, a sort of withdrawal of consolation, as if every time she went into it she had to review the extent of her capacity for repression. But she did not allow this to force her to do anything superficially; on the contrary, in that room she was capable of spending hours dusting dolls, cleaning the curtains, changing the bedclothes, beating the little carpet, adjusting slippers, refolding a nightdress or staring at where a few child's hairs were still stuck among the bristles of a brush, or catching a glimpse of herself out of the corner of her eye reflected in a window or mirror as she mercilessly swallowed her anguish and, at the same time, exalted in playing the potential executioner to the extent of denying that world the refuge of falling into oblivion.

We all cherish our own particular ghosts and evoke them in different ways. As memories, sometimes. We may dismiss them as fleeting thoughts, or accept them as things that recur in the mind unexpectedly, with the mind having done nothing to retrieve them. Thieves, perhaps, that invade us, breaking through the locked doors of our control. So far from encouraging control, Marianna had left all these doors wide open.

Her only real regret was that she had no ability to dream about her child, and sometimes could not even remember what she had looked like. Nor could she remember much about the night when the child and her father had both been killed. Though she could still remember wandering about the countryside before finding herself in a police station. That was all. She also remembered a dry sound, and the car being sucked down while their chauffeur had tried to push past whatever obstacle had been blocking their way. And the only tender look she ever had from her husband. That was all.

"Doesn't anyone ever ask you anything when you go out?"

Vincenzo looked at Marianna as if absorbing from her all the anxiety his natural mother had never been able to give him. "Who are you going to see at this hour?" she persisted, perfectly understanding the game they were playing.

"The team," he answered. "An hour at the most, just long enough for a chat." Then he added, "Nicola Serra-Pintus," as if slamming an ace on the table during a game of briscola.

Marianna did not flinch, but Vincenzo had learned that in her such stillness was always particularly expressive. An appearance of calm that concealed nerves. "Oh, yes, Nicolino, how is he?" she asked, staring through her nephew with a fixed expression. "I haven't seen him for years, not since he was five or six."

Vincenzo made no response to this. He just added, "Mimmíu Guiso will be there too."

Marianna no longer seemed fully in control of herself, as if trying to hold back tears, though in fact she was only trying to remember which precise day Nicola Serra-Pintus, third son of her husband's brother, had actually come into the world. Was it a few days before or a few days after her own child? They would have been about the same age now. "Go on, then, go . . ." she suddenly said. "But don't be late back."

"No," Vincenzo said, adding, "But don't wait up for me," though he knew there was no point in saying this.

As soon as the boy had gone out, father and daughter started arguing. They usually kept their words firmly under lock and key, but once they decided to unlock the prison cell, they talked and talked.

Michele Angelo was certainly not ready to limit himself to the part of an old man being looked after by his daughter, and Marianna was even less drawn to being the sort of daughter who nursed an elderly father. So what did they discuss? What subjects caused disagreement? They agreed on everything, surely: on the fact that their grandson and nephew must be left to live his own life, that no-one was in a position to make decisions for him because he was not an underage child, and that both father and daughter had much lost time to make up for. They agreed about that. The point could only be themselves. Michele Angelo had suffered enough hardship while Marianna had no idea what hardship her father could be talking about. To her what had happened to them now was an unexpected gift, some sort of last chance. He saw this as yet another obstacle cleverly put in his way by fate. Because, he told himself, once you had worked out how to come to terms with your own existence you could not suddenly change your beliefs and alter all your perspectives. To him, existence is like a load of bread or fruit he must bring home down a dusty road. A long way ahead he can see a small house with a roof and chimney-pot, which always produces smoke at all times of year; in stories and parables there are no changing seasons. He is walking barefoot through the dust, but the house which had seemed so near seems to get further off with every step, and his load heavier . . . His responsibility for delivering the load is the only thing that drives him on. If he were free to choose he would not be going to that house at all. If he had nothing to carry, no responsibility, he would be free and easy. But free to go where and to do what? Along the road there are people to meet, areas of shade, hollows, small troughs and crystal fountains. He often needs to stop, think out problems and avoid falling, and indeed he is always free to stop for a rest and free himself for a while from his burden, refreshing himself at a fountain or exchanging a few words with a passer-by.

As Michele Angelo sees it, this newly discovered grandson has in no way altered his perspectives, but has rather been a reason for him to continue further along the road, with no particular hurry to reach his destination. Because he also understands clearly that if he ever does reach that house he will never walk again. Surely that must be obvious?

But no sooner has he finished explaining this than he regrets it because for him such talking in metaphors can only have a limited meaning. For him things were simply things, they had always been like that and always would be, amen. It got on Marianna's nerves when her father interrupted himself in this way; she would have even liked to shout at him if she had not been unwilling to let herself go more than strictly necessary. Some boundaries could not be crossed in quarrels between father and daughter, as if quarrelling was only alright so long as done with due respect. Michele Angelo himself repeatedly risked crossing that boundary and destroying it because he was the one with a knife in his hand, while if his daughter flew off the handle she could always be silenced with the formula: "I am your father, little girl, don't you dare talk to me like that. I created you and I could squash you too! Understand?"

As for all this talk, it reminded Marianna of a story she had heard earlier in the war during the air raids on Cagliari. It was about a man who had a comfortably off but not seriously wealthy uncle, who owned the little house he was living in. The nephew wanted to get married and longed for his uncle to die so he could inherit this modest house. So began flattering the old man as much as possible in the hope that his uncle would want to leave him the house. But it soon became clear that the old man was as fit as a fiddle and not in the least likely to die any time soon, so it would obviously be a long time before what the nephew longed for was likely to happen. So, the times being so topsy-turvy, the nephew decided he might as well give nature a helping hand and poison his old uncle, so this is what he did. The old man's funeral needed to be brief as an air raid was imminent: a "pater noster" and a "requiescat" would have to suffice. But at least the young man was able to move into the house instantly, since his uncle had obligingly gone to the notary a few months before to make sure that his house, modest though it was, should be left to his loving nephew in his will, and even before his uncle's coffin was in the ground, this disinterested young man was already calculating how much he could get on the black market for the few bits and bobs his uncle had left in the house, as well as getting to work without delay on starting the large family he had planned to have there with the woman he loved. Well, it so happened that this particular house was the first in Cagliari to be hit in the next air raid. The same raid also destroyed a part of the cemetery near the house. And what do you think they found in the rubble? Uncle and nephew locked in each other's arms in death. One had been killed in the house and the other hurled back out of the cemetery into his old home. Incredible, don't you think?

Marianna is trembling, but Michele Angelo opens his arms and says, "My dear girl, what on earth can I say about a story like that?"

He is not angry, just surprised, because Marianna's mind amazes him, astonishes him and confuses him.

"It means that even if you tell yourself things are certain to go in a particular way, they may end up quite differently."

"Ah," the old man says. "An explanation even worse than the story itself. So what?"

"So if you imagine the arrival of your grandson won't change anything, you're wrong, because things will change."

Michele Angelo's defeat at this point is more like a capitulation, because he well knows that much the best thing would be to leave her story at that, pretending to understand what his daughter is driving at, but he cannot do this. So he goes on insisting, "so?"

"So, telling yourself that certain things haven't happened doesn't mean that it's impossible for them to happen."

"Well, why don't we leave the story at that, then?"

"That's typical of you."

"What's typical of me?"

"You're always like that when you're in the wrong."

"What do you mean by like that?"

"Doing what you're doing now."

"Either I'm going to bed or I'll have to kill you. Or no, I won't kill you, who knows, you could come back home to me from the cemetery!"

Even Marianna had to laugh. "Have you shut the courtyard gate?" she asked.

Michele Angelo did not even bother to answer.

At the Bar Nuovo, the only subject for discussion is the imminent referendum. And the degree of apprehension with which they discuss it depends on their perception of how important it is to them. Clearly the nation will not be the same afterwards. Vincenzo limits himself to watching and listening. Recent history seen from that bar was like a fierce argument between mother and daughter: with one side not wanting to abandon the certainties of the past because – terrible though that recent past had been – some were beginning to claim it was not right to condemn the Fascist experience as entirely negative, while others thought it would be better to try something else, in other words, a complete change. Vincenzo realised his own view was influenced by what he had lived through himself. Monarchy and Republic were much more than simple programmes for the future, they were the fruit of direct experience, whether private or public. He asked himself how many of these youngsters arguing so hotly for one side or the other, had any precise vision of the future ahead of them. A vision or an image. The war Vincenzo had seen had not been the same as that experienced by most of those now presenting their views. They might at most have seen reserve officers in the Cremona Battalion. But was not this going to be a fundamental change, an opportunity for everyone to say freely what he thought? Vincenzo began to realise he was a man, an adult in a land of adolescents, at least six years older than most of those around him. And perhaps he could express this difference by explaining the war as he had seen it.

It seemed to him that whatever of the world around them had reached the district, it was no more than a mere outline, a historical footnote. And if someone reminded them that the priest at Mass had advised that they should vote for the king, meaning the young king who had just come to the throne, well, that too seemed just a gentle nudge from History. The Monarchy, others said, was merely a system, the actual work being done by men. But in the end even the house of Savoia had to admit to having made rather too many mistakes, and the new king, young and promising though he was and a great contrast with his predecessor the timid dwarf his father, the young king had even agreed to accept the will of the people. Someone argued if he had only waited a little longer, there would have been no more people left for him to appeal to, though the idea of extending the vote to women was not a bad idea, not a bad idea at all. The priests were telling everyone they should vote on the yellow voting forms bearing the Cross of Christ, and certainly not on those that showed the profile of a woman. Or on the grey forms, which had a different symbol with a cross.

Marianna did not bother with discussions. "How should we vote?" she asked her nephew, as if it were entirely logical to establish some sort of common strategy. As she saw it, families should always act together.

Vincenzo laughed. "What do you mean?" he asked. "Surely you know how to vote? Your vote is secret."

Marianna shook her head: "Yes," she said obstinately. "Outside this kitchen it is secret." She looked round the room, as if searching for a system of thinking that had little to do with the case in question apart from the central idea that they were a family that lived together. "How are *you* going to vote?" she asked point-blank.

Vincenzo had no idea whether she was being serious or not but Marianna held his gaze to show she was being serious. "Republic," he said after a pause.

"I knew it." There was no particular inflection in her voice. "That's what I expected. You have your father's face and the head of your uncle Gavino, God save us."

"Is that so awful?" Vincenzo said, somehow beginning to be amused.

"Neither awful nor good," Marianna said, refusing to get involved in a discussion that threatened to shift away from the level on which she had started it.

"And you'll vote Monarchy, won't you?"

Marianna, folding clean clothes on the kitchen table, suddenly stopped what she was doing. "Why should I?" she said, staring at Vincenzo with tremendous tenacity.

Her nephew struggled to hold her gaze for as long as he could. "Because you will," he said after a long pause. Marianna continued to stare at him. "Because you were married to a *podestà*," he ventured.

"I was, but what of that?"

"Then it's possible . . ."

". . . what?"

"Let's leave it at that," Vincenzo said with a determination that restored a certain distance between him and his aunt. After all, he told himself, what right has she to treat me as though she has known me all my life? What does she know about me? What do any of them know about me?

Marianna understood these silent questions. I have always known you, my dear, she told herself. I knew you even when I had no idea you existed. "What time do we have to go to vote?" she said.

As could be expected, the most difficult member of the family to persuade to leave the house was Michele Angelo. That morning in June, he told himself that History had randomly swept through Núoro not as a mere echo, but as the "right that the men and women of this town have been called upon to exercise", as the future Member of Parliament Santino Carta put it to them from a makeshift platform in Piazzetta del Popolo. In church, from the pulpit, the priests took a different view. What worried them was that women were being allowed to "exercise a vote". It is well known that priests have a genetic understanding of the very essence of problems, having had more than a thousand years of such experience. The main thing for them was to explain during the Mass that this right granted to women at a civil level, did not change them in any way at a confessional level. Luckily, in Rome, the Vatican had had the happy idea of appropriating the cross that symbolised the Monarchy, to double as the symbol of the Christian Party, so all one had to do was continue to trust in the cross.

Michele Angelo's problem was different; he had convinced himself that allowing himself to be seen in public would encourage people to discuss him, and this was the one thing he could not stand.

He only agreed to go to vote at all because it was Vincenzo who asked him, and because aunt and nephew had agreed on going to the polling station so early that people would not yet have had time to come out of Mass.

And that was how it went: they exercised their right to welcome the rebirth of the nation. Washed from head to toe and wearing their best clothes, the Chironi family went off together to vote at six-thirty in the morning.

Núoro was extraordinarily quiet at that hour, the still air promising a hot day. They walked down towards Piazza d'Italia, part of the way beside a long handrail Michele Angelo had never seen before, any more than he had seen the petrol pump now at the top of what was a rise or a descent, according to whether you approached it from San Pietro or from the Dispensary. He convinced himself that this horror was inevitable if life needed to go forward in spite of everything. There were also newly built houses whose balconies were decorated with iron railings that had not been made by him. And he had certainly not been responsible for the handrail, all hundred and fifty metres of it, on the Orune side of the plateau. No, this was clearly a factory product, forged without love.

Thus, fit though tired after his unaccustomed walk, Michele Angelo leaned on his grandson for support rather than touch the ugly municipal handrail, with its joints visibly welded as if never intended to be permanent. The new times were also clear in many other small examples of negligence. Of course, as people were always claiming, everything still remained to be done. They walked in silence through this open-air construction site, which was the very earth they were treading. Where were the market-gardens that used to be a feature of the valley? And the orchard of Bainzu Pes? They were clearly planning to hide the countryside behind a bank as though ashamed of being so close to it, and this must mean a definite movement towards reclassifying the town as a city. From Michele Angelo's point of view, this was the difference. He could not imagine a history of evolution and stratification; for him "modern" simply meant something that could survive in spite of everything. Yet he was not a conservative person, he had the brain of a craftsman, and his invariable rule was if something didn't work, scrap it and start again, rather than struggling to adjust it or fix what was broken. This district, as he saw it, was something that had turned out badly and that someone was trying to fix. So he could not accept expressions like "everything still remains to be done", because though it conveyed an illusion of progress, deep down what it revealed was a fundamental fault in manufacture. It claimed that you could go ahead and remake things without being properly aware of what it was about them that had been unsatisfactory in the first place. Marianna understood at once what was making her father so angry, Vincenzo did so a bit less readily, though he too understood something of his grandfather's dissatisfaction from the way he was looking about himself. But no-one said anything or asked questions.

The term "reconstruction" was never used in Núoro, except when it came to abolishing extreme poverty. A poverty sometimes misunderstood and so not really poverty. The condition of the town's outskirts had preserved them from the bombs, but also from destitution: they had been treated as if nothing had happened around them, and so had remained as poverty-stricken as they had been before. Not more than before, though, which was in itself a notable result, paradoxically regarded as development. However, this relative unconsciousness contributed to speculation, since denying reality sometimes involves imagining wild alternatives. Fundamentally, Núoro was a village determined not to remain a village that had no idea how to become a city; it had been home to a presumptuous bourgeoisie and intelligent shepherds, after which the world had been turned upside down and history with a small h had briefly crossed the main road and created a little incipient Sardinian Athens – projected onto the world stage by a Nobel Prize winner and rebranded arbitrarily by the Fascists as a city. It was still inert with reason put on hold everywhere, like a knick-knack that had survived in the rubble of a collapsed building – this was what was now trying to become normal. As if suspended uncomfortably in middle years, neither ancient nor modern, but sensitive and vulnerable to contagion, it was in this suspended territory that a meaning needed to be found and a perspective needed to be imagined.

This, if he had known the words for it, was what Michele Angelo would have said during his walk to the polling station. But he merely commented on the strange flaming red apparatus with pipes and pumps disturbing his view of the ridges of Orune. Marianna just shook her head as if she did not know that one's sight has its own inalienable rights, but in fact she knew this perfectly well.

No-one celebrated the victory of the Republic, not least because it was so unexpected, since everyone had assumed the Monarchy would win. Rumours spread of tricks by Palmiro Togliatti, who was hand in glove with the Russians, and of a volte-face by Alcide de Gasperi, who though claiming to be a Catholic, was behaving like a Republican – as though these two things must necessarily be in conflict. And in fact they were for many people, since from their point of view it was like believing a priest could take a wife, or that a Communist would be seen in church every Sunday. At the crossroads and in the taverns, political nuances simply become coarse opposites, especially for anyone who still has faith in politics. Mimmíu Guiso, for example, was a convinced Christian Democrat, in the sense that to him the term simply meant what it stated, involving both Christian and Democratic principles. Both difficult in practice, but not to be despised for that reason. As for Vincenzo, you could not classify him as a Communist or a Christian Democrat either, but having been educated in a seminary, he did know what being a believer meant. So contradictions of this sort were the most logical way of expressing things he had not been allowed to articulate for at least twenty years.

Vincenzo, Mimmíu and others were discussing this and other things outside the Bar Nuovo when, from the end of the lane, Nicola Serra-Pintus appeared and joined them with a girl on his arm.

But do you understand who you were before?

Me? Before when?

Before everything, at the very beginning.

What are you doing over there? Come to bed.

Mercede, standing in the most shadowed corner of the room, refuses. All Michele Angelo can see of her is her white nightdress and the tip of her left foot. He knows well that when his wife behaves like this there's no point in arguing, so all he does is change his position in bed. Usually this is enough to send him back into a deep sleep, but not this time.

First you were a Godless animal, and before that a plant, and even earlier just a thought.

Why are you still over there? Come to bed, it's late, how is it possible you are still awake?

Before being a thought you were Nothing, merely a wonderful nothing. Can you remember being nothing? Of course not, because that's the state of grace . . .

Michele Angelo turns the other way, and making a kind of tidal wave of sheet presents his shoulders to the corner of the room away from the glare of the moon as it crosses the half-open window towards the wall facing the bed.

. . . and before you even deserved to be nothing, you could

have been an animal or a tree, hunted down or burned. Or stone or a lifeless rock, Mercede goes on, refusing to acknowledge her husband's distress. With you I always have to explain everything.

That's enough now, Michele Angelo whispers into the emptiness of the room. Either finish saying what you have to say or shut up.

For a very long moment a light, rhythmic sigh reaches him from the shadowed corner of the room. Michele Angelo sits up in bed and glances at the alarm clock on the bedside table: not yet two o'clock. Hearing a soft knock he rapidly turns to the door and calls "Yes?" confused between waking and sleeping.

Vincenzo comes in in his underclothes. "Alright?" he asks. "I heard voices, I was thinking . . ."

"I'm fine," his grandfather interrupts, leaning back against the bedhead. "At my age you can wake for no good reason and not manage to get to sleep again."

"Not only at your age," Vincenzo says with a disarming smile.

Michele Angelo gives him a long silent look. Vincenzo lets him look. There is no shadow of anxiety in the silence, in fact it says everything. The old man shakes his head.

"What's the matter?" Vincenzo asks, slightly awkward.

"Nothing, nothing," Michele Angelo says. "I was just thinking how like your father you are, but you're like your uncle too . . ."

"Yes, I've heard that before."

"Why are you not asleep? When I was your age, gunfire couldn't wake me. Your grandmother used to say it was more like death than sleep."

"I don't know," Vincenzo says.

"Nonsense, of course you do," the old man says, making room

for the boy to sit on the bed. This degree of intimacy disturbs Michele Angelo more than he would have expected. Deep down it involves reverting to long-dormant senses, dormant for too long. Moreover, when he feels the pressure of Vincenzo's body on the mattress, he realises for the first time that he is alive, and is even moved to tears. Mercede reaches a hand from her shadowed corner. Vincenzo turns abruptly, trying to follow his grandfather's gaze but sees nothing. Yet Michele Angelo can still hear the love of his life still persistently whispering: "But you do know who you were before?" and can hear himself, now finally confident, answering: "A father," he tells her, "I would always have been a father even as a tree or stone, I would always have been a father, my love."

Vincenzo, not understanding whatever may be happening to his grandfather, waits patiently for this vision to fade.

Michele Angelo is aware of Vincenzo sitting next to this unexpected vision, poised between himself and the answer he has just given. The old man smiles with the corners of his lips like a child caught behaving badly. "When a boy of your age can't sleep there must be a woman in it somewhere."

A laugh bursts from Vincenzo. "Yes," he says.

"How do you mean, yes?"

"What you've just said."

"A woman?"

"Yes."

But not just any woman.

It had happened a few weeks earlier. Just after the referendum. There had been other occasions too, but these no longer mattered to Vincenzo. But now he had broached the subject, all he wanted was to talk about the woman who was preventing him from sleeping. It was an instinct that might push him to do unbelievable things, and this scared him. A mutual instinct, he was sure of that, he knew it from the way she had looked at him.

Michele Angelo was well aware of what the boy was talking about. And he also understood that Mercede's presence in the room, where the two men were talking in low voices so as not to disturb Marianna, was a sort of permission for her to listen without them having to worry about her presence. "A father," Michele Angelo repeated to himself while Vincenzo searched for words. Vincenzo's words concerned a creature so beautiful she had taken his breath away, perfect in every respect, in her smile, in her movements . . . Michele Angelo listened without interrupting, there was something marvellous in the immense tenderness of this man or boy, repeating so exactly what so many before him had said of the woman they were falling in love with. It was as if this feeling so specific to him had never before been known to the rest of the human race. But Vincenzo seemed unaware of the sheer normality of what to him was remarkable. If he had been able to see his grandmother Mercede the time she looked up in the church to watch his grandfather Michele Angelo adjusting the great thurible three metres above the floor, he would have understood the force of the obstinacy, the repetition, the compulsion that traps us all. And likewise, the extraordinary blindness that can make every possible alternative meaningless.

Vincenzo recounted how the girl in question, though only seventeen, was a fully developed woman. Then he interrupted himself for fear his grandfather would misunderstand him. But if there was one thing Michele Angelo could not misunderstand, it was what he was now hearing. Certainly the girl was young, but not necessarily too young, and women grow up faster than men. Yes, yes, Vincenzo confirmed, just to see her, you could not imagine she was only seventeen, nor would you if you listened to her, she always knew just what to say and when. This was something else Michele Angelo knew only too well. So much so that he could have described to Vincenzo their wedding night, and how his grandmother Mercede had had to show him exactly where to go and what to do, but he preferred to keep that to himself.

Vincenzo did not know how it happened. He really did not know. The girl had arrived in the company of another man, and there they were outside the Bar Nuovo, doing the usual things one does there, you know how Mimmíu is, impossible to be bored when he's around. In a word, they were all there when she arrived arm-in-arm with Nicola Serra-Pintus. He had brilliantine on his hair and introduced her to everyone. "Cecilia Devoto." She had said her name and looked Vincenzo straight in the eye. The irises of her eyes showed clearly how impossible it is for ordinary humans to understand the wonder of nature. Vincenzo had no words to describe the colour of those eyes, grey yes, but more than grey: a blink and they were green, and another change of light could turn them purple. And who knew what she might be thinking, because while he was struggling to understand the abyss he was aware of having fallen into, she asked him if he wasn't the "foreigner" as though she had been curious to meet him for some time. This is what she does, Vincenzo explained, she can say things she is not actually saying. Michele Angelo accepted that as if it was not entirely unfamiliar to him.

"Cecilia Devoto." The old man repeated.

"Do you know her?"

"No, but I've heard people mention the family, they haven't been here long."

"That's true," Vincenzo said enthusiastically. "Evacuated from Cagliari, and they've settled here. But . . ."

"But what?"

"It's possible she might be committed," Vincenzo blurted out all at once.

To Michele Angelo this was a strange way of putting things, but he was only too well aware of the implication. His face darkened. "She might be engaged, you mean."

Vincenzo looked at him; he did not know what to say, all he knew was how the girl had looked at him. "No . . ." he said, as if talking to himself. "But she . . ."

Michele Angelo put his index finger to his lips to cut him short. "Don't say any more," he warned. "But the other man is Nicola?" he asked point-blank.

"Nicola Serra-Pintus." Vincenzo completed the name in a single breath.

"God forbid that your aunt should hear about this. I don't mean for your sake, but for his." Both laughed softly so as not to be overheard.

In the long silence that followed, it became clear to Vincenzo that it was time for him to go. He started to get to his feet, but Michele Angelo stopped him. "There's something I've been meaning to say to you for some time . . ." he began, then halted. Vincenzo waited.

Finally he went on in a very serious voice: "That closed forge," he said as if the forge had nothing to do with him, almost as if the idea had never before occurred to him, though his tone was that of someone repeating an old argument.

Vincenzo stood up: "I don't know."

"No need to answer immediately," his grandfather said, anticipating what his grandson might say.

"Yes," Vincenzo said. "Thank you." And he moved towards the door.

Michele Angelo was genuinely astonished. "Thank you? No . . . How do you mean, thank you?"

Vincenzo reached the door: "Let's try and get some sleep," he said. Michele Angelo saw Mercede wince in her corner of the shadowy room.

But Vincenzo had not altogether disappeared into the corridor when he unexpectedly turned, stopping in the doorway as if he had walked into an invisible wall, before retreating back into his grandfather's room. "But where does Aunt Marianna go every afternoon?" he asked from where he was standing, as if he had been turning that very question over in his mind for a long time and that it had been the main reason he had disturbed the old man in the first place.

"She goes to the other house," Michele Angelo said. "You know the story, don't you?"

"A bit."

"Don't be afraid to ask, you're part of the family, you need to know things." And before Vincenzo could say anything more, the old man jumped to his feet. "Wait," he whispered. "Wait a moment." He went to the chest of drawers and took out a folder, stroking it with his hand before he handed it to his grandson. Your father wrote this, he was educated, you understand, and he wrote down here where we came from . . . because we must all have started somewhere, as you know."

Vincenzo took the folder from the old man, just in time to realise that this was the first direct contact he had ever had with his father. Naturally he had been shown photographs of him, and he had understood how astonished others had been that he himself looked so very similar to the subject of those photographs. But he knew whatever there might be in this folder, it would be something intricately linked to himself.

"We'll sort everything out in time," Michele Angelo said, misunderstanding his grandson's hesitation. As he stood there in underpants and nightshirt, the young man suddenly looked fragile, while his reflection in the mirror on the door was as stiff as Christ must have been after He had been taken down from the Cross and the nails removed from His body.

"Yes . . . and in time, we can discuss the forge too," Vincenzo agreed.

Michele Angelo smiled. "It's going to go well, Vincé . . . everything will be fine."

So Vincenzo spent the rest of the night awake, reading. First he needed to get used to the writing of someone who had obviously made a swift copy from scribbled notes; it was neat, but still it was handwriting, thus lacking the familiar authority of a printed page.

This is how my father Luigi Ippolito wrote, he told himself. The precise result of his wrist and the pressure of his hand on the page, but also the very orderly description of an invisible world brought here to light. Vincenzo could not be sure how much the handwriting revealed of his father, but he was certain the pages must contain something of the creative act that had generated himself. And he could feel the manuscript bringing him close to his father. The pages had the particular mixed smell time brings to things, a perfume that was also a taste, a combination of sandalwood and piquancy, like a sweetened lily. As for the content, this seemed mysterious at times, partly a cloak-and-dagger novel, partly an attempt to set down a legendary chronicle in black and white. Rather too rhetorical, distinctly adolescent.

It was all about a Spanish knight called Quiròn who in punishment for his dissipated life had been banished to northern Sardinia, to the Capo di Sopra, to represent the Royal Bank of Spain and arrest an inquisitor by the name of Don Diego de Gamiz. When the attempted arrest went wrong, the knight preferred to avoid dishonour back in his homeland by vanishing into the accursed country in which he now found himself. In the course of time he became aware that his new country had changed him, and from Quiròn he became Kirone, and eventually Chironi. Just a minor example of genealogical delirium, one might say. But also containing, here and there, traces of wisdom. The section that described the officials of the Royal Bank breaking into a monastery and the fierce resistance they encountered from the guardian brothers revealed a talent for writing, and the lines that detailed the relationship Quiròn had with Sardinia had genuine visual power, rather than mere rhetoric. The rest had little value, a mere hotchpotch costume drama. Even the sense was not so much in the actual writing as in the reason why it was written. The first Chironi to be able to claim a bloodline was now in the presence of a Chironi who had had to invent a bloodline for himself, tracing this process back to its birth, even having the cheek to invent the whole process. If you enquire closely enough, of course, no orphan who ever lived can altogether be without real ancestors, including Michele Angelo Chironi and Mercede Lai, his own two ultimate ancestors. They too must have had fathers and mothers. One would only need to seek these out to be absolutely certain that the surname they keep repeating started as nothing more than a bureaucratic accident, a word on a document. But things have to start somewhere. What does it matter, in the end? Only to the extent of making sense of that accident. To make it possible for an amalgamation of chance events to make some sort of sense. This is why Michele Angelo had wanted Vincenzo to read these pages, for him to find a meaning, any meaning, even one with no rational connection to anything. Wanting to make oneself a Chironi has been an act of faith, but also a practical act. A way of being accepted in the world with one's papers in order. If you thought about it everything must have gone like this, each one of us being the result of previous assumptions. The only difference was that what had created the Chironi family had happened more recently.

In Núoro such things matter. That is to say, one's kinship relates to the land. One could say that what counts is the number of footsteps that generation after generation have trodden on this land. The Chironi family were rich but unlucky, but they were also people taking their very first footsteps in Núoro. And, even more to the point, they had been able to set out a second time on their path thanks to a grandson from overseas, which was tantamount to starting again from scratch.

The First Disobedience

ONE ASSUMES THAT SOME THINGS HAVE ALWAYS EXISTED even if they first occurred by accident. For example, the mountains look as if they have been there for ever, but once there were no mountains at all. Or if they did exist they were different, of another genre, even perhaps soft and smoking like just-heated soup. It took time for them to develop into what they are now. The enchanted spot where we stand, in what to us may be a paradise of forest, fountains and fruit, was once an inferno of incandescent material and ill-defined lava, a broth of bacteria. We are the result of disobedience and it is of no consequence that this may be told as a story of prohibited fruit. Which is why Vincenzo believes time is all we can count on, fearlessly doing our best to ensure it remains our friend and accomplice.

This determination of Vincenzo's was called Cecilia, and had Cecilia's eyes. Though young, the girl was far from foolish, and already understood perfectly well what she needed to know about "the foreigner". Yet she refused to accept, what already seemed a *fait accompli*, that she was already committed to Nicola Serra-Pintus. She did this for reasons she considered entirely her own, and certainly not because she was happy to have a virtually official fiancé. If, for example, Vincenzo asked her out she would say no, and when he asked why not, she would simply say, "I know why," which meant both everything and nothing. "I know why" was a very useful way to prevent discussion without having to give a definite answer. And at the same time it was an infallible way of leaving a door half open through which no-one could enter.

Despite the fact that he was now more than thirty years old, no-one could call Vincenzo Chironi an expert on women. The few physical encounters he had experienced so far had merely been formal acts to satisfy his basic manhood, undertaken with little expense and no emotion. He had never kissed a woman out of love. In any case, Cecilia Devoto would never have let herself be kissed. And he knew time and appearance were on his side, he was tall and good-looking, even if judging by her attitude, these qualities must almost have been considered defects by Cecilia. But this was a consequence of her being a woman of the world, that is to say one of those women who always understand the ways of the world without ever needing to have anything explained to her. "That woman was born knowing everything," people in Núoro would say, referring to the fact that her undoubted beauty was underpinned by a deep intelligence. But it would also involve a lot of to-ing and fro-ing for any poor man who got caught in her web.

In fact, you could not describe Nicola Serra-Pintus as her official fiancé, nor did she ever call him that, even if he assumed it to be the case because she allowed herself to walk out on his arm. Vincenzo and Cecilia knew they were two different species, but they shared a mutual condition of intimate foreignness in relation to Núoro; she as a refugee of high status, but a refugee nonetheless, and he plucked like Moses from the waters when the Chironi bloodline had seemingly run dry.

Once they had accepted that they had this in common, nothing could have prevented them falling in love for life.

It had only taken a second for Cecilia to understand this, so in fact she was actually giving herself to him by refusing to do so. It took Vincenzo longer to grasp the fact, since he was obsessed with her appearance, while she was more concerned with the way he breathed. This was strange to the extent that the more she pretended no relationship existed at all between them, the more he convinced himself that she must be the woman of his life. Since their fleeting encounter outside the Bar Nuovo on the evening of the proclamation of the Republic, they had only set eyes on each other four or five times. This would never have happened if he had not looked for her and she had not allowed herself to be found. But there was one occasion when she looked for him and found him without Vincenzo being aware of it.

This happened when she got Vincenzo to take her home despite the fact that Nicola had insisted on staying at the bar. Cecilia and Nicola had arrived together as usual, and formed part of a group enjoying the late summer air, but suddenly a short but frenetic discussion had broken out between the two of them, which she had cut short by turning her back on everyone and heading for home. Nicola abandoned his glass and the discussion to follow her, but she no longer wanted to be accompanied, or at least not by him. Turning to the group, she asked Vincenzo, in front of the others, if he would like to come with her. When Vincenzo looked uncertainly at Nicola, Cecilia said sharply: "No need to ask him."

So Vincenzo said nothing, broke away from the others and joined her. They walked in the dusk and *maestrale* wind towards her home. In silence, a pace apart, with Cecilia saying nothing, but watching him. He could feel her eyes on him like a diffuse tingling sensation. Occasionally he would scratch his neck and look round timidly just enough to make sure that she was still keeping her eyes fixed on him. Shortly before they reached the street door of the house where she lived, she said: "But you, did you have a girlfriend in that place where you used to live?"

"No," he said with the simplicity of extreme embarrassment.

"Really not? A boy like you?"

Vincenzo, realising he had answered abruptly because unprepared for her question, tried to qualify his answer. "Not really."

"What's 'not really'?"

"I was never really engaged."

Cecilia took refuge in a faint smile because she did not want him to see she had not understood.

When they reached her door a few silent seconds later they turned and looked straight at each other.

"Well. Goodnight then," she said.

"And you?" he said.

"And I what?" she said, though this time she had understood perfectly.

"You know."

"I know what?"

"Your fiancé."

"Nicola?" Cecilia said as if he had said the most unbelievable thing in the world. "Goodnight," she added, holding out her hand. He held out his too, but barely touched her. She pushed the door open and vanished into the house.

*

143

That evening Vincenzo went to bed early, not wanting to go back to the bar after seeing Cecilia home. When Marianna saw him come in at that unusual hour, she began asking without asking. When she started watching you, it was worse than any number of questions. So barely risking a word, Vincenzo said he was going to bed and made for his room. Marianna followed.

"Are you not feeling well?" she said before he could open the door.

Vincenzo shook his head as if she had said something totally absurd. "It's just that I'm tired."

Marianna gave him a long look. Was he really telling the truth? Here was yet another woman trying to read his mind. "Tired," he repeated with less confidence than before.

Marianna seized on this slight hesitation as if she had won a fort from an enemy. "Yes, of course," she said, pausing long enough for him to go into his room.

After standing in front of his closed door for a few seconds, she returned to the kitchen, where Michele Angelo was waiting.

What he was waiting for was clear, as always when Marianna had that expression on her face. And indeed, she sat down behind Michele Angelo in silence, but eventually, struggling to control the nervous tremor in her voice, she whispered, "Something's going on." Michele Angelo was careful not to respond in any way. "What about the forge?" she went on. "You've been saying for a long time that you'd like to open it again." Michele Angelo suppressed a snort, but made sure she was aware of it. "Alright, snort away if you like, but can't you see what's happening?"

"And what *is* happening?" Michele Angelo asked without even turning round.

"What's happening is that I don't want that woman in this house!"

"What woman, for God's sake?"

"The one they say has her eye on Vincenzo."

"Ah."

"Exactly."

"And who might she be, for heaven's sake?"

"Oh, forget it. Never mind. Everyone has been chattering about it, they say she's not even from round here. A girl with bad habits, always on the loose, out of control—" Michele Angelo burst out laughing. "It's easy for you to laugh."

In fact, Michele Angelo was laughing through clenched teeth, because he was measuring his daughter's resentment against the fact that this enemy who had appeared so unexpectedly in their lives could not even be named. But it was clear, as usual, that people knew something was up and were imagining more than what was actually going on.

"Let's wait before we get too excited," he ventured.

"No, we can't wait," Marianna shouted. "That woman doesn't even come from this part of the world!"

"Let's not exaggerate; Vincenzo doesn't come from this part of the world either!" the old man blurted out. "What's that got to do with it? Nor am I from round here and nor are you. What are you talking about?"

Marianna gave her father a seriously worried look .

"These are people from Cagliari," she specified, as if that were enough. But Michele Angelo was unmoved.

"When I fell in love with your mother nothing in the world could have made me change my mind. Can you understand that?"

Marianna covered her mouth as though her father had made some intimate and improper revelation. "We haven't reached that point, God forbid . . ." she murmured, crossing herself. She was absolutely convinced this refugee girl must have cast a spell on her nephew, and it had never even entered her head that he might be no less interested in her. But Marianna was not in the least concerned with what men thought about love. She had been taught to believe that the woman must do the choosing, but allow the man to think that it was he who had chosen her. But here was her father insisting on the opposite, something she would have been able to understand only if she had ever been sensitive to the way Michele Angelo had always looked at his wife Mercede. This revelation made her feel that her resistance was pointless. She must accept that her nephew was young and obviously had needs of his own.

However, for the moment Vincenzo was happy to imagine that his parting from Cecilia on this occasion had been sealed by a kiss, rather than a formal contact of hands that had been even less than a handshake. And his imagination communicated with his body. It only took him a few minutes to masturbate violently, but it gave him little relief. In fact, it made him feel more agitated than soiled. Not so much sinful as restless, because although his flesh had been satisfied, his breathing refused to return to normal. He looked for something to clean himself with. Outside his own room the house was utterly silent. If his aunt and his grandfather were still in the kitchen, they were not speaking or even moving. It was such a perfect moment that Vincenzo was forced to clear his throat to find out whether the silence was natural or whether his ears had let him down. Suddenly the song of some nocturnal bird made everything clear, and following that sound, as if in a procession, came everything else: leaves disturbed by the wind, cats mating, guard dogs whining in the distance, all sounds that seemed to want to contribute to creating a space and defining it.

Once clean, he took off his trousers which had dropped round his ankles, pulled up his underpants, finished undressing and got into bed.

Now that the silence had yielded to natural sounds he was able to close his eyes. But even this action, imperceptible though it was, brought him no peace. On the contrary, behind his closed eyelids the world seemed to be swarming with flesh as though the multitudes of the damned, from cathedral frescoes everywhere, were waiting naked to burn in hell, or to lie like soldiers in crammed marble sarcophagi.

The whole of that imagined world, when he thought about it, was as far away as could be from the place where he actually was, which felt as if it had been interrupted or suspended. And made silent.

Cecilia, that night, fully understood the unexpected circumstances her as yet brief life had run into. She was enough of a woman to realise the danger of the meeting she had had with Vincenzo, understanding how different it had been from anything she had experienced before. She swore she would keep well away from him, but at the same time imagined herself breaking her oath.

It had been only the day before that the Serra-Pintus family had called on the Devoto family to approve an official engagement between herself and Nicola. A strange ceremony, riddled with silences, as one might expect between people who have little in common but are forced to get on with each other. That is perhaps why such people can be described as family connections, like birds that have accidentally landed on the same branch as they obey an uncontrollable impulse to migrate. The instinct that has brought them to rest side by side has also determined that they will keep company on the next lap of their journey. This is how families grow, or at least how the more fortunate ones do.

They began by discussing their children and how important it was to take their tastes into account, but also that these children should choose their partners responsibly. The Serra-Pintus family were of entirely local stock, one could even call them autochthonous, complete and certifiable, with all four grand-parents from Núoro and with the local self-confidence that came with it. Such people were known as primary stock or "*prinzipales*". People who had been there before.

The Devoto family on the other hand were city-dwellers, a race with Levantine manners, perhaps originally from the mainland. Their women were very beautiful and distinctly bourgeois.

The two sets of future in-laws seemed products of two entirely different worlds, the indigenous family compactly built and the city-dwellers slender; the one family darkened by the sun, the others pale from desk-work; the one family quick-witted and the others naturally reflective. The one family believed themselves shrewd, while the others actually were shrewd.

At the engagement ceremony, Fausto Devoto looked into his daughter Cecilia's eyes. "These people have nothing but their name," he said, "though such a name still means something in these parts. What are your plans?"

Cecilia felt herself pinioned by her father's eyes, like a prisoner with no right of self-defence.

He woke as if from a bad dream, as though an infinite weariness had unaccountably accumulated while he slept. Opening his eyes was like recovering his balance, but he was still stunned for a few seconds as if in an empty corridor between sleep and waking. He now became aware that what had disturbed him in bed had been a premonition, as when the mind acts on one's eyelids before the alarm clock can ring, so that return to the waking world seems a sudden urge unconnected with any earlier impulse.

He felt cold. He was aware of a familiar noise coming from the kitchen, from the world of the living, but he remained completely passive, in the power of a gentle resurrection. It occurred to him that when his time came this was how he would like to die, without struggle or suffering. And that there was nothing very special about having such a thought.

Marianna knocked gently on his door.

"Yes?"

"It's ten," she said, her voice carrying no trace of reproach.

"Yes, yes."

"And there's someone here to see you."

"Someone to see me?" Vincenzo asked through the closed door, but Marianna had gone.

He could hear Mimmíu's familiar voice talking softly to Michele

Angelo. When Vincenzo came into the kitchen Mimmíu did not even stop talking to greet him, just shook his head as if to say only gentlemen of leisure can permit themselves to sleep so scandalously late.

"I couldn't get to sleep," Vincenzo apologised pointlessly, since no-one had expected him to say anything.

"Mimmíu was telling me about the malaria campaign," Michele Angelo explained. "He says they have a new product that exterminates the insects, eggs and all, everything."

"D.D.T.," Mimmíu interrupted. "The E.R.L.A.A.S., you know, the anti-malaria campaign, are looking for people, and they say they've already done a great job against the locusts. The pay's good, too."

Vincenzo glanced at Michele Angelo. The old man looked away. "There's work for you here if you want it," he said, staring at the iron tongs in the fireplace. "And for you too, of course, Mimmí." he added.

A loaded silence followed. "Is that coffee ready or isn't it?" Michele Angelo snapped at Marianna. She nodded and hurried to serve it, if only to fill the silence.

Outside the French window, a gentle wind was touching the plants without stirring them.

Marianna knew everything in that little world. She had learned how death can nourish life and her plants had even taught her the irrational movements of the human mind. This was how she knew how to deal with this particular kind of bad temper in her father, and that he was expecting her nephew to respond to a question he did not have the courage to ask directly. She added a little sugar to the old man's coffee and tinkled the spoon in the cup before handing it to him; he emptied it with a grimace in a single gulp as he always did. "Does this mean you would be away from home?" he suddenly said to Vincenzo, breathing in the sweetness from the bottom of his cup, which was ultimately what he wanted.

Vincenzo spread wide his arms.

"Like last time with the locusts," Mimmíu said, "it always depends where they send us. I think those of us from Núoro will be sent to Baronía."

Michele Angelo nodded.

They set out for Marréri. On the way they discussed the real reason why Mimmíu had come to look for Vincenzo at home. It seemed Vincenzo might be in trouble for his excessive interest in Cecilia Devoto. Excessive? Vincenzo said. Well, Mimmíu said, someone's not very happy about it and is going around saying disagreeable things. Disagreeable in what way? Vincenzo said. Mimmíu shrugged because by now he had learned the trick mainland people had of pretending to be stupid – but only when it suited them, of course. In fact, he told Vincenzo at once, this trick wouldn't work, so he might as well stop playing the fool because he, Mimmíu, knew all about it. Vincenzo burst out laughing; if there is one thing Friulians and Sards undoubtedly have in common, he was thinking, it is that they know how to tell stories; not so much in the sense of lying as of knowing when to leave out inconvenient truths. Mimmíu laughed too, almost tempted to kick this son of a bitch who was so good at exploiting their friendship. So it seemed clear the anti-malaria campaign could also be a convenient way of interrupting this love affair before it grew into a real problem. Even so, Vincenzo insisted on asking what problem there could possibly be. And Mimmíu, a little more irritated than before, said: here we go again; Nicola. Then, more forcefully: Nicola Serra-Pintus. Vincenzo protested, but what if Cecilia had been the first to insist that there was nothing between them? Mimmíu shook his head and said that may have been the explanation Cecilia Devoto had given to Vincenzo, but not to the other man whom she had accepted as her official fiancé. Now Vincenzo began to feel the discussion was getting absurd, because even if Nicola Serra-Pintus believed he had any rights over Cecilia Devoto, he only had to say so, and he, Vincenzo, would get out of the way. He said that, though he knew it was not true and, in fact, Mimmíu seemed in no way reassured to hear it. Rather the opposite, in fact. He had not taken his eyes off him or stopped grimacing, and it was quite clear that Vincenzo was lying. So Mimmíu sat down on the low wall where the road to Marréri began and asked Vincenzo to do the same, which he did after glancing all about him for a moment.

The place they found themselves right in the middle of was a sort of no-man's-land, neither village nor countryside, a district where man and nature were fighting a stalemate and taking turns to dominate. The dry wall they were sitting on had been attacked by a bramble that had crept in between the mossy stones, making it clear that the truce on that scrap of land where houses and trees imperceptibly shaded into each other would not last much longer. At that exact point the paved road dipped between the houses on its way to the church of the Rosario, merging with the grass like a muddy brook swallowed up by green. This was where Núoro came to an end physically, but it was also the exact point – from the leaden rocks of the Marréri road leading to the bottom of the valley, to the mule-track leading over Ortobene towards the little old church of the Solitudine – where the real Núoro could be said to begin. This was the kind of thing Vincenzo had understood ever since, as a child, he had been able to see from the windows of the orphanage in Trieste that his prison extended further than the building inside which he was confined. The mountains had been part of his prison too, and even the sea. That border, whether Italy as it now was or Austria as it had earlier been, defined his prison. And now here, in this raft in the middle of the sea where fate had presented him with a surname and a family, it was just the same. Looking around while Mimmíu was talking to him, Vincenzo noticed the point where the paved area merged with a field.

"You have to listen to me," Mimmíu was saying, "you do understand that, don't you?"

Vincenzo gestured that no, he did not understand.

"Things are different in this part of the world."

"Then how are things in this part of the world?" Vincenzo said provocatively. "What am I supposed to have done?"

"Nothing, so far. And nothing is how it must remain." Then he stopped abruptly and looked straight at Vincenzo. "Nothing. Is that clear?" Mimmíu added less confidently, shrugging, while a light wind ruffled the fields like a barber running his hand through freshly cut hair. "Just take care, that's all. Nicola Serra-Pintus and Cecilia Devoto get married less than three weeks from now."

The bushes around them began to scratch the silence. Vincenzo smiled bitterly. "How much are they going to pay us for this work in Baronía?" he said.

In the ground-floor office of the communal building, the same place where the market was held twice a week, a sign advertised prominently "Government of Italy – U.N.R.R.A. – Rockefeller Foundation". Mimmíu and Vincenzo went in and handed over the documents required for their names to be added to the list.

They spent the next week doing for the mosquitoes what they had previously done for the locusts. They had fumigators full of insecticide and maps. Also small and badly duplicated manuals with poetic or esoteric titles like *The Care of the Waters* and *The Cycle of the Anopheles*. They learned that pyrethrum powder was a natural repellent obtained from common wild flowers like the local *scarlina*, *fiorrancio* or marigold and the margherita or daisy. They read the unpronounceable name Dichlorodiphenyltrichloro-ethane, which everyone simply knew as D.D.T. They admired the shades of Paris green which, despite its name was aceto-arsenic of copper, for use against the dangerous aquatic stages of the mosquito. When the days started getting longer again "summer clouds of insects will descend on the population with their malarial load", warned the manual entitled *A Front against the Epidemic*, specifying which areas of the district would need to be disinfected. These areas, called sectors, were subdivisions of two square kilo-metres each within which the teams assigned to them had to apply the disinfection. Mimmíu and Vincenzo were again allowed to form part of the same team. They began on April 7, 1950, twelve days after Vincenzo and Cecilia had last met.

They had survived a cold wet March and a no less churlish April. The light, a little weaker than the lamp on his bedside table, hinted at a new day. As he went into the kitchen, Vincenzo noticed Marianna had already been up for some time and had hot milk, bread and biscuits ready for him on the table. She had also prepared bread, cheese and wine for him to take with him. He sat down without a word to eat breakfast. She only spoke to ask if he would like coffee, and when he said no, reverted to silence. She stood and watched him, wondering yet again at how generously the Creator had designed this nephew of hers who was her real son, her soul. Everything had been given to him and he had claimed nothing, she thought, suffocated by the emotion that gripped her whenever they were alone together. Vincenzo looked up and smiled, suddenly a child again, as if realising how all the time he had spent in what had once been his father's home could be defined as a sort of apprenticeship for life. Even on the verge of his thirty-fifth year, he could not claim to have lived enough to be able to call himself grown up. This conflicting and now impossible love was churning him up as though he were still a young boy, deluding him into believing he had found the woman of his life like a four-leafed clover in a huge field, what else could that be if this wasn't recognising maturity without ever having really experienced it? He told himself he knew nothing of the world. Nothing at all. And cursed himself for having only accepted real life on becoming an adult in his thirties. Because the fact was he was now back where everything had started, as though some extra time must still be waiting for him, yet another new departure.

Outside the courtyard gate, Mimmíu announced his presence with a low whistle.

"Bring him in," Marianna said without conviction. "He can have some hot coffee."

Vincenzo emptied his cup, wiped his mouth and picked up his few belongings with the packet that contained his lunch. "We're late already," he said, heading for the door.

He stopped in front of it before grasping the handle. Marianna saw his shoulders curve as he took a deep breath, as if some particularly burdensome obligation were waiting for him outside. "Go safely, son," she murmured in dialect.

Vincenzo turned to smile and gave a little wave.

Vincenzo's seniority made him team captain this time. With two other men, his team was assigned to an area that included Siniscola, Torpè, Posada and Budoni. These were the familiar names of places he had never needed to visit before, when on his initial uncertain journey towards his new home and life. And now here he was heading for these places armed with a fumigator and D.D.T. Typhus and malaria are said to be lovers, which is why he and his team were now acclaimed as saviours, with honours normally reserved for heroes or angels, in those villages and hamlets and even sheep-folds in the back of beyond. But there was not much time for being cheerful. The local people were indeed "surviving" in the extreme conditions the team had read about in the dupli-cated manuals provided for them by the Núoro office. With the locusts it had been a face-to-face battle against armoured, noisy and voracious adversaries; while the mosquitoes dealt in invisi-bility and blood. With the locusts it had been a matter of will-power, brains and physical resistance, defeating sheer numbers, as if in an arena full of screaming gladiators, whereas the new enemy had to be surprised before he could reveal himself, more like slaughtering Argives.

Wherever they appeared, the disinfection agents were pre-ceded by clouds and advanced almost imperceptibly through smoke, like warriors flushing out the voracious Anopheles and writing on walls, like the Angel of the Lord marking the houses of the righteous with the blood of the Lamb and leaving the rest to be lashed by the divine whip.

Eventually they reached the sea, where lilies adorned the sand and oleanders saturated the air with a pungent moisture smelling like almond. This was an area traditionally abandoned to the care of unmarried women, since you cannot irrigate crops or graze animals on sand, and in salt water even cows can do no more than refresh themselves.

But even here too, the invisible enemy needed to be fought because, though worthless in themselves, these coastal districts could become extremely dangerous points for the spread of disease.

Vincenzo fell in love instantly with that sea; he had crossed it, then fallen in love with it from the hillside and now he was able to touch it.

Two days previously he had forced himself to go as far as the path through the olive trees where, years before, he had nearly been hit by bullets from the priest Virdis' double-barrelled rifle. He had come again to the open space beyond the little church of Sant' Antimo where the small houses circled round and hugged one another as though embraced in a dance. He headed calmly behind the buildings where he had once washed his miserable clothes and where, one exceptionally wet morning, he had helped bury the priest's old dog. Then he stopped before the house where the priest had lived. The door yielded in the same abrupt way as when pushed by his host so many years before. Inside, nothing seemed to have changed; it smelled the same and the corner where the old dog had dozed was still occupied by the chair where Virdis had sat watching him as he left.

Outside the house Vincenzo's new colleagues asked him why on earth he had insisted on going so far beyond their sector to disinfect such an obviously clean place. He had answered that he had his reasons, and that this particular place had to be disinfected with particular care.

But now, on the beach, on this first sunny day in April, Vincenzo moved aside to let the others take off their shoes and roll their trousers up to their knees to get a touch of the water.

Suddenly feeling faint, as though he might suffocate, he walked on by himself as if casually to a point where there was a large mound of dried seaweed high enough to hide the sea from view, and let himself fall on the sand.

All around him spring was singing a song of emerald green. It seemed unbelievable that from this marvellous body of stone and earth, of flowering thistles and broom, of oleiferous bushes, of budding myrtles and twisted juniper, that all this could give rise to such a buzzing fever.

Like the fiery breath of dragons in legends, malaria passes from blood to blood in unimaginably tiny drops, invisible to the naked eye but sufficient to transport hundreds of plasmodia into an organism. If this happens all one can do is to hope for the benign tertian fever, since one cannot survive the malignant variety. Like Cain and Abel, one is bad and the other good. To begin with you think you'll get away with it, even if the infected area looks raw. Then comes a sudden fever and a terrible alternation of hot and cold, with successive fits of shivering and sweating. Then nothing more for so long that you again decide all must be well and that you will survive. This is followed by a second attack, which they say is the worst, because it proves you have not escaped after all, despite what you had thought, so that the pain in your body is now made worse by the loss of hope. In children, tears replace the stout resistance with which they had initially faced the illness. Tears when they imagined they had won the war, when the fact was that they had merely got the better of the first phase. Then a subtle desperation kicks in, with teeth chattering to breaking point and sheets soaked with sweat. Then a second respite, shorter than the first, is followed by abdominal pain so acute it is like being pushed over a precipice and falling, only to be miraculously saved by the branch of a tree that then gives way and casts the victim once more into the abyss. It is true that in many cases immunity or semi-immunity can develop, but this in itself can weaken the kidneys and liver.

Knowing all this helped Vincenzo understand he must keep his distance and develop a respect for the indescribable beauty all around him. Even so he thought himself mad because he felt unable to curb the thoughts and images that assailed him. If it had ever been necessary to judge how much of his childhood still survived dormant within him, it would have been enough to see his expression as he observed the soft piles of seaweed on the furthest reaches of the beach where he had decided to hide while trying to battle his disquiet. Soft heaps said to have been dumped by a storm that had mown down immense underwater fields of seaweed. It seemed every beautiful object must also carry its share of violence and sickness, and it was precisely this that made the beauty so wondrously extreme and significant in itself, beyond any need for explanation. Where he grew up your way of seeing had to contain a magnificence, something graphic, terse and sharp, but here – with his bare feet buried in the white sand and the rest of his team trying to lower themselves gently into the fountain-clear water between the rocks and calling him to come and feel the cold shock for himself – Vincenzo understood that his vision was inadequate, because it was a vision of tiny things, at the same time over-inflated yet faint, seemingly insignificant but in fact agitated in essence.

When Mimmíu came up behind him it made him jump: "Easy!" he said, to reassure him. Vincenzo shook his head. "Come and join the others," Mimmíu said, "or they'll think you're in love."

Vincenzo threw a fistful of sand which his friend evaded, laughing but saying, "What day is it today?"

The laugh on Mimmíu's face faded. He sat down and looked at Vincenzo. "You know quite well," he said drily. "But let's not talk about that."

"Cecilia's wedding day," Vincenzo persisted.

"Exactly." Mimmíu tried to sound aggressive. There was a short silence. "But why bring that up?" he said suddenly, genuinely disconcerted. Vincenzo looked at him without answering. "What's the point of saying that?"

"What?"

"What you've just said. What difference can it make?"

"To prove it's really happening."

"No," the other man said. "That just makes it uglier." He timidly reached out to touch his friend's shoulder. Vincenzo pursed his lips.

A little further off the others had improvised a bivouac.

Mimmíu got up: "Come on."

Vincenzo looked at him and blew away the lock of black hair that had slipped across his face.

"I'm coming, I'm coming." He didn't hurry.

Two months after this, well into June, Vincenzo finally went home. He had never taken any sort of leave from his work, just sent back clothes to his grandfather and aunt for washing via other members of the team who, unlike him, went home at least once a week. In return, Marianna had sent back food and clean clothes, and her anxiety.

Coming into the courtyard now he found Michele Angelo; Marianna had gone to the other house. The two men looked at each other, then agreed it was getting hot now, in the manner of people who want to say something simply to overcome an initial awkwardness. In any case, he and his grandfather were never inclined to unnecessary talk. Even if they did not greet each other at all after not seeing each other for a long time, it would mean little because nothing important would have been left unsaid.

"I was thinking of selling," the old man muttered at one point, just as if he had been discussing the subject a minute earlier.

"Selling what? Vincenzo asked, though he knew the answer perfectly well.

"Everything," Michele Angelo answered. "All that stuff in there." He nodded towards the forge.

"Why sell it?" Vincenzo said.

Michele Angelo did not answer. All he could think of was that he had let too much time pass before facing up to selling his rights in the forge, and that there was no sign that his grandson had any interest whatsoever in taking on the family business. "I knew you'd be back, I told Marianna you'd come back." Vincenzo waited for him to go on. "She's gone to her own house to do some cleaning. She was worried you'd never come back. But I knew you hadn't gone anywhere," he said.

"Here I am," is all Vincenzo replied, going to sit beside his grandfather.

"Are you hungry? Would you like a wash?"

"Yes, but there's time. I like sitting here." As the last words escaped him, he stared at the absurd twists and turns of the wild jasmine.

Michele Angelo looked in the same direction: the plant bowed the end of one branch as if it knew it was being watched. "That plant has just been asking if this is how the created world responds to our presumptions," he remarked. Vincenzo allowed himself the ghost of a smile. "You frightened your aunt," the old man whispered. "She was certain you'd never come back again, after everything that's happened."

"Happened? What has happened?"

"What?" Michele Angelo asked. "Don't you know?" Vincenzo shook his head. "The marriage," his grandfather specified, "the girl you fancied?"

"Cecilia?" Vincenzo was worried.

"Yes, her: they say she wrecked everything at the last moment. So your aunt was sure the two of you must have run off together. But I knew you'd be back."

"Wrecked everything" simply meant that Cecilia Devoto had left Nicola Serra-Pintus standing at the altar. Not by accident, or just in a manner of speaking. She had done it deliberately. She had stood before the priest, supremely beautiful in the white dress bought for her in Cagliari, like a bride in an illustrated magazine. She had crossed the aisle elegantly on her father Fausto's arm, with a large veil of tulle arranged like a compact cloud over her shoulders so as not to hamper her walking. Anyone interested in the symbolism of her appearance could have said that everything about that veil already signified a burden. They say she moved with determined steps, a little out of breath, with her father almost struggling to keep up by the time they reached Nicola at the altar. At that moment he looked a desirable husband, dressed perfectly in an iron-grey double-breasted suit with padded shoulders, his thick hair plastered with brilliantine. But dressing as a man made him look more of a child. It was that Sunday in April when Vincenzo had suffered a fit and collapsed on the beach behind the mountain of seaweed. The morning when Marianna had forced herself out to the main road to watch the wedding procession go by and crossed herself in relief that that particular peril had passed.

Cecilia reserved the only look of love she ever gave Nicola for that moment in front of the altar. She had not even removed the veil from her face, yet he was able to see her clearly and it frightened him.

The very day when Mimmíu, joining Vincenzo at the end of the beach, had understood how far resignation could conceal suffering. And when Marianna had seen a neighbour who, like herself had been waiting to watch the bridal procession go by, had failed to smash the traditional congratulatory plate of grain and sweets despite hurling it against the pavement with all her strength. The plate had not broken until the third or fourth attempt, causing the procession to stop and the good neighbour's congratulations to change into a cry of helplessness and shame.

At the altar, the bride had turned her back on the groom without further ado, and faced her father, searching carefully for words, knowing that if she failed to make the most of this particular moment of disorientation, she would never have another chance to do what she had decided.

It was the first sunlit Sunday day that April. Marianna, opening the windows of her house to air it, thanked destiny for blessing the day with good weather. A Sunday when the troops of warrior angels enjoyed a break and unconsciously rendered thanks for the marvel they were contributing to by making that house habitable. When Michele Angelo, burrowing in the left pocket of his lightweight jacket, found the keys of the workshop which he had not expected to find there. When Marianna decided to spring-clean her already spotless house, turning it upside down to wash curtains and pelmets and all the towels from the trousseau nobody had ever used.

At that moment Cecilia angrily lifted the veil from her face, glared at her father and told him that she believed herself a good daughter who loved him enough as a father to make her want to die rather than say what she was about to say, and that till now she had always obeyed him in everything, in absolutely everything, but this time: no. That refusing to marry a man she knew she could not love must be her first act of disobedience.

Her father gazed at her as if to imprint a permanent memory of her on his mind, then said: "You say you would rather die than displease me? Well, you have displeased me, severely. And as far as I am concerned, you are now dead."

His Real Place

CECILIA AND VINCENZO SHARED THEIR FIRST REAL KISS IN broad daylight. It was a very hot morning in July. He had had to search for her until she let herself be found.

Cecilia had stopped at a shop not far from the Chironi home, knowing Vincenzo would soon pass by. She also knew he would walk straight on pretending not to have seen her and swearing not to give in to her, only to turn back cursing himself a few seconds later. She would then wait for him near the shop window. And so it happened: when she saw him turn back, she walked on and passed him, watching him from the corner of her eye and making as if to continue straight on so that, exasperated, he was forced to catch her by the arm, blatantly, in full sunlight, near Vincenzo's home and with the shopkeeper watching from inside her shop. That is to say, Cecilia let herself be stopped while Vincenzo pretended a rage he did not feel but thought he should have been feeling. In fact, the only emotion he was really feeling was elation. It was enough for him to have touched her and that she had let herself be touched, no matter that he could no longer remember any of the things he had sworn he would say. Confused, he just stood still, and she just stopped and looked at him.

"What have you been doing?" he said. Not a real question, and with none of the dramatic effect he had intended, devoid of authority or manly detachment. Cecilia knitted her brows as if she had not understood his question, simple though it was. She had become even more beautiful, if that were possible; her face an alternating harmony of light and dark: raven-black hair above a bright forehead, eyebrows seemingly drawn by hand, shining grey oval eyes and near-violet lips. What should he do? And how should he do it? Had he not just emerged victorious from a battle with the biblical plagues, he would have kissed her on the spot. She was wearing a purplish dress with short sleeves and a pleated and flared skirt almost down to her ankles. Her delicate shoes were hardly more than babouches or Turkish slippers. Her hair, held at the temples by two bone combs, fell loosely down her back. If he had thought about it, Vincenzo might have realised it was extremely unlikely she would have dressed like that just to go shopping – if he had thought about it at all. But he was not thinking. Overcome by nervousness, he began buttoning up his shirt which was open at the collar, then thrust his hands into his pockets. He made another attempt to speak: "Where have you been?" But his voice escaped from his throat like a whistle.

"Rome," she said. "I've been in Rome on a course. I have an uncle and aunt there."

"On a course," he repeated.

"Yes. Puericulture." She stopped, knowing he was not likely to know the word and with no intention of yielding her advantage. "Looking after children," she explained after a suitable pause. I start work on the first of September at the O.N.M.I."

"You mean at the nursery school?" he said.

"At the nursery school." She nodded.

168

Silence. This should have been the cue for him to move on. But nothing happened.

Cicadas were chirping loudly all around them like a deafening rumble of kettle-drums, reminding Vincenzo that the rest of the world still existed like a welcoming room from which Cecilia must not be allowed to escape. "All this time and you never looked for me," he grumbled, finally striking the right note.

"Why would I have looked for you? What I did, I did for myself, it had nothing to do with you." She looked at him.

It was only then that he seized her by the shoulders and kissed her as though hungry to eat her, and hugged her as if he wanted to glue himself to her for the rest of his life, though he used no force because she was not trying to escape.

Bright daylight, on a hot morning in July.

News of this public kiss in full sunlight reached the Chironi court-yard in no time at all. This apparent return of a problem, as reported to her by eager neighbours, nearly killed Marianna. The pious women had run to her with phoney embarrassment, claiming to be her sisters in arms, to give her the most intimate details of how the two had embraced, so as to leave no possible doubt the kiss could not by any means have been an act of politeness. In fact, one woman, as big and fat as any of them, insisted I've never seen anything like it before, excuse me for having to tell you. Of course, I understand him, said another, you know the way men are, but the girl . . . and she paused, knowing any one of them could have completed the sentence. The most convincing version of the story was that she, Cecilia Devoto, having made a fool of her unfortunate fiancé, had moved on to the innocent nephew of their dear friend Marianna, and now of course it was the unhappy duty of her sisters to tell her everything before she learned of it from strangers, since the news was circulating everywhere and it was impossible to hide it. Marianna listened with the resigned but undefeated expression of Saint Cecilia, who having made a vow of perpetual virginity had persuaded her husband to respect her determination to remain chaste for life. But this Cecilia was of course from Cagliari and the very opposite of the virgin saint in every respect; a woman to turn men's heads and, of course, everyone knows how men are made. It had little relevance that after the scandal of her abortive wedding, her parents had packed her off to relatives on the Continent – on the Continent, really? – to Rome, to be precise, where her mother had a brother. But young people nowadays no longer had the sense of shame that used to be such a distinguishing feature of the way they were brought up. As Marianna, of course, would know only too well; having been an important woman in her time and an extremely considerate one, and having survived the cruellest trials with remarkable courage – a husband and daughter slaughtered like cattle before her eyes. Well. It would have been enough to drive anyone mad. And now, just when the poor woman finally seemed to be finding a little peace, here was everything starting all over again with this nephew.

There could be no doubt, times were changing fast. Life changed from one second to the next. Freedom had suddenly become what everyone insisted on. Avalanches of votes were given to the Christian Democrats in 1948 in the parishes, but out in the countryside the Communists were raising their heads. Walls once papered with crossed shields had been redecorated with hammers and sickles, then covered with crossed shields again and so on, telling a story of political tension but little conviction. The young did not want to hear about hunger and sacrifices, and how could one blame them for that? Naturally they wanted to be up-to-date, to feel they were living in a real nation, but they failed to take their host into account because they had not asked whether the nation wanted to be incarnated in them. A balance had to be struck between confusion and courage, the confusion of the old and the courage of the young. Now some people were saying that Cecilia Devoto should take a job outside the home like any man would. But her real loss of value, according to this senate of confused women, lay not so much in the fact of her having to work – after all they themselves being women had always worked like mules – so much as in her abdication of her status as a woman. How would she ever be able to control the world beyond her own kitchen? To whom would she able to entrust family, home and tradition if she went out to work? The world of women like her is one of paradox, the paradox of being brought up to command in exchange for accepting a life of slavery. Women behaving like men and kissing in public, wearing trousers and going with bare arms may well be modern and the way things are done on the mainland, but here it causes disorientation. Changes are indeed inevitable, and it would take more than that to get the women down. Yet Marianna does feel a certain anxiety, because it is all very well talking about things in general, but when these things involve something that directly affects yourself and your own family, it is no longer a distant matter that you can discuss with detachment. These pious women are fully aware of this, and in fact they are careful to stress a series of basic facts that have

171

to be taken into account: that the girl is not of local birth and was educated goodness knows where in the depths of southern Sardinia, where they don't really care about certain matters; and the man too, although for heaven's sake, no-one can deny that he is a hundred-per-cent Chironi from the ends of his hair to the tips of his toes, he is another who grew up with other customs in a far away place. All this talk reaches Marianna like the indistinct buzzing or humming of an orchestra tuning its instruments. The passage about using spurge to soothe Suor Chiara's wasp sting in Puccini's opera "Suor Angelica" runs through her head:

> Here, take this spurge,
> bathe the swelling,
> use its milky juice,
> as a potion . . .

Meanwhile the pious women make clear they consider Cecilia Devoto's trip to the Continent suspect in every respect, and here she is strutting around as though nothing had happened; as if the scandal she caused had nothing to do with herself at all. And Nicola Serra-Pintus? Well, his family are almost Marianna's relatives, people she must know well, and she must understand she will never be able to count on them, especially seeing how they treated her after the tragedy of what happened to her husband and daughter.

> Tell Sister Chiara
> it's very bitter
> but will do her good . . .

Then the discussion shifted to the sufferings none of us can avoid in this vale of tears; the women conscious that they have all been marked with deep stigmata caused by the loss of husbands and children, and the collapse of buildings. The only happiness they can conceive of is getting together to tell each other how the world should be rather than how it actually is. They like to imagine a serious, reliable future for themselves rather than the infantile buffoonery they have had to put up with so far, which gives things to them then snatches them back again at random. They like to imagine a peace constructed from nothing, if they ask for nothing more than they need. This is what they talk about: how little they need in order to be happy: health for themselves and if possible for their children too, with enough food on the table every day. They have stored up years of reflection in this way. Feeling History touch their backs, without even asking whether it has been malicious in what it has denied them or benevolent in sparing them. But not Marianna. Her mind is obsessed by that kiss. These pious women, professionals of phoney astonishment, look as if they have no idea what might be tormenting her soul. What's wrong, Marià? they ask, and when she does not answer, they look surprised. She simply shakes her head to show that in fact she too has also learned to show astonishment in a way they can understand:

> and tell her too
> the stings of wasps
> are small suffering . . .

So now it was time to settle for a peace that was no peace at all. People called the end of the war peace. But these new times, in that distant place, have if possible become even more turbulent than the years of conflict. Now people kiss in the street, and distances have grown greater for grandparents and grandchildren without parents, and mothers who are widows. For Marianna the blessing of her rediscovered nephew is changing into the curse of a life that has taken him away from her again . . .

Nor should she complain,
which just creates more pain.

With the pay from his work on the anti-malaria campaign Vincenzo bought himself a Guzzi 500 Falcone motorbike. For the moment, the fact that he had no idea how to ride it did not seem relevant: Mimmíu would teach him. He could not quite believe he had made such an extravagant spontaneous decision. Not even when the excitement of a brighter future tormented him and his mind would not stop hooking on to all sorts of new ideas – had he ever imagined he would one day be in a position to buy anything so impractical. But, watching Mimmíu giving the bike a test run, he suddenly felt at home in a way he had never felt before. He was in love and had a home, a surname and possessions. Everything he had lost had now been repaid.

When he got home he said nothing about the motorbike so as not to fill Aunt Marianna's head with unnecessary ideas. But when they sat down at the table, he could not help at least alluding to it indirectly.

"They've asked me if I'd like to be a candidate in the municipal elections," he said, cutting himself some bread.

"Oh, who asked that?" Michele Angelo said without moving a muscle. Marianna began to look apprehensive.

"People you know," Vincenzo said.

Michele Angelo put down his spoon. "Do what you think best," he said. "Personally, I've always tried to keep well clear of politics."

"I know," the young man replied, but with no sense of irony. "I know how you feel about it, and I've said neither yes nor no."

" – which they would take as an answer." Michele Angelo said firmly. "Isn't that what politics is all about?"

"Of course it is," Marianna intervened.

"I've got the point," Vincenzo said, his expression darkening.

"What do you mean by that?" Michele Angelo said.

"That you don't approve."

Michele Angelo gave a light laugh. "Let's see," he said, leaning towards his grandson. "I've never entirely approved of anything apart from the fact that you once walked through that door. But it doesn't bother me. If you want to be a candidate, do as you please. But don't come and complain to me afterwards that politics is a dirty business. Have you realised what kind of people you'll have to deal with? Politics here takes no account of what is in everyone's best interests; we're all just a lot of poor devils and each of us is only concerned with himself. We all put ourselves first, my boy. Miserably selfish, all of us."

"I'm well aware of that. Especially now with so many people hoping for construction contracts. That's something else I wanted to talk to you about." Vincenzo stopped, waiting for Michele Angelo to settle his back in his chair. "Did you know they've already divided the whole area above Istirítta into plots?" Michele Angelo shook his head, but Marianna said she certainly was aware of that. "Affordable housing all the way to the Nuraghe," Vincenzo said. Michele Angelo grimaced with astonishment. "But the most important thing is that they've secured the site and found the money to finance the construction of a new Le Grazie church, which will go in front of the new workers' centre at Ponte di Ferro, and behind the old one."

"Yes, yes, I know where Ponte di Ferro is. Well?"

"So that contract, the site for the church in particular, will be worth quite a few million."

Marianna started at the word "million".

"Yes, yes, but what of it?" Michele Angelo said, but as if fully aware of what Vincenzo was leading up to.

The excavations are starting within four months, and the elections are three months from now."

"Ah," Michele Angelo said.

"What?" Marianna sighed.

"That's why they've asked me if I'd like to be a candidate," Vincenzo said, as if the situation required him to be a bit more specific. "I asked myself whether to accept or not, especially since once they've finished their excavations they'll start on the upper work." Michele Angelo shot up in his chair like a puppet on a string.

Marianna looked worried. "What's going on?" she asked.

"Nothing," Michele Angelo cut her short. "We understand each other, Vincenzo and I."

"What do you think they're going to need for the pillars, aunt?" Vincenzo said. "Iron, of course!"

"Iron," Michele Angelo repeated. "Iron."

The three apprentices who cleared the lemon plants from the entrance to the forge were Paddeu Erminio, Bosa Bartolomeo and Tanchis Giuseppe. Michele Angelo would remember them like this, surname then first name, for the rest of his life. If you had asked him the names of the three boys who moved the lemon plants, he would have been able to repeat them without hesitation, even with his very last breath, surname first, like a roll-call at school or in the army. The three apprentices had no idea that they had become the heroes of a new narrative. The workshop had been shut up before they were born, but now it was to be opened again, and they were silently taking their place in the sombre saga of the Chironi family, master blacksmiths.

Modifications needed to be made: things shifted, new machinery bought and part of the courtyard cleared to make the workshop more accessible. In this new period of sacrifices, Marianna was ready to part with a few of her plants since life needed to return to her house. The changes would also involve interior improvements with up-to-date bathrooms, and the kitchen completely refurbished with a new gas cooker and refrigerator.

Vincenzo and Cecilia continued to meet discreetly as lovers, trying not to go much beyond kissing. It was also discreetly that Michele Angelo, aware of his grandson's frustration, one evening gave him the keys to the other house without letting Marianna know.

Quite apart from its obvious significance, this gesture made Vincenzo nervous. He took it as a sort of legacy or bequest or even an entreaty, since his grandfather's eyes seemed to be asking something unspoken of him, as if expecting him to add substance to the miracle of his return home. He looked uncertainly at the old man.

"Here, take these keys," Michele Angelo encouraged him.

"I'm not sure." Vincenzo hesitated.

"Come on. Though if your aunt catches me giving them to

you, being the daughter she is, she'll strangle me with her bare hands. Don't do anything rash, either of you. Tread carefully."

In the end Vincenzo took the keys, though not without a certain awkwardness. But take them he did.

If everything was beginning again, Michele Angelo reflected, it might as well begin properly. In the forge, the three apprentices, Paddeu Erminio, Bosa Bartolomeo and Tanchis Giuseppe, were cleaning and setting up the new machinery. And at the forthcoming council elections Vincenzo Chironi, son of Luigi Ippolito Chironi, hero of the Carso, would stand as a candidate for the Communist Party and perhaps even be elected a councillor. In which case, the old man decided, finally pressing the keys to the via Deffenu house into his hand, the boy might as well learn what real loving involves. "If you take that step forward you'll never be able to turn back," he told his grandson.

Vincenzo looked at the bunch of keys. "I know," he said. "I know."

So the first time that Cecilia and Vincenzo made love was like when a peasant or shepherd looks up at the sky wondering if it will rain and decides to rely only on experience and trust his instincts. Things like the direction of the wind, the height and position of the clouds and the colour of the air can only mean something to those who have good ears, sharp eyes and an alert mind.

This is how events unfolded. They kissed again, and he told Cecilia that if she liked, they could go to the house in via Deffenu. And like an experienced peasant or shepherd, he said this without further explanation. She looked at him as though unsure what he expected, since male wisdom never quite matches what women instinctively know. Her face red, Cecilia feigned surprise as if to say: what is there to do in the house in via Deffenu? When he did not reply, she held out her hand as if to a drowning man, and whispered, "But I've always been curious to see that house . . ."

He would not have been able to describe how he took her. He was a man who combined the instinctive gestures of a boy with a natural awkwardness she found irresistible. Once they were in the austere and functional hallway, he realised he must kiss her even before he put the keys down on the briar and ebony hall table. So he kissed her, and she perfectly understood that the new, more forceful quality of his kiss, must clearly be a prelude to something more. Her first emotion was akin to panic; she was paralysed by the realisation that they had come to the point. Yet she never worried she might find herself adrift on an open sea, because she was ready to go anywhere without fear in the arms of the man she loved. No, she was more afraid of herself, and knew that once what was about to happen had actually happened she would no longer be free to give up this man under any circumstances. So she felt both strong and vulnerable. Now that he seemed to be taking the initiative more forcefully, she let him do so through devotion and gratitude, as these were the feelings that came first to her, in the way that bridesmaids serve to announce the bride and the first complications of love. Feeling her breasts in his hands for the first time, she suddenly felt intensely beautiful. Looking back later to that precise moment, she was always sure nothing could have been more urgent. And his breathing also told her how beautiful she was, a warm breath from half-open lips like a combination of honey and must. And the shudders shaking his tall slender frame paid tribute to her beauty too.

He pretended to murmur something, though no words could have expressed his feelings. She seemed more compliant than he had ever known her, thoughtful and docile. As if she had understood and accepted that this was now his moment in the game being played out between them. And even if he was not fully aware of this, he let instinct lead him forward so gradually that she never felt assaulted in any way. They could not know it for sure, but the bedroom where they undressed may have been the one where Biagio Serra-Pintus and Marianna Chironi had conceived their daughter Mercede, named after her grandmother though she was always called Dina. Even the sheets, so carefully preserved for so many years, may have been the same. In any case, it was where Cecilia Devoto lost her virginity, and in a sense, where Vincenzo Chironi lost his too.

They also generated new life, but that was not something they were aware of.

They dozed in each other's arms, until woken by a noise in the entrance hall. Vincenzo jerked up into a sitting position and looked around for his clothes, but he was still completely naked when Marianna appeared in the bedroom doorway.

His aunt assumed a look such as the one the archangel Michael must have had on his face when he came to Eden looking for the missing apple. Cecilia faced her just like Eve thousands of years before, while Vincenzo, for obvious reasons, put his hands over his genitals.

"Don't waste time tidying up," Marianna said simply. Then turned her back and left the room.

Back at home, she said nothing to Michele Angelo. And when a

181

few hours later Vincenzo came in, she spoke to him as if nothing had happened. During dinner they discussed the forthcoming election and how someone was already begging for votes for all the candidates, and that though the whole thing had only just begun everyone had already had enough of it. Vincenzo could not help saying that no doubt for his aunt, things were often at their best when they were at their worst. But she, once again, as if unwilling to blame anyone for anything, said that all the evidence seemed to indicate that her nephew had not grasped what she had been saying. Michele Angelo understood the too obvious calm in the way that cuckolded men suddenly realise what is happening to them. So he gave Vincenzo a secret questioning look and Vincenzo raised his eyebrows to admit yes, he had understood perfectly. So his grandfather raised his shoulders as if to say: blessed woman, you can never hide anything from her. Marianna pretended not to notice this mute exchange, but tried to control her nerves by showing irritation that someone had trampled on her basil plants with his boots while leaving the workshop. After supper Vincenzo said he would go to bed.

"Not going out this evening?" Marianna said.

"No . . . I'm tired," He was not finding it easy to stay calm.

"I can well believe it," she said, not giving an inch.

When Vincenzo moved towards his own room, Marianna, with apparent innocence, followed him along the corridor.

"When are you getting married?" she said before he could disappear.

Vincenzo turned: "Excuse me," he said.

"For what?" she scoffed, but finding it hard to hide her pain. "In any case that house was yours."

"No, it's not mine. We should have asked your permission."

"Your grandfather knew about it," she said in a firm voice, then repeated, "when are you getting married?"

"Soon," Vincenzo said, attempting a reassuring voice. Marianna stopped and stared at him, as if to fix the moment and his answer firmly in her mind. Then she turned back to the kitchen.

In the months that followed, Vincenzo Chironi missed election to the local Council by forty-seven votes, but Mimmíu was elected. It was said two factors were equally to blame for Vincenzo's failure: the people of Núoro still regarded him as a foreigner from "the Continent", and the Serra-Pintus family held him responsible for Cecilia Devoto's failed wedding with their relative. But the real reason was probably different, since those in the know said the Communists, consistently in a minority, even before the guaranteed victory of the Christian Democrats, had agreed to accept a fixed number of council seats. Their reward for being content with a seat or two less was to be an acceptable proportion of the now generous local building contracts. From Vincenzo's point of view, this pulled the seat from underneath him, so to speak, but secured the contract for building the new church.

Meanwhile he had learned how to ride his motorbike.

The Chironi forge now began feverishly producing the iron-rod reinforcements, some equally shaped and some not, needed for the new church. The courtyard had suddenly become such a hive of activity that it was driving Marianna mad, but also thrilling her. Her enthusiasm was all the greater as Vincenzo seemed to be keeping his promise to arrange the marriage as soon as possible.

What Marianna did not know was that the marriage could not be taken for granted. Not because of the wishes or otherwise of the would-be bridal pair and their relatives, but due to the obstinacy of the parish priest at the Rosario, who had discovered something both Vincenzo and Cecilia had so far kept secret from everyone: that the would-be bride was already pregnant. In fact, hardly anyone knew it, but this "hardly anyone" threatened to scupper the whole thing.

When the couple had presented themselves to the priest, Don Corràine, not realising their secret was out, he assailed the girl verbally. And Vincenzo in turn attacked him unfortunately not just verbally. It was now a question of finding out whether it was possible to get round this obstacle by turning to another priest or giving up the idea of a religious marriage altogether, something that seemed not a problem to the would-be husband, but was not at all what Cecilia wanted. But it was clearly going to be very difficult to find a priest in Núoro willing to marry them, despite the fact that the Chironi family, no less, were making the iron foundations for the new church. The problem was to establish the degree to which this paradox could either be explained by the new times, or accepted by the old.

The fact that Cecilia had started work made her doubly vulnerable, without taking into account the rumours circulating about how her family had sent her to Rome not so much to distance her from the scandal of the failed wedding, but so as to arrange an abortion.

Vincenzo felt he must respect her decision to work, though he would have been happier to have her at home. As for abortions, he was certain she had been a virgin when they first made love.

He understood only too well the extent of the marvellous curse he had inflicted on himself.

On August 29, 1953, when everyone else in Núoro was distracted by the feast day dedicated to the Redeemer (to whose statue Michele Angelo had contributed a substantial sum more than fifty years before), Vincenzo arrived in front of Cecilia's house on his motorcycle. Mimmíu had gone to pick up Marianna and Michele Angelo in his car, with the excuse that Vincenzo needed them. And a few metres further away two of the workshop apprentices had done the same for members of the Devoto family.

It had been an unusually stable month, a year when the weather had not deteriorated after Ferragosto. It was a very hot day. Vincenzo, in a dark blue double-breasted suit, waited on the saddle of his Guzzi for Cecilia to come down, one foot on the pedal and the other holding the bike upright.

She arrived wearing a bright grey tailor-made suit with close-fitting dress, and to see her you would say she had grown only a trifle rounder. She climbed onto the back and put her arms round her partner's waist. They went down by the curves of Marréri. Parched by the heat, the dwarf oaks edging the road were beginning to smell like dry leather. They branched off at the Valverde fork near the little sanctuary dedicated to the Madonna. When Vincenzo stopped in the shade of a yew to allow Cecilia to dismount, she stood up and automatically began to adjust her hair, her high heels piercing more than a few dry leaves. In his turn, he got off his motorcycle, shook out his trousers to restore their crease, and took a small comb from the inside pocket of his jacket to arrange his forelock.

Cecilia looked at him with no particular surprise; this was

just Vincenzo, someone who had odd ideas when everyone else was enjoying a holiday. But she asked, "What are we doing here?"

He finished combing his hair. "Have you never seen the inside of this church?" She shook her head. "I know someone who can open it for us."

"Alright," Cecilia said.

He offered her his hand and she took it.

The small church door was open. Inside it was dark and cool. "I'd rather die than see you unhappy," he said just as they began to get used to the absence of direct light and became aware of a simple, meagre interior, its altar unadorned apart from a few clumsy statues of saints. Having eyes just for Vincenzo, she did not notice a man in ecclesiastical dress standing near the altar.

The priest Virdis seemed not to have aged much; he was just thinner. Two days earlier, in Mimmíu's car, Vincenzo had sought him out. He had not been easy to find until someone pointed out the road to Torpè, saying they would find him there at the church of the Madonna degli Angeli.

"Have you brought everything?" the priest immediately asked Vincenzo.

He nodded, pulling out two sheets of paper each folded into four.

"What's going on?" Cecilia said, and from her tone it was clear she had her suspicions.

And then, a moment later, accompanied by Mimmíu, Michele Angelo and Marianna came into the church.

Here were two people who were never "astonished" by anything. Marianna looked around and saw that as far as cleaning and decoration went, a lot of work was still required in that little church to make it suitable, in her opinion, for the rite about to be performed there.

Michele Angelo remembered his own clandestine wedding in the days when he had been poverty-stricken, and how they had had to organise it early in the morning to suit the priest and witnesses.

From the Devoto family, only Cecilia's youngest sister was present and, out of sight of the bridegroom, her mother too, unbeknown to her father.

Vincenzo went up to his relatives. "I know this is not how you imagined it," he said.

"If it suits you, it suits us," Marianna said, speaking before Michele Angelo, who looked at her with surprise, knowing how much saying such a thing must have cost her. Whether she was being sincere was not the point.

"He never said anything to me either," Cecilia broke in. "And of course I should have been told, don't you think?" Her forced smile faded as her mother and sister entered the church with the apprentices.

Despite everything, it proved to be an extremely beautiful ceremony, simple and full of warmth.

Years later, in the way that we are always forced to weigh things up, Cecilia was forced to admit that that August 29, 1953, had been one of the happiest days of her life. Because on that day the man she loved – and would have loved in any circumstances – had decided an imperfect ceremony must be better than an imperfect marriage. Because she had understood where she wanted to go with her man the moment she had caught sight of him from her window, so handsome in his double-breasted blue suit, waiting below the house on his motorcycle. So she had hastily removed her flowered suit and open shoes and put on her pearl-grey tailored suit and more elegant shoes, and had thrust a small veil for the church and kid gloves into her bag. It moved her to think that he had decided to ignore all rumours being spread about him, not because she cared a hoot about any of that nonsense, but because he feared the opposite.

Cecilia went over to explain to her relatives that she and Vincenzo had only decided on such a hurried ceremony because she was pregnant. She said this quite naturally, in a way that did not require a response. She told her mother and sister that this man loved her so much that he didn't want to subject her to the prying eyes of those who would have crowded into the church to see whether, dressed in white and standing before the priest at the altar, she dared repeat the spectacle of her notorious refusal.

There was indeed nothing else to say. Vincenzo had shouldered responsibility for the choice, so she would never have to tell her children that she had ever disgraced herself in public. But he did not know she would never have been ashamed anyway, because Vincenzo had been hers for ever even before she knew it.

The ceremony was quick and silent, without hurled handfuls of grain or neighbours ready to smash plates loaded with sweets and flowers at their feet.

Mimmíu was the bridegroom's witness and Cecilia's younger sister Francesca the bride's. Despite the simplicity of the ceremony, Virdis included a sermon, in which he recalled how, when out hunting hares in the year of the famine, he had nearly shot a young man who was wandering around near an olive grove.

Vincenzo had bought two bulky wedding rings, asking for the

most expensive, and having had his name inscribed in hers and hers in his.

"There can be no doubt the boy's a true Chironi," Michele Angelo remarked at one point. "When he gets something into his head . . . how did we never notice?"

"He definitely is a Chironi," Marianna agreed. Which effectively explained everything. Then she thought of the great difference between this ceremony and the one that had sanctified her own union with Biagio Serra-Pintus in the year of the march on Rome. That foul May day, when the sky had been like a sheet of inky paper and rain had threatened to ruin everything. Yet everyone agreed that had been a real wedding, a memorable one, with a few of her friends still able to remember the wonder of her wedding dress and hair even now. Subsequent events had led Marianna to forget these details.

"Stop there, don't move!" shouted one of the apprentices, holding up a camera for snapshots of the little group.

They all stood still, trying to see themselves from the outside as if their own eyes had actually been those of the boy behind the camera lens. Offering an image of themselves to outlive the passing moment and enabling them to remember themselves, years later, mirrored in that photograph just as they were then, neither ancient nor modern. More serious than posed, more excited than happy, more childlike than adult. They knew they would want to be able to look back on themselves with affection at that future date, and be surprised how much their "authenticity", or in other words their strength, would still mean to them. Serious faces of women and men half-way between themselves and the world. They knew these photographs would reveal a beauty they were in the process of resolutely abandoning. They would have to explain – even if they would not have known how – that their pride was changing, at first unconsciously, but later from familiarity. So the real purpose of their solemn pose was to preserve the importance of the moment rather than provide material for nostalgia.

Thinking back in old age to such moments they would identify indelible furrows in them, moments that if not captured at the time would have been lost for ever. "Don't move," the apprentice said again, then clicked.

After the ceremony they went to eat somewhere near Oliena.

And in the evening they walked arm-in-arm on Corso Garibaldi, no longer called via Majore, to see and be seen, their new rings shining on their fingers.

When Cecilia felt the eyes of passers-by on her she would discreetly caress her belly for their benefit.

The widespread wonder on the faces of those who saw them pass was the only public celebration the newly married couple allowed themselves.

Entering the house in via Deffenu as a married couple was no mere formality. Marianna wept bitter tears as she filled the old chest of drawers in the bedroom with Vincenzo's things. But these were tears for herself, certainly not for her nephew. He had learned to interpret her tears. They were the result of feeling that every change would inevitably lead to being uprooted again. Part of the subtle torment that comes with every disconnection, large or small.

In any case, a little time had to pass before the new couple could live there together, because a good deal of work needed to be done inside the house, and no-one wanted its new inhabitants to see it as a sanctuary that must at all costs be preserved. So the plumbing was renewed, and the kitchen entirely modernised with a lot of American electric machinery, like houses they had seen at the cinema. Even the room where little Dina had lived was transformed.

It dawned on Marianna that keeping everything intact had been pointless. But not to Michele Angelo, who felt his daughter had been a custodian, ensuring that whoever lived there next would inherit a cared-for environment, rather than a relic left to go to rack and ruin. A marvellous gift she had kept untouched for her nephew, as the old man saw it. But she felt she had not done enough. Because she believed everything should be for those yet to come, not those already alive. And she also insisted that the arrival in their house of someone not yet even known to them could never be adequately provided for. It was like a dry branch, she said, or a barren plant, not uprooted earlier simply out of carelessness or laziness, that then produced a gem, a sign of life, where nothing had been expected but inevitable death. This perfect nephew had turned out to be the shoot that persuades the gardener to save the whole plant after he has already written it off as lost.

When it was finally possible for them to move into the finished apartment, Cecilia went through it, throwing open all the doors, pulling aside the spick and span carpets and walking on tiptoe as if in church to avoid making any noise with her heels. The windows were so clean there seemed no glass in them at all, so she walked with her hands held out before her so as not to risk walking into them. Finally she went into the kitchen.

"Do you like it?" Vincenzo said.

Cecilia nodded, almost as if afraid to appear too enthusiastic. He gave a slight smile, lest she should think he was teasing her.

"It's all been changed," she said. The modern perfection of the room enchanted her, the gas rings and the oven, and more than anything else the refrigerator with its bulging belly.

"We are the only people in Núoro with one of those," Vincenzo said. "Aunt Marianna had it sent specially from Cagliari."

Cecilia touched everything as if she wanted to get used to it more tactually than visually. When Vincenzo held out his hand to her, she pulled herself closer to him. "Thank you," she whispered.

"What for?" he said. "Thank *you*."

"What for?" she said in turn.

They laughed and embraced. Outside, beyond those windows so perfect that it was hard to believe they existed at all, a light breeze had blown a few early fallen leaves between the houses and along the lanes, while the sky was constructing what seemed to be threadlike spider's webs from the slenderest clouds.

It was the precise moment when summer asks autumn permission to stay a little longer and autumn agrees; Vincenzo and Cecilia kissed.

It had been several weeks since the brothers Gavino and Luigi Ippolito last called on their sister Marianna in her room. This in no way surprised her, considering the sense of disquiet that had afflicted her since the afternoon after her discussion with their father, and considering how much time had passed in her mind since the brothers had last appeared to her.

So it was a real relief to see Luigi Ippolito sitting on the edge of the straw-seated chair and Gavino standing near the milky surface of the window. It was quite clear from their faces that this was no courtesy visit.

What's been happening here? Luigi Ippolito started.

We've changed a few things, Marianna said, playing for time. Luigi Ippolito nodded to his brother.

What about you two? she asked.

Gavino looked at her like someone pointlessly trying to avoid bringing bad news.

We are suffering for you, he answered.

Marianna risked a smile: We're fine, she said.

My dear, Gavino began, then looked at his brother, waiting for a sign from him before saying more: You know as well as we do . . .

Marianna involuntarily started shaking her head. Is it me? She asked hopefully.

Gavino waited a moment before denying this with a sharp movement of his head. Luigi Ippolito nervously pushed his hair away from his brow. No, my love, it's not you, he confirmed.

When? Marianna asked, a hint of resistance in her voice.

Now, Gavino answered.

Luigi Ippolito seemed to agree.

Marianna leaped out of bed.

Got dressed.

Ran along the corridor.

Went into her father's room without even knocking. The old man was lying quite still. Asleep, he seemed unexpectedly docile, his brow smooth. His daughter shook him until he woke and sat bolt upright in bed. "What's going on?" he asked, his mouth still full of sleep.

"Oh," she said. "Thanks be to Heaven!"

"What's the matter?" Michele Angelo continued, staring at his daughter.

She did not answer, but fell into a chair in the corner of the room. "So you're sleeping on Mother's side?" she said.

Michele Angelo shrugged as though to shake off the embarrassment of this sudden intimacy. "So what?" he reacted. "But what's been going on?"

Now Marianna faced up to her duty to warn the old man that the Nothingness so long evoked must be about to end and that the icy glare of destiny was once more hovering over their home.

But Michele Angelo understood everything without her having to force herself to extremes. He could see she was dressed as if for early Mass. He got out of bed, displaying with a certain pride the physical decline that had made his legs thinner and his belly more prominent, pulled trousers over his woollen underpants as if alone in his room and finished dressing with careful precision. He knew he had to be ready quickly.

They calmly went to sit in the kitchen. She asked her father if he wanted anything. He said no. It was still two hours before dawn.

They could smell a new season, the time when foxes mate and oranges ripen, and the sky smells of cinnamon and embers.

Then came a violent knocking.

By the time Vincenzo reached home, it had already happened. Cecilia had somehow managed to drag herself back to bed, and now seemed unconscious. He was more frightened by her empty expression than by the blood as if from a slaughterhouse that had soaked the sheets and carpet and the whole floor as far as the bathroom. "I'm cold," she said when aware that her husband had at last come home. He wanted to hold her close, but realised her nightdress was sodden. So instinctively he backed away from the bed and looked around for the first time.

He had been late. It was a couple of hours before dawn.

"You weren't here," Cecilia was saying.

"We have to keep calm," Vincenzo murmured, more to re-assure himself than her. "I must call someone." Confused, he took a woollen blanket from the wardrobe and put it round her shoul-ders to stop her trembling. Then went out of the house by the front door.

Once outside he knew he must run. The darkness was of that intense quality that precedes first light. There was a smell of baking and roast coffee, and a few stray dogs were out scavenging. Sensations were piling up inside him as if fastidiously trying to distract him from the absolute imperative of reaching the one place where help could be found.

So once more he found himself in front of the gate he had first found ajar exactly eleven years previously, and knocked with all his strength.

They opened at once.

She was taken to hospital. They said that, in her twenty-second week of pregnancy, she had had more of a premature birth than a miscarriage caused by cervical insufficiency. And also that her copious haemorrhaging had necessitated curettage and a blood transfusion.

It took Marianna and Cecilia's sister Francesca a long time to get the blood out of the sheets, curtains, floors and bathroom tiles.

Cecilia said she had just fallen asleep when she felt humidity, and almost without waking touched herself between the legs and found she was wet. She had tried to stand but failed, because as soon as she was out of bed her legs gave way and it was only as she fell, that she realised she was fully awake. She had tried to drag herself to the bathroom propped on her elbows, but had to fight a terrible instinct that seemed to be trying to force her to contract her muscles so as to expel a foreign body from her belly. More she could not remember, just that her lips had seemed cold and unresponsive and her head very light. Reaching the bathroom she had grasped the edge of the basin and tried again to stand. She thinks it was then, during that struggle, that she felt something inert slide down the inside of her leg, cushioned by the wet nightdress.

She could not say more than that. Instead she wept, and whoever was with her wept too.

Vincenzo, in the days that followed, explained over and over again why he had not been at home in such a crisis. He had been detained at a long meeting of the Federterra, the Union of Agricultural Workers. They had all heard how the Piano di Rinascita, the regeneration plan, was leading to a lot of swindling there and, Well, he had said, this was causing discontent because, though Fascism had officially been abolished five years before, it was not really a thing of the past at all, since those who had previously worn black shirts had now simply changed them for white ones. That was why he had been so late home that night, he said, because even those working for him at the church of Le Grazie were just poor devils without proper support who, once they had finished that particular job, would find themselves once more with no guarantee of further work, while those who knew the right people would be able to profit from the inflow of cash from Rome. There, that's how it was, just that. Finally someone said, "Look, Vincé, nothing's changed, what matters is that your wife gets better." So he hastened to reassure them, "Yes, yes, she is getting better."

He felt a huge sense of gratitude to the man who had spoken to him, whoever he was, allowing him a moment of normality in the midst of his terrible distress. He had a horrible, vague feeling of being stunned, almost as if understanding for the first time that everything he had found could be snatched away again in a single instant. As if a hand were grasping his throat without exerting pressure, just as a warning. There he was, ready for anything, and whenever he had anyone to talk to, he would talk about the dreadful night when Cecilia had suffered, had suffered so terribly . . .

*

While his wife was recovering he had gone back to sleeping in his former bachelor room at the old house.

On the second night he heard a knock. It was Michele Angelo, carrying a photograph album. The old man sat down on his grandson's bed and held it out, waiting in silence for Vincenzo to open it.

"These are your uncles Pietro and Paolo," he explained, pointing to the first picture. The two little boys were sitting on a donkey. "They died not long after that. There are no other pictures of them, people didn't take many photographs in those days."

Vincenzo looked closely. The boy in front seemed to be trying to hold back a smile while the other, behind, was making no effort to hide a sulky expression. "How old were they?" he said.

"Ten years old."

"Twins?"

Michele Angelo said yes. They turned to the next photo. "Your father," the old man said quietly. "You've already seen him."

"But not this photo."

"He can't have been more than seventeen here." Luigi Ippolito was trying to balance on a rock with a row of vines behind him.

"Where was this?"

"A place that doesn't exist anymore," Michele Angelo said, turning the page. "And here's your uncle Gavino, just out here in the courtyard."

Vincenzo couldn't help laughing: Gavino was pretending to look like a caveman. Michele Angelo smiled. "This is how disasters happen, my boy," he said, suddenly serious. "Look carefully: your father, your uncles, and now look at this one . . ." He leafed through the album in search of a particular photograph. "Your aunt in her wedding dress." Vincenzo looked up from the album. Behind his grandfather, as if on cue, Marianna herself had appeared in the room.

"Unbelievable, don't you think?" she said. Michele Angelo swung round towards his daughter, following Vincenzo's eyes. "I mean, that could be me . . . I really can't believe it now." She looked at herself, happy and beautiful in the photo. "And to think I thought it horrible to be dressed up like that." She allowed a long pause. "I know what it proves," she began again, turning directly to her nephew. "I have had so many moments like this, when I have felt certain I was losing in every respect, when I felt all the best things of life slipping through my hands. Never waste your time looking for reasons and trying to find explanations. There." She stopped. "You see how it ends? It ends with leafing through an album of photographs that show you when you thought you were ugly but when you in fact were very beautiful, without wrinkles, slim and with perfect hair. But it can also end with you seeing yourself again when you thought you were utterly beautiful and as elegant as a queen but instead were clumsy and ugly. Everything passes, Vincenzo, when you think you have things in hand they will be mercilessly snatched away from you."

"You saw him, didn't you? My son."

Marianna shook her head. "Never mind that now." She knew she would never be able to tell him about that tiny being, so perfectly formed but no larger than a fist, that she had picked up from the bathroom floor.

"He was my son." Vincenzo sobbed, trying to hold back his tears.

"Yes," Michele Angelo said.

Marianna nodded, waiting in case what her nephew might say

would need any further comment. "But you must understand that having children never makes you stronger. In fact, it makes you weaker, revealing depths of fear inside you that you never could have imagined," she finished in a single breath.

A long silence followed. Indeed, everything had changed: If you looked around, you would not be able to claim that even that sacred room had remained unchanged, despite everyone's efforts. Even those photographs, so full of life, were beginning to mist over and fade. This realisation surprised Michele Angelo and Marianna, who had always before found consolation in their way of remembering, but that day, abruptly, they could only find reasons to fear that all the pain that had forged them was obstinately returning to its true home.

Life went on, and the episode of the stillbirth began to seem ancient history.

It was a melancholy Cecilia who went back to work, because the children she looked after were all other people's children. She felt empty, and she told anyone who asked her so. When those working with her saw her pass by they looked at her with understanding, as if the only path open to her must be victory over misfortune. Other women would have accepted defeat, but not Cecilia. Not she. She had a beauty in her that rejected defeat. Her white uniform, much like a nurse's, though complete with cap and apron like a high-class waitress, made her look even more beautiful if that were possible. Spectacular rather than modest, perfect in every detail, from the turn of her lip to the jut of her chin, from her luxuriant hair to arching brows: some unexpected detail would always surprise you.

Only Vincenzo worried her. He insisted on meeting her every afternoon at four-thirty when she finished work. When she turned towards the gate he would be there across the road, sometimes on his motorbike and sometimes on foot, as if he had just happened to be passing. He would always watch her take leave of her colleagues before going over to meet her, waiting a moment before crossing the road. When she reached him he would wrap an arm round her in front of everyone, like a former Siamese twin who missed their lost joint existence. Her colleagues would envy her luck in having found a man to love her so much.

But Cecilia was not so happy. It seemed unnatural that he should always want to escort her the short distance from the O.N.M.I. to their home. She felt her husband must be suffering in some way from her apparent freedom. But she was too intelligent to say this out loud.

During the short journey home Vincenzo seldom spoke.

Their conversation never got beyond the fact that Cecilia's work colleagues had fewer problems than his wife because they were unmarried and had no house to run.

And it could not be said that Vincenzo was implying that, unlike the others, Cecilia had something rather more than a simple home to look after.

"Is there anything you need?" she would ask.

And he would say, "No, we misunderstand each other."

"On the contrary, we understand each other only too well," she said.

"I'm saying this for you," Vincenzo said, not making clear if he was being serious or not, because instead of stating it outright he whispered it.

"For me?" she said, but without it coming across as a question.

"Because you're getting tired," he said, making things worse.

The nervous laugh that escaped her seemed more of an un-spoken answer than a direct reaction to his remark. "Relax," she told him, while he fussed at their front door.

Inside it always smelled of quince, real life and fresh air from the wide open windows, whatever the season. Of olive-oil-based

Marseilles soap on the floors. Of sheets changed at least once a week. A steady persistent natural smell with no ingredient ever missing, whether it was Sunday morning, Saturday or Monday. The table was never left uncleared after lunch or dinner, and the kitchen was always as clean after a meal as if it had never been used at all.

That interior, that scent, summarised the answers Cecilia did not know how to give Vincenzo. And he certainly realised that when she asked him if he was in need of anything, she was referring specifically to her devoted and irreproachable housekeeping. Certainly it could never be said that her work at the O.N.M.I. ever caused her to neglect home or husband, and in fact this was never suggested.

"I ask myself how you do it, how you manage so much," Vincenzo said as he hung up his jacket.

Cecilia waited for him to go on, but he said no more. "Is my work a problem? Even now?" she said, to change the subject.

"Your work is looking after other people's children," he said finally. "How do you manage it?"

"I'm not ill," she said simply.

"That's not what I was trying to say."

"Whatever you meant, the fact is I'm not ill."

This insistence upset Vincenzo. "Come here," he told her. Cecilia went up to him and he hugged her, in the space between the fridge and the table against which he was leaning. He whispered, "My love." Words never frightened him. He was deeply in love and understood how much she needed to feel loved. They stayed embraced and motionless, silent for a long time.

Then she said, "I'm really sorry," before touching his chest lightly with her lips.

Autumn 1956 arrived without warning on September 20. Vincenzo could not help noticing, because while the *solette* – the stone slabs for the new church – were being set in place, the workers went from vests to sweaters and gloves in the course of a single day. You could not say the light had changed, just that the sky seemed to have moved much closer to the earth, as if it had become heavier, sticky and cold.

From the top of the church, the city-cum-building-site seemed to have turned to stone in the unusually solid air. The level expanse now stretched over the whole area from the narrow-gauge railway to the south-east slope, where small detached buildings were beginning to spread, encouraged by a swelling flood of investment. It was a time of consolations and duality – shepherds versus peasants, bosses versus servants, bourgeoisie against working class, all in their first decisive confrontation. The revolution here was based on the illusion that equal opportunities were open to all. They just had to believe in the perverse mechanism of compensation for this to kick in. The more the town grew, the less of a city it was. And, so long as no-one tried to invent it, there was very little History available for anyone to take into consideration. And what there was happened to be so ancient as to be of very doubtful relevance.

That sudden autumn, hour after hour, became a point of no

return. The folk who had made the place pulsate with life looked about and did not recognise themselves. They were changing without knowing it. Their instinct for resistance had gradually given way to imagined acceptance. How could one say one must cure people who were ill but unaware of it, or that new times had created new pathologies never previously labelled as such. Certainly people had got richer, but without ever really knowing they had ever been poor. And they had become more impatient in demanding what they had been promised. That early autumn marked the passage from active memory to passive memory, carried by a selfish fury, a deep and widespread malice that turned friends into enemies, and the simple-minded into cunning schemers. Under the living crust of people who wanted to enjoy life after twenty years of mourning, were others brooding in immaturity without any methods or even real motives to lift themselves out of the same grief. They believed they deserved to eat with the rich, but never having been invited to the table were unaware that they had been making do with crumbs. The new rich were just as they had always been, only seeming different now because they had stopped mingling with the poor and were no longer content with the patched-up trousers of past years. Because this was a bourgeois age. A time for showing off. Traditional clothes were now considered relics from a distant past, and they wanted to get rid of handmade furniture and have dining suites manufactured in factories.

From the top of the new church one could see clear evidence of the spread of all these shortcomings, of these inadequacies. A rapid and violent transformation had occurred. It was like discovering that you had to go to the barber from one day to the next – like going to bed with perfect hair and waking up with uncombable locks. Proof that even the most sudden changes are not, in fact, that sudden. The only sudden thing is the moment when one becomes aware of them.

Vincenzo's eyes swept over the mass of prefabricated new houses already beginning to decay and at the same time "spreading" endlessly in accordance with the inevitable process of infinity. He shuddered because his clothes were not warm enough; who could have thought it would get cold so suddenly?

Mimmíu engaged the third gear, grinding the motor. "It won't last," he said. "I tell you, it'll finish badly. One step forward and two back: the point is that, in proportion to what they have been allotted, the land round here only yields the half, and to improve it will cost double to anyone wanting to cultivate it. It's pretty obvious you can't carry out reforms without taking into account those most affected by them, isn't it?" Vincenzo looked thoughtful, but said nothing. "It's not just a matter of poor productivity, it's basic inexperience. They haven't had the training, Vincé, they lack skills and old-style co-operation." He approached a curve. "So the only people who will profit from this so-called reform will be contractors from the mainland and, even then, only those who already owned something or have seen their land increase in value without having to pay their dues to the syndicates. It's when we get past the crazy idea that everything is possible that you'll see the real trouble begin, Vincé."

"Of course," Vincenzo finally answered, bracing himself with both hands against the dashboard to absorb the abrupt braking of the car.

"Sorry." Mimmíu pulled his keys out of the ignition.

They had stopped in an area of sparsely planted young pines. The rumble of the sea was not far away. Mimmíu got out of the car and took a few steps. He had grown fatter, but this had only increased his seeming authority. He was wearing high-waisted trousers and a rust-coloured autumn jacket over an ivory-coloured shirt.

"You look like a fashion model," Vincenzo said.

"O.K., have your joke," Mimmíu grumbled. "I know I've put on weight. But this is the site," he added, indicating a precise section of pines that opened like a wedge between two horns of rock.

Vincenzo examined the place. "Can one build here?"

Mimmíu looked at him as if at a child. "The commune has no interest in what you do here. If you buy it, it's yours, end of story."

"But what about water, power and drainage?" Vincenzo insisted.

"All taken into account, but the point is that the authorities are only bothered if it's worth their while . . . understand?"

"So in practice I buy without thinking twice, and they know they'll make a fat profit."

"Vincé, if I wasn't sure it was a bargain I would never have suggested it. I know important people who've already invested in big plots of land round here."

"Listen, you know how much respect I've always had for you, it was you who first brought me here, but what on earth can I do with a scrap of sandy pine forest like this."

"How do you mean, what can you do? Build yourself a little house. The sea's beautiful round here."

"I know the area well, Mimmí, it's barely five years since we rescued the people round here from the mosquitoes."

"You're quite wrong, things are changing fast now. People want things that didn't even exist a short time ago, my trade union friends tell me that in the north in Gallura, mainland folk and even foreigners are moving in to buy land by the sea."

"Let them. If I go home and tell Michele Angelo I've thrown away a hundred thousand lire on a scrap of pine forest he won't even let me back into the house."

"Just think about it, Vincé. I tell you, you'll be sorry if you don't."

"You talk so much, Mimmí, have you bought a site for yourself?"

"Well, I might buy this one."

Vincenzo gave him such a long stare that he looked at the ground as though searching for something. "I've never had a real brother, Mimmí. You are my brother. So as your brother, let me tell you, find yourself a good girl and forget this other stuff."

Mimmíu smiled with a slightly twisted mouth and lit a cigarette. He inhaled with pleasure because the scent of the pines had drenched the breeze with a syrupy sweetness one could almost taste. A little further off, the sea was like satin stretched over a tailor's table ready to be shaped, and the sand could have been ashes. "There are no more good girls, Vincé," Mimmíu stated rather bitterly. "But guess who's just got married in Sassari?" He paused. "Your relative, Nicola Serra-Pintus. He's landed a job in the Agricultural Inspectorate, even though he has no educational qualifications. How about that?"

Vincenzo laughed. A late turtle-dove was still complaining among the pine branches. Dry pine needles had softened the sandy soil. The sea was slowly sighing like the breath of a dying man. Cecilia's expecting again, he revealed. Nobody knows, we haven't told anyone. But now you know, and so does the doctor, of course.

Mimmíu's lower lip trembled. He held his breath as if trying to control something uncontrollable and tensed his eyelids as if attempting to stop tears bursting from his eyes. Regaining control, he hugged his friend and buried his head in his collar. "Yes, yes," he said. "Well done!"

They had decided to announce the pregnancy at the end of the fifth month. Mainly because by then it would be visible, but also because this was the critical phase which had previously ended in stillbirth. It was not easy to say how Cecilia was feeling: she did not seem anxious, though not particularly confident either. She told everyone who asked that she was readying herself for the moment when the doctor would order her to stay in bed so as to discourage her slack cervix from rejecting the foetus again. She seemed docile in a new way, even resigned to having a metal ring inserted to keep her body firmly closed. Yet she found it hard to understand why her body should try to reject something she so much wanted. She was certainly not afraid of losing Vincenzo's love. She knew well that discouragement was not a word he understood, and also that he would have loved her no less if she had been as arid as a desert. She had indeed been lucky to find such uncommon love, and he felt a similar good fortune. But she was afraid of missing symptoms she had been too inexperienced to understand on the previous occasion. That constant pain in her loins, for example, had she felt that before? And the numb sensation in her legs when she spent any length of time sitting down? And a certain confusing vagueness of thought? Or being thirsty at night? Or the burning in her stomach? Was it all happening again, or was this different?

For three months she moved as little as possible. Outside, snow began to fall gently but persistently. Everyone said the whole nation had been gripped by frost of a kind never seen or felt before. In Núoro snow fell without stopping for two weeks and the temperature dropped to minus nine or ten. Total peace and utter immobility dominated everything. Never in human memory had there been such snow. Schools and offices had to be closed and all life was subjected to a white dictatorship. It was the first time Cecilia had ever seen snow. She watched the flakes accumulate silently on the window sill of her room, and little stalactites grow downwards from the gutters. The euphoria that had first driven everyone out of their homes to play like children again had changed to stupor and disquiet. Those daring enough to venture onto the streets had to climb heaps of snow up to two metres high. Warm under her bedclothes, Cecilia began to be afraid the silence would never end, and that everyone would be dazzled by the clarity that filled even moonless nights with a blinding glare.

Vincenzo had had a telephone installed in both houses so there would always be a way to keep in touch.

Having a telephone in the house took Marianna back to the old days. She had had one in Cagliari as far back as 1928, which seemed a lifetime away. Now, as she watched the workmen attaching cables and testing the instrument, it occurred to her that her widowhood had somehow taken her back to her origins, and that this had been a way of saving herself. She had made an effortless and instantaneous transition back from wife and mother to daughter; all it had needed had been a hail of shot into the face of her husband Biagio, and a stray bullet in the forehead of her little girl Dina . . .

But now the snow outside saddened her, bound her to the logs crackling in the fireplace, and reminded her that one day a silence would begin that would never end. The quiet in the kitchen was overwhelming. Michele Angelo had made himself a path from house to workshop, and was constructing firedogs for himself in the flames of the forge.

When Dina sat down beside Marianna and stretched out her little hands to warm them, Marianna instinctively shooed her away to prevent her from speaking. Dina looked crossly at her mother, stood up and put her hands over her ears. Outside the French window, the path just trodden by Michele Angelo was already covered by fresh snow. A strong certainty had settled on Marianna's mind, but she pushed it aside, unwilling even to consider it. She felt weak and sorrowful. She was thinking of going over to Vincenzo's house, but when she turned back to the fireplace she saw that Dina had not moved, realising that speaking would be pointless. In fact, words hardly ever came from the world where she lived now.

Marianna began to work out how to get to via Deffenu. Perhaps pulling on a pair of over-long country trousers belonging to her father, as she would need to gather the strength to open the courtyard gate when the moment came to thrust herself through it. And once through it, she would need to make her way through the icy froth that now covered everything.

But she must do what she had to do, and since Dina had raised no objection she convinced herself she was doing the right thing. She found some suitable trousers and some enormous boots that needed three pairs of wool socks. When ready to go, it occurred to her she should tell her father and telephone Vincenzo. But no sooner had she lifted the receiver to her ear than she realised the telephone was dead. So she wrote a note to tell Michele Angelo she had gone out and that his supper was ready for him in the oven.

Vincenzo also banged the receiver down on a dead telephone. The weather had interrupted the line. Cecilia had been asleep for at least two hours, in a deep torpor from which he could not wake her. He tried three times, and each time she protested almost to the point of losing her temper. He imagined her wonderful body warm, soft and tense under the covers. Her big belly and the life swelling inside it dominated his thoughts. But he could not wake her. She was pale and her lips were tightly closed. He tried again: "My love," he whispered. "My love." She grimaced and tried to open her eyes, but failed. So he took her by the shoulders to help her tenderly raise herself into a sitting position without suffering discomfort, but she resisted him with exceptional strength. He was too surprised to be alarmed. Years later, remembering that moment, he would tell himself her strength had been unconscious. "My love," he said again, louder. Then he turned back to the telephone in the corridor and repeatedly dialled the doctor's number which he knew by heart, but it was useless.

Beyond the window, in an orgy of silence, the frost was reaching its peak, as if it was never going to be possible to return again from that whiteness. Vincenzo began to lose control of his breathing. A doubt was growing inside him, with the same subtle but obstinate power as the relentlessly falling flakes of snow. Terrified, he went back to Cecilia, gently moving the covers back to see what he dreaded above all else. So he covered her again, telling himself he could not believe it, that it was too unbelievably cruel that natural conditions had combined to make it utterly impossible for anyone to come to the help of his child.

He stood in the middle of the bedroom while Cecilia slept on, frowning as if she was having a bad dream. He wanted to shout, but was restrained by the fear that she too might have realised what was happening, or had already happened. So he sat back on the carpet, to be able to think better and more quickly, to stifle any doubt, to reinforce every certainty, to preserve every memory, to lament anything forgotten, to define every substance, to console himself in his distress, and to pray every prayer. Thus he realised that despite his upbringing, he had never really learned to pray, and that this failure had imprisoned him in an unprofitable farce. He could see himself again as the child he had been, on the end bench at the orphanage where the kneeler had no cushion, and feeling again the old pain in his kneecaps. He remembered the cutting way Father Vesnaver had invited him to pray as best he could, which would be good enough. So now, at the foot of the bed where his wife was sleeping her unnatural sleep and where in all likelihood the worst thing possible was happening without anyone being able to do anything about it, he mumbled the only prayer he had ever learned at the orphanage, the Lord's Prayer in Trieste dialect:

Pare nostro che te sta in zel
che fussi benedido el tu nome
che venissi el tu podèr
che fussi fato el tu volèr
come in zel cussí qua zo.
Mandine sempre el toco de pan

e perdònine quel che gavemo falà
come noi ghe perdonemo a chi che ne ga intajà
No sta mostrarne mai nissuna tentazion
e distrighine de ogni bruto mal.
Amen

A tremendous silence followed.

Then Vincenzo heard knocking.

Nobody knows how Marianna, unrecognisable in her borrowed clothes, reached her nephew's house; even managing to drag the doctor with her, no better dressed than herself, each of them a shapeless bundle of garments and shoes. Once out of their cocoons they got Vincenzo to take them to the bedroom where Cecilia was still asleep. The doctor felt her pulse and took her temperature, with Vincenzo impatient to lift the covers to show them what he had seen.

What he had seen was just a trickle of blood, enough to soak the fine fabric of her underwear and stain the sheet. But the doctor felt her stomach and understood.

"We must wake her," he said to Marianna, avoiding Vincenzo's eye. "And we'll need some hot water," he added, turning to Vincenzo.

Marianna, who had understood more than she would have liked, nevertheless raised her chin as if to ask the doctor a silent question. The doctor barely shook his head, so that Vincenzo, running to fetch hot water from the tank in the kitchen, should not realise there was nothing to be done. Clearly the dead child must be expelled by any means possible, since it was out of the question to take Cecilia anywhere else with the streets in their present state.

217

"I didn't expect it, I really didn't expect it," the doctor murmured.

Vincenzo brought a steaming basin of water. Now he was no longer alone, he seemed eager for action and was full of expectation. He was well aware that the particular way the doctor drew back was far from promising, but he kept telling himself there was no reason to expect the worst and that nothing should be read into the simple fact that his aunt had managed to reach the house.

"Here's the water," he announced.

The doctor called Cecilia by name and patted her gently. "Cecilia, good girl, wake up."

But it was as if her sleep had saved her, as if it had been fundamental to her life. "No!" she roared, aware that the doctor, unlike Vincenzo, would not give up, and almost as if that "no" had been yelled by someone who had been fully lucid since the start and only pretended not to be.

"We have to get on with this, Cecilia," the doctor insisted. "When did it happen?"

Vincenzo looked at her, puzzled, coming forward as though to the edge of an extremely high cliff. Marianna put one hand over her mouth to shut the agony back inside her body, and reached out her other hand to touch her nephew as he passed.

"The heart of the foetus has not been beating," the doctor explained, finally looking Vincenzo in the face. "The child must have been – dead for several hours, I would say."

"But I never moved from here," Vincenzo said, almost as if the doctor had been accusing him. "Oh, dead?"

The doctor nodded, but Vincenzo's face was so stricken with grief that, for a moment, he too seemed about to break down.

"We can't leave it in there," the doctor said, trying to soften the phrase to make it sound less ruthless. "We must take it out before it can be noxious to the mother."

"Noxious," Vincenzo repeated.

"Yes, before antibodies begin to mark it out as an extraneous body. Do you understand?" the doctor said, turning to Marianna.

"Why is she still asleep?" Vincenzo insisted.

"Because she has understood what has happened," the doctor answered.

The grief of the world was now this dozing woman, surrounded by an absolutely silent pure-white mourning earth. Around it the stupor of branches needed to conserve their strength. The tomb-like obscurity of seed longing to bud and grow towards the light. Utter humility like a whispered prayer, a liturgy of rejected pain.

The child was a boy weighing nearly two kilos. Vincenzo wanted to see him, but Marianna kneeled before him like St Francis and begged him not to look.

It was six in the morning now and Cecilia's eyes were wide open; she looked around as if wanting to say something important, but no words came. She did not want anyone to touch her, including Vincenzo. She had to be taken to hospital to have her uterus scraped and did not want her husband with her.

After ten days Cecilia was able to return home. She told Marianna who had gone to fetch her that she wanted to walk, after all it was not far. Warmly covered, they made their way slowly back. The cold air did not encourage conversation.

"Vincenzo?" Cecilia asked.

Marianna shrugged. Cecilia knew she never let inessential words escape her lips. "He's been sleeping at home recently," was all Marianna said, as if not understanding the woman had been asking why her husband had not come to take her home. "How are you feeling?" Marianna asked, noticing the younger woman had slowed down and almost stopped.

"I'm fine," Cecilia said sharply. "But Vincenzo?" she asked again more insistently.

"Things like this frighten men," Marianna stated. "It has not been a good time for him."

"No? Really?" Cecilia sneered. "It was a nice little break for me, of course."

"It was best I came to fetch you. He wanted to come, but better not."

"But why? Is he so sensitive? Poor thing. Then you'd better tell him he needn't show his face at home either."

"My dear." Marianna was playing for time."If you take things like that it'll only make them worse, believe me. Neither of you is going about this the right way. What happened happened, and when you told him you didn't want him to come with you to the hospital, it nearly drove him out of his mind."

"But what about me?" This seemed more of an exclamation than a question. Marianna looked at her. "It nearly drove me mad too, didn't it?"

"You must know, dear girl, husbands can sometimes be more difficult than children, much more difficult . . ."

"Forgive me, I've never had much chance to compare," Cecilia cut in sharply, starting to walk faster, so that Marianna had to hurry to keep up.

The house was extraordinarily tidy, just the way Marianna liked to have it: with everything in its place, Cecilia noticed, immediately realising that during her convalescence Marianna would have had plenty of time to make sure everything was put back the way it had been before Cecilia came, with Vincenzo single again and the house entirely her own.

"I'll make the bed up for you," Marianna said.

Cecilia sat down. "Don't worry about me."

"Are you warm enough?" Marianna asked.

"I'm fine." The afternoon was like a dirty rag; it had stopped snowing and the whiteness was now mixed with the reappearing ugliness of the world: animal faeces, rotten leaves, hard-trodden earth, mud and black footprints. The two women sat facing each other like widows sighing before their husbands' graves.

They heard the door open: Marianna started, but Cecilia did not move.

*

Vincenzo looked as if he had just woken from a coma, his face showing signs of forced sleep. Presumably directed by Marianna, he had shaved and put on good clothes, and was even carrying flowers.

All Cecilia said was, "Your eyes are swollen."

He lowered his head, so that a brilliantined lock of hair slipped down from the smooth mass at his crown. He looked deeply embarrassed as he stood there holding the flowers.

"I brought you these," he said, giving the bunch a shake.

"Yes," she agreed, making no attempt to put him at his ease.

In the silence that followed the light began to fade beyond the windows and afternoon started rapidly turning to evening.

Marianna stood up. "I ought to go now," she said, "or my father will be getting worried."

No-one spoke as she went out.

Alone with his wife Vincenzo put the flowers on the table. "If you're hungry, there's food ready," he said.

Cecilia went on staring at him; in fact she had not taken her eyes off him since he came in. "You've been drinking," she stated simply but firmly.

Vincenzo nodded like a guilty child.

"I can take anything else," she said, getting to her feet. "Anything else," she insisted, "but not drunks."

"I'm sorry," Vincenzo whined, following her into the kitchen.

As if forcing normality at all costs, Cecilia began laying the table. "I've seen too many drunks where I work, and their wives and children too. Especially the children, that's what I've seen!"

"I'm not a drunk." Vincenzo was tentative. "I just felt confused."

"So you drink." She attacked again.

"It just happened, alright?"

"You never came to the hospital once!"

"You didn't want me there!"

"I *what*?"

"You didn't want me to come."

Cecilia looked at him, shocked. "But who on earth are you?" she asked. "What are you? What sort of a man are you? Thanks to you, I no longer have a family, and you allow yourself to say things like that!"

It is not possible to say Vincenzo was not telling the truth, and he stared at his wife, feeling seriously disoriented. "Do you think it's been easy for me?" he floundered, as if to fill the silence.

Cecilia allowed herself an uneasy laugh. "Well, that makes us equal then. I'm sorry I was ill while you were having such a hard time."

"That's not what I was trying to say." He was desperate to soften the effect of his words.

"Look, it's best if you shut up. Just be quiet, is that clear?" Vincenzo was about to answer, but again his wife spoke first. "*Quiet!*"

He stared at her in astonishment. He had been ready for anything except such rage, such spite. He knew things would not be easy, but could not have guessed they would be as difficult as this. So when she told him yet again to be quiet, emphasising her words by pointing at the sky, he swallowed any possible response, tried to thump the table, and left the kitchen.

Cecilia released the tears she had been holding back for so long only after she heard the front door slam behind him.

*

At three that night Cecilia nerved herself to telephone Mimmíu and explain that Vincenzo had not come home. Mimmíu said not to worry, she had done well to call. He would go out and look for Vincenzo, and as soon as he had found him would ring back.

He called half an hour later. Everything was fine, and he was taking Vincenzo to sleep at his place.

The next afternoon Vincenzo waited for his wife outside the O.N.M.I. as usual. He had not even changed his clothes. She went over to join him, as always. They stared at one another as if facing their destiny, something they would never be able to turn back from. It was as if a casually flung stone had hit the most sensitive spot on a glass window. Isn't that what they say? That there is a single point at which even the most solid glass will shatter?

"I couldn't believe you had gone back to work already," he said.

She did not answer, letting him follow a step behind her. It was exactly as if the tip of a walking stick dug into the ice had caused a cobweb of cracks across a frozen surface. They reached home. Inside, the kitchen was the same mess as when he left her the previous evening.

There, thought Vincenzo, how little it takes to turn the world upside down. "What shall we do?" he said.

"You can do what you like," she said. He hugged her, without warning, from behind, but she tore herself away as if that was the last thing she wanted. "Don't you dare touch me again," she said. "I've made up your bed in the other room."

The thaw was followed by evidence that the white sheet that had covered everything for nearly a month had been concealing colour. As if a room long uninhabited had been aired, freeing furniture from beneath swathes of clean fabric. A deadly pallor was gradually dissolving to reveal a pink skin underneath.

The saturated earth discharged fountains of water. In response the grateful land sprouted leaves, while a precocious warmth deceived a few almond trees into adorning themselves too soon with flowers.

March was euphoria after mourning.

Or consolation after terror.

Vincenzo and Cecilia adjusted to their new life, pretending they too had been part of a temporarily interrupted mechanism that had now returned to its normal state.

She, slimmer and stronger, continued to care for children born into families contending with such difficulties that in many cases they might have been happier to have had no children at all, which was why they had sought government assistance. The children of penniless mothers and alcoholic fathers, or fathers who did not even know they were fathers. Rather than saddening Cecilia, this work seemed to inspire her. Perhaps giving her an excuse to get out of the house, or perhaps because such deferred maternity acted like a consolation.

Vincenzo did not look forward to going home after work either. He would come home late, more often drunk than would have been the case previously. He frequently had to be fetched from a bar or tavern and taken elsewhere to sleep, since he seemed to have difficulty finding his way home on his own two feet. More than once either Mimmíu or Marianna had had to scour the city to discover where he had crashed out.

The cause of this was clear, or should have been to anyone with a modicum of compassion. But compassion is a finite sentiment that can soon turn to reproach.

Everything had been given to Vincenzo Chironi, that was what people said of him. But now he was going to pieces because of the one thing he had not managed to obtain, something that had nothing to do with his qualities as a human being. He had been good-looking, but now he was developing a paunch and dark shadows under his eyes, and his hair was receding.

He drank to avoid going home.

Drink never made him violent, but often melancholy. No-one ever feared that, once deposited at his front door, he would go in and beat his wife. Rather, when back in their joint home, he seemed bent on proving he was absolute master of himself by moving as steadily as possible, and it was only a particular habit of moving the fingers of his right hand that revealed the effort it took him to seem sober.

Cecilia did not speak to him, letting him find his dinner cold on the table, where he would, very often, leave it untouched.

Yet, he continued to work well, lending substance in every way to the legend of the Chironi family as people destined for prosperity as well as suffering.

In fact, no matter how unreliable he might appear in the evening after several glasses too many, he was always in perfect shape the following morning, sharp and efficient. And he never failed to meet Cecilia outside the O.N.M.I. at four-thirty each day, so that everyone could see that despite the gossip they were still a couple.

A strange way of loving, everyone said. And when their previous understanding turned to scorn, people said if he was a beast, it was a beast remarkably good at playing the attentive husband.

Sometimes he did manage to honour his daily vow to stop drinking, periods that usually coincided with enthusiasm for some new project. The construction of a new workshop on agricultural land just outside the city, to take one example, a place equipped with every kind of up-to-date machinery, and big enough to give work to twenty men. Vincenzo was the first Chironi to run a family business without ever having to lift a hammer himself. An honest employer, you could say, and a decent man.

But racked by great pain.

Part Three
(December 24 ,1959)

My world was in ruins
as if wrecked by a worm.
NOVALIS, *Among the Thousand Happy Hours*

Tempora

THREE YEARS LATER WHAT WAS BOUND TO HAPPEN,
actually did happen.

It had been a relatively calm period, with life settling into a sort of permanent truce. Vincenzo was forty-three now, Cecilia thirty. Mimmíu had found himself Ada, a wife with a simple name, who in May 1958 made him a father. Marianna was still solid as a rock, and still conversed with her dead relatives. Michele Angelo was eighty-nine.

But things changed, without anyone being able to stop them.

It was not a generous age.

Christ and the Merchants

BEYOND THE WINDOWS, A BURST OF CONTROLLED ACTIVITY, Vincenzo Chironi was putting on a coat, for a Christmas so mild that there seemed no need at all for such a garment. It was an autumn coat, draped over his shoulders like a discreet encouragement, not offering the warmth or protection of a proper winter overcoat. He was willing to go out again but not entirely happy about it, as he had been out all day and was tired. But some things were still needed for the Christmas dinner party, a few forgotten presents, and he had also to fetch Cecilia. Since early afternoon, she had been at the hairdresser's having her hair set in a perm, leaving him with a list of things to "complete", though making clear that she had already done most of the work herself, which was why she was now enjoying an hour or so relaxing at the hairdresser's.

Even for driving the Fiat Millecento, this autumn coat was better than his winter coat, much better. But Cecilia had barely got into the car, coiffed in a fantastic confection worthy of an Ancient Roman matron, when she asked Vincenzo if he wasn't cold in that light coat. Meaning she disapproved of it. She had always tried to keep him looking decent, but no sooner was he out of her sight than he reverted to being the same mess he always was.

"When was I always a mess?" Vincenzo said, his eyes on the glittering street.

"Ever since I first knew you." She studied her nail varnish, newly applied by the manicurist.

The huge decorated fir in the square in front of the new church of Le Grazie looked as if it had been struck by an epileptic fit. Goodness knows, Vincenzo wondered, what forest could such a vast tree have come from? And how many years it must take for a fir to grow to such a size. It must be older than I am.

"I'd like . . ." his wife began, watching the avenue slip under the car. It was as if they could feel the tyres scraping the grain of the road sixty centimetres beneath them. "I'd like it if . . ." She paused.

Vincenzo kept his eyes on the road. "What would you like?" he said a trifle sharply.

Cecilia sighed. "I would like it if when Mimmíu and his wife and their child come, Vincenzo, you would at least make a bit of an effort . . ." she blurted out in a single breath.

Then nothing more.

Christmas was a sordid muddle of shop windows, a confused flutter of mawkishness. Everyone was wearing a private smile. Oh yes. At Christmas you must have the strength to resist both the mistletoe of professional affection and the honey of seasonal benevolence. Permed hair should not be allowed at Christmas, nor should wives who behave too much like wives.

When they got home Vincenzo remembered his wife's warning. "I spend my life making efforts, Cecilia," he said, as if into thin air. He said no more. For him Christmas Eve meant he could not wear slippers or take off his tie.

It was seven in the evening now, an evening with the regretful bitter-sweet taste of an old liqueur made from nuts. His stomach was trying to subdue a bilious melancholy.

Michele Angelo, nearly ninety now, was driving Marianna mad because he was determined not to move from the old house. He had become increasingly obstinate with age and his face clouded over whenever it occurred to him that longevity was no more than a subtle revenge inflicted on him by those who would like him to live long enough to see his bloodline dry out. From the vantage point of his great age, he could now see that even Vincenzo had not come up to scratch. Every time Michele Angelo mentioned any such thing, Marianna lost her temper and threatened to have him moved to a care home. Vincenzo believed his grandfather should spend his old age somewhere where he could enjoy unending Christmas make-believe tempered by committed affection. Vincenzo was the only one who believed Marianna really meant what she said.

"Surely sooner or later she really will do it?" he said, hanging up his coat.

Cecilia shook her head. "Eh," she said, "spare the poor woman a thought, she's no longer young herself, someone should be looking after her. Did you get anything for the engineer?"

"Some aftershave," Vincenzo said absent-mindedly. "Do you really think she could do that?"

"No, of course not," Cecilia said sharply.

"And I suppose you remembered the children?" he asked, meaning Mimmíu's son and Cecilia's sister's young twin daughters.

Cecilia nodded, and went into the kitchen.

To him, it was like watching Euridice's shade vanishing back into the underworld. He knew he was living a narrow life. Thousands of years seemed to have passed since the days when he thought he would die if he could not always have her close to him. Yet he was certain he loved her no less now than he had then, just not in the same way. They had adopted a warmer way of being together now, less belligerent, and this had made things easier. You could say they had found a way of accepting their problem without really facing it. They never discussed children anymore, or made any reference to physical intimacy. But, this did not necessarily mean they had lost their deep love for one another, just that it had changed. Perhaps they now loved each other more – or perhaps not at all.

In any case the table had been carefully laid in the smaller room, with the best cutlery and plates, and glasses for wine and water and flûtes for *prosecco*, and – ready in the kitchen – special cups for *spumante*, and napkins folded like fans on the red tablecloth.

Michele Angelo, over-dressed like a sculpture about to be recast, cursed Marianna silently for trying to make him look like a beau. He came in grumbling: it was too far to come, there were too many stairs, and none of his own things were here. An armchair had been put in front of the fire for him.

With her hat off, Cecilia's curls looked like little pastry *cannoli* filled with custard, but she was never less than beautiful.

Mimmíu hated the thought of having to make comparisons. He knew, like it or not, that he would spend the whole evening brooding over whether being a parent was important or not. He would do anything for Vincenzo and Cecilia, yet the prospect of going with his child to a party at their house disturbed him. Luckily Domenico was an unusually calm boy. Mimmíu never revealed anything of this to his wife Ada. It was a point of honour with him always to be open with her, but he never said anything about "all this", because he did not know how to find the right words. On the other hand, he never had trouble finding words at trade union meetings. And he was never at a loss when he saw possible pain in the eyes of a supply worker about to lose his job at the milling machine, or read an unspoken insult on the lips of a secretary who had just been told that her pregnancy would cause issues, or when stretching his arms wide while others argued about work, or when he was looking for the right words to express his gratitude for his annual Christmas bonus.

But nothing terrified Ada more than fear of poverty. Nothing in the world. When there was a charity appeal for starving children in Africa, she could not understand why such misery had to be mentioned in church, especially at Christmas, because surely

Christmas is a time for poetry and children, for crackling fires and goose quills and flannel nighties, and of course the important thing was the feast on Christmas Eve.

"Please, Mimmí," Ada murmured, struggling to fasten a shoe buckle. She looks like a stork off balance, he thought, as rather than bending nimbly like Cleopatra's curling asp, she stiffly lifted her foot to one side.

Mimmíu was rubbing his chest with a towel.

"And watch what you say with engineer Bernardi," Ada reminded him, afraid that otherwise he would start a political discussion as usual.

Mimmíu silently stroked his wife's buttocks with the palm of his hand. "No, stop that," she said. "How come you're still not dressed? I have to get Domenico ready, so hurry up, and don't put on that grey shirt because it doesn't go with your brown suit." She chattered on and went to the child's room. Mimmíu contemplated his unappreciated erection.

How much better if they could have stayed at home to make love, but Ada thinks it is not nice to talk about such things, or even to think about sex at Christmas, because Christmas is white and virginal, chaste like a novice, more a time for teddy-bear cuddles.

Inside this uniform of a man well past thirty, inside this envelope of a young husband and father, Mimmíu was able to cloak himself in how he believed he should be. He had no idea whether his excellent health related to no conflict between doing what he wanted to do, and doing what had to be done. But he had decided to find out one day so he could tell his son.

Leaving his home, he had no sense of Christmas at all. Closing the door of the flat while Ada called the lift with their child in her arms, he could only regret being forced temporarily to leave their apartment. He consoled himself that at least the apartment had been paid for.

"I know Mimmíu doesn't seem a particularly affectionate father, but that's his nature," Vincenzo was observing as the guests were about to arrive.

Cecilia gave him an ugly look. "What makes you say that?"

Vincenzo shrugged. "These shoes hurt my feet, and when my feet hurt, it puts things into my mind."

"You say things like that about him, but have you ever been a loving father yourself?" she said pointedly. Clearly she could not forgive him for having raised the subject.

"We can never know," he said firmly.

"No," she agreed.

This Christmas dinner was designed, among other things, to bring Vincenzo and Mimmíu together again, because the twists and turns of life had recently been pulling them in different directions. The affection between them remained unchanged, but recently they had had less opportunity to spend time together.

Mimmíu and Ada were sighing when they reached the house in via Deffenu. Ada was struggling not to drop her parcels, while little Domenico was listening to laughter from the far side of the front door. Ada looked at Mimmíu, who shook off his negative thoughts like a wet dog shaking his fur, and pressed the bell.

When Vincenzo found himself face to face with Mimmíu, he imagined he was falling and struggled against the feeling. It was like dreaming you were falling without actually falling, almost an anticipation of death. Meanwhile words echoed obsessively in his head as though spoken by a ventriloquist: "Why not put your arms round him? Why not put your arms round him?"

Meanwhile the engineer Bernardi had arrived. He secured an armchair for himself as though he assumed it had been put there specially for him; being of course from a family of bosses. He had come to honour his friend Vincenzo Chironi, and to confirm their collaboration in shared building contracts – *shared*, it should be noted.

Mimmíu advanced into the sitting room followed by Ada and her parcels, while Domenico clung to his mother's skirt. Mimmíu bowed so low to the engineer, that his forehead nearly touched the man's wrist. Vincenzo waited behind him. And when Mimmíu stepped back, he and Vincenzo caught each other's eye, conscious of the alienation into which they were falling. "Happy Christmas."

Michele Angelo announced he was hungry and tired.

Cecilia's sister Francesca and her husband were the last to arrive. But they had only called in to say "Happy Christmas" because the twins were unwell. Even so they wanted to come for five minutes.

After exactly five minutes they left. At least there were still a few people in the world whose word you could trust.

Plates came and went from the table, Domenico was getting bored, while Ada's attention wandered because she was trying so hard to listen to everyone at once. Someone said Mother Teresa was not Indian as people thought, but Albanian.

The engineer thought this a huge joke. "Are you trying to tell me Mother Teresa of Calcutta is really Mother Teresa of Tirana?" he said.

"Perhaps heavenly geography is different from earthly geography," Vincenzo said. His remark happened to fall in a moment of total silence. In the silence Mimmíu suddenly laughed. Vincenzo looked at him: Mimmíu seemed as uncomplicated as fresh water, but Ada had a strange expression on her face.

The discussion next turned to Marianna, who had retreated to the kitchen to eat by herself . . . at Christmas, of all times.

That's just the way Sardinians are, the engineer declared. After a year in Sardinia, he had got to know quite a few through his business.

"Extraordinary!" Mimmíu burst out. The engineer stared at him, puzzled. Mimmíu looked for help from Vincenzo, who nodded. "Extraordinary there are so many Sards in Sardinia, isn't it?" Mimmíu said in a solemn voice. Ada and Cecilia look disapprovingly, but soberly at the two "children", because if anyone got a fit of the giggles there would be real trouble.

Hearing her name spoken, Marianna shot them a withering look from the kitchen before going back with a smile to her bowl of broth. Cecilia's voice rang out from the dining-room.

"Give me an example of something Christ said that is no longer valid today," Cecilia was saying. "I'm waiting to hear," she challenged her fellow-diners, now leaning over steaming plates of lamb.

"Well," Ada reflected, "these days we can't all be expected to be poor."

241

Cecilia finished serving the food. "But, my dear, the poverty Christ was referring to had nothing to do with economics."

"Luckily," the engineer Bernardi guffawed.

Vincenzo closed his eyes for a moment, and Mimmíu looked over at Domenico.

"Well then, what kind of poverty does it refer to?" Vincenzo said unexpectedly.

Ada wiped her mouth.

Cecilia held her husband's gaze.

"Poverty of spirit, perhaps?" she asked, making the question a statement.

Michele Angelo had stopped eating and was drowsing off. Marianna, appearing from nowhere, moved him to his chair and arranged his head against the arm.

"Yes of course, poverty of spirit," the engineer Bernardi said approvingly.

Vincenzo nodded; he felt himself sinking deeper, his feet hurt, and his tie was throttling him.

"Poverty of spirit," Ada repeated.

"I'd be really curious to know if spiritual riches paid for your hairdo, Cecilia." Vincenzo's voice was ominously calm. Ada winced and Cecilia shook her head.

The silence around the table was growing heavy, so the engineer Bernardi decided to break the ice. "Have I ever told you the one about the man who insisted on having a loan?"

It was time for the presents now, fortunately.

Cecilia looked coldly at Vincenzo: "Oh, a pressure cooker, how could you have guessed?"

"You look so distinguished in that felt hat and soft brim . . ."

The scarf for *nonno* Michele Angelo was still in its wrapping, he would see it tomorrow morning. There was also a blender and a regimental tie and tennis shoes and a little picture of the Madonna of Fatima. And another tie, some eau de Cologne, and after-shave – "Oh, you really shouldn't have" – and a paper-weight, and some crayons, and a book of adventure stories, a pair of tongs for serving roast meat, a hotplate, a silk scarf, a toy track, and then . . . Marianna brought in her present for her nephew . . . a picture, a so-called artistic reproduction of a painting by Caravaggio: *St Matthew and the Angel*, showing the angel dictating the gospel to the saint.

Panettone or *pandoro*? A problem quickly solved.

"*Pandoro*'s as good as *panettone* but lighter," the engineer began.

"Hard to say." Cecilia considered the question. "To me this *pandoro*'s like the work of the devil . . . I mean . . . the tradition of eating it."

Vincenzo found it extraordinary how useful such a pointless discussion could be.

The table was covered with used glasses; Marianna had spirited away the dirty plates and surreptitiously busied herself tidying up in the hope that Cecilia would not chide her. The table was now strewn with nut shells, the remnants of a frenzied pleasure.

The company was beginning to move from the table. Domenico was falling asleep on his feet. Vincenzo had loosened his tie and undone the top button of his shirt. Mimmíu and the engineer were talking politics.

Soon it would be time to get ready for midnight Mass. But not for Michele Angelo, because Marianna was taking him home.

"No, no," Ada said, struggling to get her son into his coat. "Do you want to go to sleep on the very night Jesus was born? This is the one night you can't sleep. We're all going together now to see baby Jesus born."

Domenico shook his head. "Leave him alone," Vincenzo said, coming into the room. "Settle him down in the guest bed. I'm staying here."

"Aren't you coming to church with us?" Ada was astonished. She was about to give in and leave the little coat on the armchair.

"Get that coat on him! Finish dressing him!" Mimmíu commanded, arriving at that moment.

"He's tired," Vincenzo protested without even turning round. "Leave him here, I'll stay with him, the rest of you can go to church."

"That's generous, but . . ."

"Generous?"

The two men stared at each other without saying another word.

Ada looked around as if searching for support. At the end of the corridor near the front door, Cecilia and the engineer were sharing jokes as they put on their coats. Ada imagined herself as a film star, an Indian slave in chains and facing down a ferocious tiger.

Vincenzo tried again, but not as calmly as he would have liked. "Why insist when there's no need . . . leave the boy here to sleep."

Searching for appropriate words, Mimmíu bowed to his son like an adoring Balthasar. "Baby Jesus is expecting you," he murmured.

From the other end of the corridor, Cecilia called out to ask if they were ready.

This was how things happened, and the weapon would often be no more than a smile of capitulation. If only I could bring myself to hug him, Mimmíu thought. But in fact he just went on staring at Vincenzo. And all Vincenzo wanted was for Mimmíu to give in.

Mimmíu grabbed Domenico's coat and shouted at his son, "Stand up at once!" in a tone precluding any answer. The tug-of-war had to end.

"Stop it!" Ada tried to exert authority, but no-one was listening.

"What's the matter?" Cecilia asked, coming in from the corridor. "Are you still not ready?" she asked Vincenzo. "And what are you two waiting for?" she added, turning to Mimmíu and Ada.

Vincenzo imagines Christ smiling furiously as he approaches a perfume-seller. "What have you done?" says the Messiah. The other, from behind his stall, stares at the Messiah with the look of someone who has no idea what to say. "Join the queue like everyone else," he imagines a gentleman in a coat saying . . . but the Son of Man keeps asking, "What have you done?" . . . "We did it out of love," comes the answer. "We did it to show our gratitude . . ."

"You have lost yourselves, you have turned my temple into a den of thieves . . . feeding on all the love in the world and setting a price on it . . ." Vincenzo said suddenly into the silence.

Cecilia gave him an ugly look. "Love, love . . . you're always using that word in unsuitable circumstances. What do you know about love?" Vincenzo looked down. Then she asked him bluntly, "Are you coming to Mass with us, yes or no?"

Just that.

"No." Vincenzo's voice was like the gasp of a dying man.

"Then I won't go either," she said, taking her coat off again, before calling out to the others waiting in the hall: "The rest of you can go now."

The others went.

Vincenzo and Cecilia returned together into the house.

For a while they said nothing. For some time now their silence had become an almost unbearable burden, so different from the days when they used to talk together for hours without even opening their mouths. Cecilia had no idea why she decided to stay at home. She just acted on instinct, perhaps hoping to annoy her husband. Because nowadays the victory of one of them meant defeat for the other.

When she broke the silence it was like a liberation. "Well, what shall we do?" she asked.

Vincenzo, looking out of the window, did not even turn. "Sleep," he said. "Isn't that what you usually do?"

A strangled noise escaped her, as if he had punched her hard in the chest. "I meant the two of us." She could hardly get the words out.

"So did I," he said sharply.

Cecilia joined him at the window. "Beast!" she whispered as if trying to hold back tears. "Beast!" steadily louder. "Beast! Animal!"

Centuries seem to have passed since they had been ready to die rather than offend the love each felt for the other.

"Alright," he said. He saw her raised fist reflected in the window and grabbed her wrist. They stopped like this, she with her arm raised and he holding her back. "I was there," Vincenzo said. "I was there and you were asleep!"

She was surprised by the huge sob wrenched out by her effort not to cry. Her husband was before her. Looking him in the eye she had no doubt about the reality of his spite. She tried to jerk her wrist free, but he gripped her harder, and pulled her closer. "No." She shook her head, then cried out: "No!"

But he was not listening, pulling her against him, cold and decisive, twisting her arm. "No!" She panicked because he would not speak, but was fingering her like a whore, reaching under her dress to clutch her underwear. "Why?" she cried. Vincenzo seemed able to communicate only with his body, in a silent, impassive frenzy of violence. Brutal and determined, with the cold fury of three years of silence. He wanted to hurt her, bruise her and fuck her. She realised he would not stop. "Not like this," she protested uselessly. He threw her on the divan, twisting her arm, forcing her to bend over, ripping off her dress, pushing down his trousers, and thrusting himself roughly and deeply into her body. She cried out because this hell made no sense. Then fell silent, while he needlessly pressed the palm of his hand over her mouth. Panting heavily, he ejaculated, holding back a ferocious groan, then collapsed.

She had to push him off like a dead body, heavy with the full weight of what he had done.

She rearranged the torn edges of her dress, aware her lower lip was bleeding, that there was a round bruise on her arm, and that her neck hurt.

Staggering into the bathroom, she saw her contorted face and still intact permanent wave in the mirror over the basin. She locked the door.

The sound of her weeping seemed to revive him. Slowly he got to his feet and decided to join her in the bathroom, but made no effort to open the door. Her crying was different from anything he had ever heard before, a sort of angry braying. He had ruined his home and destroyed his love. It was too late for weeping. He hurried across the corridor, took his coat from its hanger by the front door and put it on. He waited a few seconds more, then opened the door.

He wished he could tell a different story, something that never really happened, but which might help to explain the inexplicable. Perhaps something never said before about Christ and the merchants, perhaps he might even now recover from his anger. He imagined Christ, after his outburst of anger, helping the merchants to get their goods back, then maybe going off together with them to enjoy something to eat and drink. To understand the full force of forgiveness.

But the increasingly desperate weeping from the bathroom grew ever louder.

It was too late for forgiveness now.

He left the house.

Nothing

THEY SAID HE HAD STOPPED, BUT THAT WAS NOT TRUE. I knew he was still drinking, even if only in secret. I ask myself how he could go on like that, a man of such distinction, tall and impressive, with a good head of hair now turning grey. A one-hundred-per-cent Chironi. Of course, the reason he took to drink is because none of us is ever really happy, and we imagine we have nothing even when the fact is we actually lack nothing. Tell me what more that man could have needed? He wasn't short of money or a home – and what a home.

The house belonged to his aunt, the old Fascist. She was mad about her nephew and never gave a thought to anyone else. It's impossible to imagine how it must have been for her when they couldn't find him. It seems they all had a nice Christmas Eve, eating dinner together. I can't imagine how much money they must have spent on presents alone, because such people do not scrimp and save. Yet as you see, even when it seemed nothing could possibly be missing, something was missing. But just think, what sort of a marriage could it have been with the wife out all day? I know times are changing, of course they are, I'm not trying to say women should be slaves to their husbands, but all the same. These matters do need some attention, because if you don't hang on to your husband he will slip away from you, and then you'll be in no position to complain about misfortune. What? No, you tell me, why did that woman have to go out to work? It's not as if they were short of bread, my God, with all that stuff they owned. But that's always how it is: some have too much and others nothing at all. If you only knew the sacrifices I have had to make with having four children.

They searched for him everywhere, which can't have been easy. First they assumed he must have gone back to his grandfather's house, but no. Then they looked in all the bars and taverns. Nothing. No-one had even seen him. The car had gone, so he could have driven out of Núoro. But they had no idea why he might have done that. It was said things were going badly with his wife. I believe she wanted to be a modern woman, and he was not too happy about that. With the best will in the world you can't have everything. You know as well as I do what running a home involves, so you tell me whether it's possible.

Oh what a fuss; he had taken to drink, but what can you expect? When you put your drinking and your friends before your family that's how it goes, believe me! And he had too many interests, too many activities, he was someone with more than one head. It was quite obvious he had not been brought up in this part of the world. Such things do matter, of course, in the long run having a different head can make all the difference. Like all the Chironi family he loved money, in that respect he was typical of them. But they are real workers, that family, you could never accuse them of thieving; whatever they achieved was always honestly earned – by the sweat of their brows. But the situation was not too distressing to begin with: remember that for a couple of days no-one was particularly worried because he had often disappeared for short periods. It was only on the third day they began to worry. But those who had been at the dinner on Christmas Eve said he had seemed wholly normal, a bit on edge perhaps, but no more than usual. He was a typical Chironi in that way, serious, though some-one you were wary of. But this apart, he had seemed normal. They said the meal had passed quite peacefully.

Very peacefully, I can confirm that. A faultless evening. It was extremely pleasant at the dinner table. Did I notice any special irritability? I don't think so . . . I would say Vincenzo Chironi had generously invited me to what was a private family party, knowing I was alone in Núoro. As you know, I don't come from these parts, but my work has brought me here. And Chironi, with whom I had work contacts – I work in the building industry – asked me to spend Christmas Eve with his family. A gentleman, a real gentle-man, and with an exquisite wife. I can't say more, his disappearance took me entirely by surprise. I'm appalled, I really can't say more.

On the third day they began to be really worried, as I said. Even his aunt Marianna, the old Fascist, began searching everywhere for him. Then she said that when she went home, she found him sitting in the kitchen as if nothing had happened. Any of you who have ever temporarily lost a child will recognise the situation at once. A mixture of relief and rage. So she began shouting at him: disappearing like that was no way to behave! Driving everyone mad! And Mimmíu too had been looking for him everywhere! But he never answered his aunt, just bowed his head as if knowing his game had gone a little too far. Then, getting closer to him, she realised he was wearing the double-breasted suit he had got married in, and that his hair no longer had any trace of grey, and that he was once more as slim as a fashion model. What more can I say?

It was Mimmíu who eventually found him. In a place no-one had thought of, if only because Vincenzo Chironi had always liked to do everything his own way. Those who had seen him knew something was not right, but could not put a finger on it. When you have been brought up in an institution on the mainland, you can't expect to be an ordinary person. Anyway, on the fourth day of the search Mimmíu remembered Vincenzo mentioning a workshop he had recently bought, a sort of mixture of garage and general store somewhere near Predas Arbas, where they had constructed buildings for E.R.L.A.A.S. during the anti-malaria campaign. Mimmíu was not sure exactly where it was, but imagined there could not be too many similar buildings in that area. In fact, it did not take him long to find it, because the Fiat Millecento was parked outside. The place was locked from the inside, but after two or three sharp jerks, the lock gave way. It was dark inside. Mimmíu went in and called, "Vincé, Vincé, are you there, don't be silly . . . Vincé, are you there?"

He was there, in the office. Hanging from the iron grille on the high window.

They say Mimmíu fell to the ground as if punched in the solar plexus. And that he then studied the hanged man's highly polished shoes, suspended motionless a metre from the floor. At such times one's gaze tends to rest on details rather than the general picture. When you cannot accept what is before your eyes, there is nothing else you can do. They say Mimmíu fixed his eyes on the highly polished toes of those shoes which, who knows how long before, had stopped swinging. At first he did not even weep, just found it progressively harder to breathe through air that seemed to be becoming as solid as rubber around him. Then he realised he must eventually give way to his feelings, and that alone in that shed, he could weep unseen and curse the whole world and every creature in it and, if possible, torment himself even more by reminding himself of the day when Giovanna Podda had asked him to give a tall stranger a lift to Núoro. And when he, damned fool that he was, had agreed. One of those moments when you say "Yes" and regret it for the rest of your life. But regret Vincenzo? No, he told himself. How could he regret the most tormented creature he had ever known on this Earth?

Outside the night was more silent than ever. Winter had paralysed all forms of life, shattering each attempt at resistance, reducing everything to a stupefying muteness. The body hung motionless. Perhaps in solitude, days or possibly hours before, it may have swung convulsively for a while, then more and more slowly, until finally it hung still, as if an external life had decided to take over control from its internal life, which had departed with the last breath. So Mimmíu decided to weep alone close to his friend, the man most starved of love he had ever known, so taciturn that no-one could understand what was going on in his mind.

*

When Mimmíu reached the house and told Marianna, she already knew everything. I'll describe it to you the way they described it to me. When he came in; she looked him in the face and spoke before he could open his mouth. She told him that, the day before, Vincenzo had come home utterly beautiful – but then he had never been ugly – and sat down in the very chair where Mimmíu was himself sitting now. And it seems that Mimmíu confirmed everything, every detail, his eyes dry as if he had finished his weeping. Now all that remained was to tell Cecilia. Marianna explained that things never happen singly and Cecilia had had a fall at home, her face and arms bruised where, it seems, she had tried to save herself as she fell. And now she was busy. When Mimmíu asked what he should do next, Marianna simply shrugged: Marianna Chironi, formerly Signora Serra-Pintus, a woman now beyond being affected by tragedies. Her eyes calm with a heart-rending unflappability. But it was important to say nothing to Michele Angelo. Nothing at all! Was that clear?

So they decided to hide the circumstances of Vincenzo's death and pass off his suicide as an accident. They moved heaven and earth to make this possible. Mimmíu went to Torpè to fetch the priest who had married Cecilia and Vincenzo seven years before. Vincenzo had a real Núoro funeral, what more can I say? During his address the priest Virdis recalled that he had known Vincenzo since 1943 and told the story of how his dog had died and how they had buried the animal together, in the terrible year of the malaria epidemic, which Vincenzo himself had helped to fight. And then the priest added that, without telling a soul, Vincenzo had had the roof of the little church of Sant'Antimo repaired at his own expense, and also spent money on the country sanctuaries where he had been welcomed when he first arrived in Sardinia.

The only way the funeral Mass could be allowed was for Virdis to go straight to the bishop's palace in Núoro where he knew a certain Monsignor Melas, and explain that what technically may have looked like a suicide, had in fact been the last act of an alcoholic no longer in control of his own actions. He begged his friend to put his hand on his generous heart and grant forgiveness and an official authorisation for a funeral Mass for that suffering soul and others who like him are still beloved children of Mother Church. Thus, thanks to Virdis, this was granted and also a pardon that Vincenzo had never asked for.

They buried him forty-eight hours before New Year 1960. Cecilia, dressed like a professional mourner, arrived at the cemetery with her sister and brother-in-law, where she was joined by Marianna, who kissed her on the forehead in front of everyone. Room was made for the new incumbent in the family tomb near the twins Pietro and Paolo, the stillborn Giovanni Maria and Franceschina, not forgetting Gavino who had been buried on an island somewhere in the far north; and grandmother Mercede, who was represented only by her name and photograph, because she had disappeared twenty-four years before and had never been found, while Luigi Ippolito, father of Vincenzo, lay close by under the war memorial.

After the stone closed over the late Chironi Vincenzo, Cecilia placed on it a photograph of her husband smiling. She had had it printed on ceramic and framed in marble with one word carved on it in capital letters: PADRE.

Part Four
(1972 and 1978)

Indifferent to fate, as though asleep.
F. HÖLDERLIN, *The Song of Destiny*

First Person

IT SEEMS I COME FROM A VERY ANCIENT FAMILY. PEOPLE originally from Spain, who changed their name and customs over the centuries either from destiny or choice, but even this is not clear. The Chironi were once called Quiròn, or so my great-grandfather Michele Angelo used to say. I never knew my grandfather Luigi Ippolito or my father Vincenzo, but I'm told they were very alike in every respect.

As for me, my name is Cristian, Cristian Chironi.

Why they gave me this name is another story, a narrative in itself: but according to the doctors in the hospital obstetric department where I was born, I was not likely to survive my first night, and my mother wanted me to have a name that would look suitable on the list of our ancestors and their spirits. Risking an unsuitable name on a moribund newborn baby could seem to be courting bad luck.

But one thing at a time. When my mother found she was pregnant, my father had already been dead two months. Of course she may in fact have known about her pregnancy from the very first. Women have an instinct for such things.

She had been pregnant twice before me, but it went badly each time because it seems she had a problem carrying her pregnancies to term. That is to say, the foetus would grow to a certain point, after which it appeared to be in a great rush, and being in a rush is not good with these things. So when she realised she was pregnant yet again it was as if she had unexpectedly been given another chance, when she had just lost my father.

She worked at the O.N.M.I., looking after babies and young children. I know that because she looked after me there and it became my kindergarten. It had also been a good place for us both before I was born since there were paediatric consultants there. One of these, a Dr Gabbas, told my mother that since she suffered from cervical insufficiency, it was necessary to be aware that the date of my birth could not be predicted, and by the sixth or seventh month of pregnancy, nature would have to be challenged and the birth triggered so her own body would not kill the foetus, though this had to be kept in place as long as possible to make it viable. He told her that great strides had been made in obstetrics in the last few years, and now it was possible to keep premature babies alive in something called an incubator, which was in fact an artificial womb.

At seven months, Dr Gabbas said they had waited long enough, and that the birth must now be induced. My mother was immediately admitted to the San Francesco Hospital at Núoro and there I was born, a breach birth into the bargain. Not easy, but at least I came out alive. Barely alive, they said; my weight and size were not promising. It seemed unlikely I would last the night, so they sent for the hospital chaplain to ask my mother whether she wanted her child to die in the grace of God. This would necessitate a baptism "*in articulo mortis*", as the chaplain put it. So a ceremony was arranged. My mother did not want anyone to know, so a nun attached to the ward was called in to be godmother. But what name to choose? My mother had lived long enough with the Chironi family to know that we are a race apart, with as fixed a grasp of life in all its turbulence, as are painters of battle scenes, and that she had to make a major decision.

She wavered between giving me a family name, like Luigi or even Gavino, or sending me off to the paradise of the newborn dead with an everyday name so that anyone would be able to address me in whatever way they wanted.

She went for the second option and chose Cristian, not a common name and in fact the name of the hairdresser who had set her perm on the Christmas Eve when my life started. I like to think she wanted the name to link me to something sweet, like the contentment she must have felt when she was well groomed and beautiful, with her curls newly in place, and my father outside waiting for her in his car.

But I did not die after all on the night I was born. In fact, I grew steadily stronger inside my incubator.

I was born on July 29, 1960, and seven days later I was taken home. My mother could not breastfeed me and probably soon needed a hysterectomy, but I was a child of the new age and flourished on artificial milk.

When my great-aunt Marianna discovered I had already been baptised and given the name Cristian, it was like the end of the world. A totally meaningless name that meant absolutely nothing!

The miracle of my survival was not enough for her, the natural order of things had to be re-established. Cristian was intolerably exotic, like something from the illustrated magazines, worse than death. Aunt Marianna was like that because she had suffered so much, that was what everyone said. As tough as iron, but utterly set in her views. My mother sometimes used to say it was the only way Marianna had been able to survive so long. She had become more tenacious than the dead, sticking out her tongue at the old skeleton with the scythe. And being totally fearless, she decided that since I had been born and was male, my name must be changed. No discussion possible. When I was brought home she refused to look at me, but went to the church, where she explained the situation to the priest, asking him to baptise me again with a different name. The priest had to tell her that the hospital baptism was valid in all respects and the name could not be changed, and the most anyone could do was to celebrate a rite of thanksgiving and perhaps, after a comma, to add extra names of better omen.

Marianna decided this was better than nothing. So after the comma I was given the additional names Luigi Vincenzo Giovanni Maria.

From then on, as decreed by my great-aunt, no-one where she lived was allowed to call me Cristian, but Luigi, or better Gigi.

The other name came back to me on my first day at Elementary School, when I was told my real name was Chironi Cristian. I nearly had a fit of panic: it was like someone I did not know coming to sit permanently at my side.

But I was a much-loved child. My mother took me with her to the kindergarten until I was too old for it. Then, from the age of five, I lived with my great-aunt Marianna and my great-grand-father Michele Angelo.

This was where I learned all the things about my family's history that I mentioned earlier: that we had come from far away, and are proud but discreet people.

I knew my father had fought locusts and mosquitoes, and had provided the iron-work for the new church of the Madonna delle Grazie. And that even though he was not born in Núoro, no-one considered him a foreigner because eventually, in that happy burning-up of time, during which everything seemed to have come to an end, it was my father himself, a mixture of Sardinian and Friulian, who had got everything started again: forge, black-smith business and family.

My great-grandfather and I loved watching television together as though we were the same age, and perhaps in a way we really were; when I was nine years old, he was nearly ninety-nine, still straight as a pole, with nothing to remind you he was carrying a whole century on his back. He had enormous leathery hands, and my hand in his was like a baby rabbit in an eagle's talons.

I loved him with my whole being. We never spoke, just watched television together. We saw Robert Kennedy shot, and when the astronauts landed on the moon he said he couldn't believe it, there must be some mistake, while my great-aunt said things like that were wrong, and what had been created must be left untouched and secret, or we humans would be made to pay for our presumption.

They had put the television where the stove and oven had been before, and there was also a camp bed on which my great-aunt Marianna would sometimes settle my great-grandfather so he would not get too tired. In their house I had the room where my father had once slept. An almost empty room, with two beds and a little table.

In the other house, in via Deffenu, my room was full of toys and books. And there was a picture hanging over the bed showing an old man called Saint Matthew listening to an angel. The angel had come from on high and seemed to be counting on his fingers just as I did at school. My mamma and I always laughed about that.

Then there was Uncle Mimmíu who wasn't my real uncle but Domenico's father, and I called Domenico my cousin though he wasn't really. My real cousins were two girls who were twins, but I saw very little of them because they had moved to Cagliari with their family, my mother's sister and her husband.

The only time I really cried was when my great-grandfather Michele Angelo died. I was twelve years old at the time, and he was a hundred and one. We were watching television, a programme explaining how bees build a hive and then fill it with honey. He was watching and nodding, as if to say, yes that's just how it's done. Because he knew so many things, he had made the most beautiful balconies you see on the Corso. I mean, he was watching the queen bee who was sitting there in comfort while the others, the worker bees, were all driving themselves mad to honour her because she was the queen. And he was nodding in agreement. Then, at a certain point, he was not nodding anymore. He said he wanted to go to his room where his wife was waiting for him.

This is just as it should be, a season of predictable immobility. Each body comes closer to its soul, each heavy object closer to its lighter side, flesh closer to dissolution, harmony to disharmony, and fact closer to memory: everything needs the right season for such metamorphosis to be possible.

Michele Angelo walks slowly, but he is still walking. As he reaches his own room, and comes closer to his Mercede, he is aware of the dense, bitter smell of oleanders. He understands that this precise moment between spring and summer has been assigned to him, when plants breathe a little anxiously as they anticipate the heat to come and give off traces of scent. When wind shapes the beaches and sea thistles lay siege to lilies. He fully realises what is happening and is calm just when he would have expected to be agitated. Now that he is on his way, he repeats to himself what he has said a thousand times, that the one thing no-one can avoid is death. But being certain that this is true, surprisingly, does not frighten him. He does not know how to explain it to himself, but he is certain he is now leaving the world in exactly the same way as he first came into it. Breathing deeply, he considers the ambiguity of flight, and how you can never know if it is pushed from the ground or pulled from above. He will enjoy what still remains; the air is warm, thank God. He will keep moving forward but not hurry.

So as he walks towards the season of oleanders, Michele Angelo looks at his hands and reflects that they are the only truly immortal thing about him. He squeezes his life in his fist as if it were a twitching goldfinch. From these hands have sprung not only heavy thoughts but the lightest possible wefts of iron: gates, balconies, railings, grilles and fire dogs. Every one an exercise in survival, like perfect poetry. Or like a secret memory that seems strong but still cries out in magnificent weakness. Like a targeted project of revenge against solitude. Opening those gates, leaning on those balconies, caressing those railings, grasping those grilles, anyone can feel the warmth of the hands that produced them. His hands.

The Lostia house, for example, its ironwork resembling twisted cotton thread apparently embroidered like lace; as if spun in a frenzy of slender filaments, a lace to be held up to the light, a netting seemingly sensitive to the wind. A balcony balanced on its base as if completely unsupported. Now, as he goes forward, Michele Angelo can see it more fully, can understand how far his vision was ahead of his ability when he made it, how far his hands rather than his head did the thinking. He understands everything now, can see every single scroll, remember each blow of the hammer that produced it. That was a beautiful time in his life, paradise on earth: the twins just born, everything stemming from the marvellous chaos his happiness had created.

Then the Tangianu house, its ground-floor windows with huge grilles swelling like enormous pregnant bellies about to deliver up their burdens. For that façade he forged three unpretentious female guardians, all dense, heavy curves as though cast in lead. A grey curtain built against a fate that had hit him without warning. Mercede had miscarried, and everyone looking out through those windows would have understood the sickening bitterness of that pain after the magic, the moment the glass is smashed. A shattered smile, expectation disappointed.

His whole existence had recorded such impressions, leaving a mark, breathing life into the inanimate. Because he knew how to respond bravely to problems no matter how atrocious, with the blind obstinacy of a man never afraid to face the unknown.

Then the firedogs at the Mastino house, which the lawyer himself recognised as works of art and liked to show off to his guests, people who had known Rome and Paris, but never before seen iron worked like cloth, twisted and as if sewn again, stretched out to its maximum, as if it had never been solid or rigid even when tempered.

And not forgetting the railings at the Triscritti house, black as the Day of Judgement since the metal had been mixed with soot when hot, and swarmed like a basket of eels, fluid and lucid, viscous and spiral, and now reflecting in those spirals the chiaroscuro of shadows cast by every breeze through the leaves on the trees. Never still for a moment. More sensitive than anything even Michele Angelo could have imagined, quivering like harp-strings.

And the iron bars on the civic centre, ripped out of the ground and now perhaps about to be replaced by a modern building contained in an aluminium frame. How to account for the tenacity with which the old building had fought the machines diligently tearing it down, almost as if it had been a line of poplars with roots clinging to the earth like claws? There had been a pattern of handmade bars, their linearity interrupted by a central bulb cast when hot and filed down until bars and bulb coalesced in a single flesh.

And so now, with the light finally right, he could accept his defeats without regret. The goldfinch was still alive in his hands, but no longer struggling to beat its wings.

And what of his house? A fallen house. The great doorway to the forge blocked for years, as happens when places once full of life have drawn their last breath and slipped into the darkness of absolute silence. That doorway had seen the laughter of his children, Piero and Paolo first, then Gavino and Luigi Ippolito, all dead now. To Michele Angelo they had been like a pergola of vines: leaves, clusters and curls. As he walked on, he could see it all clearly, still beautiful though now attacked by rust and creepers. A doorway that had shut out a season of light, but had still allowed hell to rage madly, the hell of eternity.

So returning to the forgetfulness from which he had started seemed a distinct advantage. It consoled him, that no matter how hard he tried, he could not now remember what the very first thought of his existence had been. He could remember nothing before the corridors of the orphanage from which the widowed blacksmith Giuseppe Mundula had rescued him when he was nine, to give him a family and an occupation. Before that nothing.

But he must go back to this time.

But do you know who you were before?

Me? Before when?

Before, at the very beginning.

Why are you over there? Come to bed.

Mercede, in the shadows in the corner, shook her head. Michele Angelo forced himself to sit up.

Look what you're making me do, Mercede Lai, you stubborn

woman. He said this without resentment, but went on to explain: All my bones hurt, have you no idea how old I am now?

She smiled, once again the young girl she had been when he had first set eyes on her from the top of the ladder while adjusting the big thurible in the church.

He would have liked to tell her that if she went out of that room she would be surprised by all the changes that had taken place around the house. We're modern now, my love, he would say. There's a television. And miraculously you have a great-grandson called Gigi but whose real name is Cristian, which is a modern name.

You began as a godless animal, and before that you were a plant, and even before that, only a thought. And before you were a thought you were nothing at all, a remarkable nothing. Can you remember being nothing? Of course not, because that is the state of grace . . . she insists.

He is beginning to understand, it is years since he has felt so well. His legs feel powerful and his arms are strong.

He leaps out of the bed, he can even run to catch up with her.

We found a letter among my great-grandfather Michele Angelo's things:

I, the undersigned, Chironi Michele Angelo,

hereby declare I do not wish my relatives when I die to dress me in black – no mourning. Mourning my Beloved Ones does nothing for me mourning is in the heart. Another point I don't want masses said if I am not present. I don't want to be put in a tomb like my Grandson, my Son and all the others. I don't want little orphan girls to mourn. Masses if you can, but be careful where you give charity. Please don't turn off the television alright? Not for eight days. The television is not just fun, it will pass the time for Gigi. Please show respect and don't displease me in life or death. I thank you from my heart for all the love and affection you have given. I've been taken like a child. I thank the Lord for giving me such a good family may the Lord give you the same and health and fortune as I wish you. Treat others well, after all what do we have in this world? If some person treats you badly, do good to them if you can. If I can't do it myself please thank all who come to see me. I thank everyone from deep in my heart, no flowers just a bunch in the coffin.

I, Chironi Michele Angelo,

April 24, 1967

Now it's your turn

MY MOTHER CECILIA WAS ADMITTED TO THE CANCER Hospital in Cagliari in August 1978. It was already an important hospital then, in fact it was now called a Clinic. The wards were small rooms even equipped with colour television. I was eighteen years old and I had never seen colour television before.

Do you know the first thing I did? I switched on the television. I asked myself how come there was no volume, then I saw a cable leading to a pair of headphones plugged into the set. But I was too tired to do anything about it, so I simply started watching images without the sound. Frantic silences sprang from the screen. I felt how the apostle Matthew must have felt before he became a saint. At the beginning, long before he was converted and wrote his Gospel and was martyred in Ethiopia.

At the beginning, before all this.

But after Christ had chosen Matthew despite himself.

Telling him: Now it's your turn.

My turn? Matthew said.

There, that was my main feeling, but not until the Messiah looked at him and told him it was his turn now. That was how I was feeling. And I suppose there was the same silence before the angel's intervention at the writing desk, at the very moment when it was revealed to the moneylender apostle, that no matter how much he pondered and stared at the blank parchment, his message was already there inside him.

That was how I really did feel, not stopping to ask myself how fate could have possibly linked me to the image of that old man struggling with his own great frailty. The angel threw him to the ground and stamped on his chest, breaking his ribs. In fact, I too began to feel a terrible weight between my own throat and stomach and, for a moment, imagined I was suffocating. I had switched on the colour television, not even knowing why, and it was showing me silent scenes of slaughter. Or more precisely, the pictures were watching me. What I was watching was like the wisp of a murmur passing through the room.

Inevitably, subjected to such a hail of blows, the old man was forced to admit he did not matter. And lying exhausted on the ground, apparently at the point of death, he could not help being aware of the persistent murmur: Now it's your turn.

He had to surrender and agree: My turn.

Then he struggled up despite the pain when he tried to breathe, despite his listlessness and the weakness in his chest; as if recapturing his infancy or an unborn hope, he made his way to the writing desk and, without further ado, dipped his pen in the ink.

I'm well aware I've never been special, I've loved the same things as everyone else: the quietness of mornings, freshly laundered sheets. I have loved falling in love and being loved. I have loved holding back my tears but loved weeping too. I have never been in any way special. I have loved fresh bread and the purity of certain shapes. I have loved loving. And hating sometimes, too: I'm nothing special.

Not even now, in the depths of night.

I was never a special child, I was quick to leave my first home, straight after my great-grandfather died.

You are not special, though in a way you are. Mamma, you often told me that. But perhaps it was simply because you were my mother and did not want to admit that either of us were failures. Or maybe you were just thinking of all the things I could have been but clearly wasn't. Or perhaps you really did see something in me no-one else could see, or even remotely imagine.

You took me out of myself. With a precise gesture you placed the open palm of your hand on my chest. And now I think I understand: you were trying to reveal a secret place, a jewel-case, a treasure.

And when I understood that, I stood up suddenly, and do you know what I did? I switched on the television. Colour television, incredible, in that place of suffering. The gloom was suddenly lit by speechless images from a picture I knew only too well: St Matthew being inspired by the angel to write his Gospel. There, I told myself, and I watched without even having the strength to reach for the headphones. All I could hear was a light irregular sound that clashed with my breathing, as if a weight of revelation had suddenly been emptied over me.

I understood how Matthew Levi, at the moment when they told him it was his turn, must have suddenly felt immensely old, almost near death, feeble, extraordinarily weak.

The images on the television watched me relentlessly. And I watched them. You're eighteen years old, I told myself. And now it's the middle of the night, I told myself, trying to taste a new silence that depended on the rapid dissolution of that final murmur.

It's your turn.

My turn.

You can't claim the old man was already a saint when the angel visited him. Such judgements can only be reached in hindsight. And we compliment ourselves on having foreseen things which in fact took us by surprise. What we have been warned of seems less threatening than what we are unaware of. That was why, despite the agony of his mission, the old man had to accept being ambushed. Self-confident, he had prided himself that with his long experience nothing could ever surprise him, and when the angel stamped on his chest he was not so much afraid of death, as that the terrible pressure might force him to reveal everything he had kept hidden inside him over the course of a long life. I believe this is also why I acted as I did after listening to the busy stillness of sleep reaching me from the other end of the ward. That was why I had switched on the television. The colour television. Which showed me Caravaggio's worried-looking St Matthew when he did not yet know he was a saint and had no idea he would ever come to write a Gospel.

And with the image having neither music nor voice, I realised the more I imagined myself looking at the picture, the more it was looking at me. Almost as if it knew there was a clear reason for me to be pitied. You are eighteen years old, the picture was saying: Now it's your turn.

It wasn't that I didn't know it, but in the instant between things happening and me understanding that they had happened, my whole life passed prosaically before me. I remembered grass staining my hands; and saw myself on the pony-shaped seat at the barber's while my skin responded to the cold touch of his razor and when, without being able to name it, I was nonetheless able to experience what I would later understand as the torture of separation; when perfect happiness expressed itself as uncontrollable laughter. All these illusions, these false conclusions, were things I needed to keep inside me where they formed a perpetual unconscious awareness. Because one must come from somewhere in the first place, and eventually go somewhere to die. And go somewhere else again after death. After death, that's the point.

I have explained what I did. To begin with, I was not even aware the images had no voice, I just thought I needed to wait until the sound came, but nothing came. Then I saw the headphones were plugged into the set, but did not feel equal to walking the couple of steps needed to reach them.

I should of course have realised that in that place of silences no television should have voice or sound, but it certainly did have real light. As if left in a ship's wake at sea and reducing all concepts of stability to nonsense. Now it's my turn? Your turn. Really your turn.

Yet it seems this will never happen. A night like this must be the final result. Just think, I am wrestling with my angel, or with my demon if that's what it is. And he faces me without either showing what weapons he might wield, or reaching out his arms as if to invite me to a harmless embrace; no, he comes from a place that does not exist, but possesses flesh, bones and weight. That is how the angel I must fight is made. Or the demon, I don't know: at one time they were the same thing. I am in no way special, even if I have vague memories of the classification of celestial beings. I know the seraphim lose themselves in God and carry that ecstasy in their eyes while the cherubim are cheeky and luminous. But further than that I cannot go.

In any case, though the figure that faces me bears no weapons, it is as if he were armed to the teeth. He looks at me and I have to accept every blow, because this is a struggle that is not a struggle, it has no ritual or respect, only the obscenity of death. That's how it has to happen, surely. Everyone will have to look their dying mother in the eyes. Even if some do not keep the appointment. That can happen, for sure.

No, I don't want to pass judgment, there are some things that you cannot be aware of until they happen, just as you don't notice thistles until they prick you. You cannot anticipate them. You may be doing something entirely different at the time, pretending all is well; enjoying a meal out perhaps, or criticising someone who works for you, or being insulted by your boss; or perhaps waiting for your child to finish his training, and he seems so slender and small to you, still in need of you – unlike all the other children. Or perhaps you are making love, or perhaps writing to a wife you fear is unfaithful. It may be midday, or late afternoon. You may be enjoying the lazy uncertainty of evening light touched by a twinge of melancholy. Or perhaps you are half-naked in full sunlight, exposed to the stares of other half-naked people. It's just that your life is racing past. You have opened the French window in the kitchen to let in light and fresh air, when a lizard comes in and runs to hide under the refrigerator. You have tidied the empty garage and gone back to looking at old photographs from a time when you thought you were hideous but were in fact perfectly acceptable to look at, even handsome, with a full head of hair and no sign of a paunch; then, proceeding with this stripping away of layers of the past, you turn to photographs from a time when you really were beautiful, irresistible, elegant, and you understand that there is nothing for you to be ashamed of but yourself. To sum up, you have realised that what you thought was under control has definitely set off on a path of its own; and it is at this point that the telephone rings.

Don't worry, the voice says, but the voice I am hearing sounds far away as if it has just departed on a journey without return. Like when your little girl turns back to wave goodbye as she goes into school. Like when you decide to tear a sticking-plaster off a scab. Don't worry. Of course I'm not worried. Why should I be worried? I'm face to face with an unarmed figure who is showing me his bare palms. There is nothing to make me feel threatened. Nothing. Yet those hands before me are as terrible as the words I heard from her on the telephone: Don't worry.

To be exact, a few days earlier there had been a message on the telephone answering machine: This is Mamma, everything's fine here. Spoken as if she might have some reason to suppose I might think otherwise. But I had no reason to think otherwise. The old apostle could not know he would become a saint, or understand why the angel looked concerned. It took him completely by surprise when he realised those bare hands with their insubstantial pallor could cleave flesh like the sharpest knife. Then he understood in his own flesh that the burning sword was simply an image of the heat of hell emanating from the angel's hands. The angel had looked at him and held out his hands as if to say, You have no need to worry, old man. And he had looked back as if to reply: Why on earth should I worry? But an instant later, smashed to the ground by a terrible blow, he began to look on the angel with terror. And when this angel, who seemed little more than a boy, began jumping on his chest, Matthew became aware of how painful it can be to discover what we have been hiding inside ourselves. And how easily, how very easily, our future can attack our past.

Terrible revelations had emerged from this ambush when greed had taken Matthew over, how thanks to the cunning and repetitive use of an ingenuous expression of his, insolvent debtors had been dispossessed, and how he had cheated about the weight of some metal or about the current exchange rate, or how he had lost no sleep at all while ruthlessly deceiving other people again and again.

He was forced to regurgitate all the documents hidden in his heart, so ruthlessly swallowed but never digested. Because of this cursed boy – waxen, soft but cold and incorruptible as marble – his old body was now being forced to make room for a higher class of document, something more nourishing than any he had ever yet taken responsibility for.

Perception is the curse. Worse than knowledge. Worse than ignorance. Having a whole army of words and connections on one's side: This is Mamma, everything's fine here. Then why that tone of voice? Perhaps it was just the desperately poor quality of sound from the answering machine. It certainly seemed to embarrass her to have to record intimate things onto a magnetic tape. But that was how she was: usually, at the first sign of the answering machine, she would ring off. So the fact that she struggled against every obvious sign of embarrassment to leave a clumsy message was reassuring, but for the same reason deeply disturbing.

Of course, there had been the whole merry-go-round of premonitions, so you tell yourself you were not unprepared for it. You had had a bad dream – for example, that you were swept away by a river in flood while trying to cross it in a car, but what car? You had been in a bad mood all day for no obvious reason; it had got off to a bad start – bad weather rather than sunshine, the shirt you had planned to wear turning out to be indelibly stained; the work shifts in the bar in front of the house meant it was closed, and no-one was looking on you with love; even unknown passers-by seemed to know you were about to fall into an abyss. To my great-aunt Marianna all such premonitions were entirely logical.

There; you came home working your way through this turmoil of irrelevant connections, ready to claim that for once you must be mistaken, but there was that message on the answering machine.

This is Mamma, everything's fine here. Spoken as if by a little girl at her first public performance at kindergarten: an embarrassed silence, a sigh, then the first words of a prepared recital: This is Mamma, more silence because, she must be telling herself, presumably he can't answer because he must be out? Why do I have to suffer this humiliation of talking to nothing as though there were someone there to answer me? So, hearing silence, she is strongly tempted to ring off. But then, she tells herself, if I ring off he may worry and maybe think goodness knows what. Everything's fine here. That's perfect, then she hangs up.

*

On that particular day Matthew Levi had come to hear the latest messiah, one of the many who liked to announce good news from the steps of the Temple. But this one had said something to the effect that he had come into the World to set father against son, brother against brother, and blood against blood. As he passed by, Matthew had shaken his head hearing such terrible things spoken in such a calm voice. And it was just this clash between tone and content that had frightened him. But he had walked on without turning back, though still feeling the eyes of that umpteenth messiah on him, so much so that for an instant he was afraid this one might even be the real one.

A little later, when he was able to look at him, he realised the force of what he had heard walking past the Temple. He became fully aware of the curse of perception. Understanding this will kill me, he told himself. Things cannot ever be the same again. And this seemed so obvious as to allow no further uncertainty. He told himself this in a very calm voice, experiencing in himself the atrocious separation of self from self. It was as if someone else were talking to him.

There is no remedy for this condition: you realise it can happen and then it happens to you. First you say it, then someone else says it to you.

Now it's your turn.

My turn.

It's your turn. My turn, at this moment, is to fake a sort of smile. Burying dumb pain under a shrug to pretend that what has not been said outright does not exist at all and is not screaming at me. Am I dying? You asked at one point. And I shrugged, as if that was the most unlikely thing anyone could ever have imagined. Yet death and the throes of death were there, curled up at your feet like a cat refusing to be driven away. As happened one night, when after many days of silence you asked in a new voice: Am I dying?

The angel said no, you're not dying, old man, you're being reborn.

And I? I answered we are all dying. And we tried to smile.

Then you looked at me and I became aware that your veiled eyes had suddenly cleared again like the eyes in that hand-coloured picture that had always hung in the bedroom.

What an extraordinary woman you had been. Even now, when reduced to the condition of a small girl with skin hanging loosely from her skeleton. Your hair lifeless but still thick.

Go and sleep now, you tell me.

And I say no, I say, if you don't sleep I won't sleep either. And you answer: Soon I shall be sleeping a very long sleep.

Though I don't understand how, I realise everything is changing. You are awake now, responding to my tone of voice. Alert. Your heart beating normally.

For an instant I feel better, then realise the cursed angel has covered my eyes. He has torn my body to shreds. He has crushed my vanity so thoroughly that I long to feel pain inside myself. He has muddled me to the point of being afraid of something there is no point in fearing.

In fact, suddenly I see with clarity, it is as if I were the one dying and you the one watching over me, Don't be afraid, you say, to reassure me: You tell me I am a child, and that I have had to grow up too quickly.

*

The angel gestures to the old man to get up. And he realises that contrary to what he thought, he is able to get back to his feet, no longer weighed down by his secrets and his years. He really does seem born again. The flame running over him ignites his hair and eyebrows, but it is a blaze that does not consume him.

Now, for a moment, I have no more fear: everything appears to have recovered the harmony this very long night had seemed about to shatter. Your face is smooth and relaxed. For five minutes we talk closely of our shared but very divergent memories. We both remember my first day at the Ferdinando Podda school, when I cried because I did not want to go into the classroom, though I remember you cried too and tried to hide it from me, when you were forced to leave me in the playground. It's quite clear to me that my "disappearance" was just wanting to escape for a few moments from your controlling gaze; whereas what you remember is searching for me for hours. What laughs now, mother and son, we are so closely aware of one another, our relationship has reached a climax. But never again, except in a list in some registry office, will our two memories lie close together again in such dignity. We have brought ourselves to the exact point where we are now.

Now you can be reborn and I, little by little, must die.

Bloodlines

FROM THE COLOURED SCREEN HE REMEMBERS A PARTICULAR detail of Saint Matthew's expression, as imagined by the painter: the moment when, having finally surrendered, Matthew listens with the greatest attention as the angel enumerates the genealogy of Jesus Christ. Abraham begat Isaac, Isaac begat Jacob, Jacob begat Judah and his brethren, Judah begat Phares and Zarah of Thamar, Phares begat Esrom, Esrom begat Aram, Aram begat Aminadab . . . And so on until from Abraham to Christ twice fourteen generations passed, first from Abraham to the captivity in Babylon, then from the captivity in Babylon to Christ.

Have you got that, old man? Matthew says yes, that's quite clear, and in any case, lists and statistics are what he is familiar with. But he knows not to allow himself to be distracted in any way. He is as attentive as a young schoolboy and has lost all his self-sufficient conceit: the angel has reconciled him to his duty. After the moment for action comes the moment for listening, and then vice-versa from listening to action, and so on.

In celestial reasoning we are little more than children to whom the same concept has to be repeated incessantly. A repetition with variation, so we can all imagine ourselves living individually what is in fact universal. And in this constant repetition we discover when old that we are less special than we ever imagined ourselves to be. All equal in dying, with this infinite repetition simply a denial of the evidence. Repeat that, the angel tells the old man, now it's your turn. So he repeats it: Abraham begat Isaac, Isaac begat Jacob, Jacob begat Judah and his brethren, Judah begat Phares and ... Alright, alright, the boy interrupts him.

Sometimes, by chance, we would meet someone you would say I ought to recognise. And I always denied I knew them. This time too, you easily recognised the passer-by and I claimed I did not know him, but only because you had started smiling again. For a long time, you insisted on watching a corner of the room and frowning. As though extraordinary things must be happening in that invisible corner and you didn't want to be distracted from them . . . you seemed to be following a thread and hearing a voice. As if listening to the completion of your own story: Michele Angelo and Mercede begat Pietro and Paolo, then Giovanni Maria and Franceschina, Luigi Ippolito, Gavino and Marianna; Luigi Ippolito and Erminia begat Vincenzo, Vincenzo and Cecilia begat Cristian ...

Cristian and Maddalena begat Luigi Ippolito.

Alright, let's start again.

It is possible that in the course of this story you may have hit upon real combinations of Christian names, surnames and circumstances. If so, these are purely coincidental.

M.F.

MARCELLO FOIS was born in Sardinia in 1960 and is one of a gifted group of writers called 'Group 13', who explore the cultural roots of their country's regions. He writes for the theatre, television and cinema, and is the author of several novels, including *The Advocate* (2003), *Memory of the Abyss* (2012), and *Bloodlines* (2014).

SILVESTER MAZZARELLA is a translator of Swedish and Italian literature, including of stories by Tove Jansson and novels by Davide Longo and Michela Murgia.